Parallel Secrets

by

ML Barrs

Parallel Secrets

Cover Art by *Debbie Taylor*

The Wild Rose Press, Inc.
PO Box 708
Adams Basin, NY 14410-0708
Visit us at www.thewildrosepress.com

Publishing History
First Edition, 2023
Trade Paperback ISBN 978-1-5092-4978-7
Digital ISBN 978-1-5092-4979-4

Published in the United States of America

Vicky wasn't entirely proud she'd find opportunity in a kidnapping, but this was also the perfect time to follow up on the levee girl mystery and find out, once and for all, whether her actions affected whatever became of little Lisa Dee.

Pete passed an old station wagon. "I checked out Google Earth. It's mostly swamp and wild land outside town. Maybe she just got lost."

"Don't think so. She disappeared from in front of her house."

"Do you think the cops will talk to you?"

"Hope so. It'll be different not working for a news station." Vicky's voice was light, though her lips tightened and her gut clenched. "It's been a few years, but I still know people."

"Sounds good." Pete didn't seem to notice her disquiet. He was usually attuned to her moods, one of the many things she enjoyed about him. She had never liked so many things in one man before.

Now, however, he apparently had something else on his mind. "There's not a lot to see right around Walkers Corner. I might take a couple of side trips to Civil War sites."

"Good. You should. I'll be busy." Besides, she'd rather not have anyone, not even Pete—or especially not Pete—looking over her shoulder as she poked around in the past.

Her past.

Praise for ML Barrs and Parallel Secrets

"…Tense, heart-wrenching and heart-warming as well, *Parallel Secrets* kept me up late, praying Rose would be found alive and well, longing for the perpetrator to be brought to justice, and hoping Pete's heart was generous enough to understand and stick with Vicky. I expect ML Barrs' next book to be equally enthralling."
~*Roxanne Dunn, Author of Murder Unrehearsed and Murder Undetected*

~*~

"… A reporter with a secret, attempts to uncover the dangerous secrets of others. A harrowing tale."
~*Susan McCormick, author of the award winning mystery series, The Fog Ladies*

~*~

"… Vicky is a compelling character. I'm fascinated by how she melds her skills as a journalist with her quest to find answers to long-unsolved mysteries—including the one that has the deepest hold on her heart. In reading it, I couldn't wait to see what happened next…"
~ *Suzy Hopkins, author of the What to Do series.*

Dedication

To my family—my heart overflows with love for each and every one of you. To my friends and colleagues in journalism—stay strong.

Chapter One

Rose
Walkers Corner, Sunday, November 2008

Rose Willwood loved being the fastest kid in fifth grade.

"Told ya!" she whooped, gloating. She rode her bike on a victory lap around the overgrown bushes in the center of the cul-de-sac. Faded yellow and red leaves danced away as she passed.

"All right, stop!" Aaron Dankin gasped. "This is so dumb."

He was ten, same as Rose, but big and blond instead of small and brunette like her. They both wore jeans and sweatshirts. It got chilly this time of year in Missouri.

Her aunt Sara sat on the covered porch, yakking on the phone as usual, with her feet up on the rocker and a ratty, stretched-out sweater pulled over her knees. Aunt Sara stayed with her every Sunday afternoon, even though Rose was too old to need a babysitter. She figured her aunt agreed with her on this because she usually ignored Rose the whole time she was over.

Aaron dropped his bike and crawled into their hideout. Rose followed. Under the bushes was a perfect little hut, big enough to fit four or five kids sitting down. Aaron sat right in the middle, his gray sweatshirt, pale hair and face barely visible in the dark.

Rose pushed his shoulder. "Move over. You're taking up too much room."

"So? I'm bigger than you."

"So? I'm faster than you."

"No way. My bike chain got messed up." He fake-yawned. "I'm bored. Let's go to the school."

"I'm not supposed to leave the circle."

"Come on. Tim might be there. Your stoner aunt won't even notice we're gone. You're just chicken."

"Am not," Rose said. "I'm not allowed to ride on big streets."

Aaron crawled toward the hideout's opening. "Then we'll walk. I'm going."

"Oh, all right." Rose started after him. "Just for a minute."

They peeked through the bushes. Rose's aunt was still on the phone, paying no attention to them. They duckwalked around the back side of the circle and ran down the block, sticking close to hedges and trees and laughing their butts off. They crossed the county highway and walked the few blocks to their school playground.

"Good. They're here." Aaron trotted toward two boys on the climbing dome, sword fighting with sticks. Rose trailed after him.

"Hey, Tim."

The smaller boy jumped down. "Hi, Aaron. That's my cousin, Lee."

Lee slid off the play structure and pointed his stick at Rose. "Who's she?"

The way he stared at her with creepy, half-closed blue eyes made her stomach hurt. Plus, he was older; big enough to be in high school.

"That's just Rose." Aaron waved dismissively. He picked up a stick and thrust it in her direction. "On guard!"

The boys launched into a pretend sword fight, complete with sound effects. They whipped their sticks like light sabers, like movie swashbucklers, pointing them toward Rose.

She tightened her fists. "Leave me alone."

"Does this tickle?" Aaron poked his stick into her side. "Does it? Huh? Huh?"

"Don't! Leave me alone."

The boys all jabbed at her, laughing, Aaron the loudest. And he was supposed to be her friend. Lee used his branch to try to lift up her shirt. She pushed it away. But they only poked harder, hard enough to hurt.

"Stop it! Leave me alone!" she yelled and ran.

"Get her!" Tim waved his stick overhead as the boys gave chase, spreading out to corner her. They trapped her in an entrance to the closed school building. With her back against the door, she had nowhere to go. The three of them faced her, jeering.

"Don't be such a crybaby," Aaron sneered as Lee jabbed her chest with his stick.

"I hate you!" Rose screamed through her tears. "I'm going to tell!"

"Aaron!" A man's low voice came from the woods behind the playground.

The boys paused mid-torment to listen.

"Who's that calling you?" Tim asked.

Aaron shrugged. "No one."

Tim and Lee poked Rose again.

When the voice called his name again, Aaron said, "I gotta go," and turned toward the woods. "See ya later."

The moment there was an opening, Rose shoved past Aaron and ran. When she was almost to the big road, she ducked behind a bush and looked back. Tim and his cousin stood on the sidewalk outside the school. They still carried their sticks.

She had to wait to cross the busy highway. She sprinted across as soon as there was a break in traffic. She didn't see the boys. Thank God. Rose redid her ponytail and zipped up her thin sweatshirt against the cold November wind. Tears blurred her eyes as she stalked home, jaw clenched so hard her teeth ached, hating those boys, hating this place, hating her life.

Rose slowed her walk. She breathed in and out, nice and deep, like Mom said to, so her face wouldn't be bright red. She hated the way it did that when she got upset. She hated those horrible boys. She hated it here, hated everything about it. Why'd they move to this stupid place anyway? And now she'd be home alone with weird Aunt Sara. She didn't need a babysitter! Sara would probably say something mean about her red face. She hated her, too.

She dropped to one knee to tie her shoe and glance around. She'd go straight to her room so she wouldn't have to talk with stupid Aunt Sara. They'd probably just have cereal for dinner again. She was hungry. She'd skipped lunch when Aaron showed up on his bike. What a traitor. He acted weird around those boys. That big kid was mean.

Her stupid eyes finally quit crying. She wiped her face with her sweatshirt cuffs and scanned the neighborhood. No one around. She turned past the tall hedge at the corner of her street.

A deep voice drawled, "Hello there, Rose."

Rose jumped, looked, and walked faster. Then she was fighting, kicking, trying to scream as something grabbed her from behind and she fell softly, softly into a pillow of darkness.

Chapter Two

Colorado, Tuesday, November 2008

A veil of heavy, damp evening air draped the tangled trees surrounding the nearly deserted campground. Vicky Robeson relaxed in her camp chair, feet propped on an ice chest, tea at hand, enjoying autumn in Eastern Colorado and the very fine view of Pete Harris as he stoked the fire. As always, the pungent smell of burning wood sharpened her senses, pleasantly this time.

Her brand-new smartphone buzzed. A news alert: missing girl, possible kidnapping, Walkers Corner, Missouri. A harsh wave of memory surged through her body as it did whenever she learned of a lost child. She shivered and zipped up her hoodie, barely breathing as she waited for the story to load. The alert was one of dozens she'd signed up for over the years, one of her many newsgathering habits.

Walkers Corner. She'd never expected, or wanted to, hear the name of that tiny town in Missouri again.

Her eyes burned. The campfire smoke now smelled dangerous. She lifted her camp chair away from the fire, away from the heat and light, closer to the RV so she'd have something solid behind her. She read and reread the short article about the missing girl. Ten years old, disappeared from in front of her house while playing with a friend. No witnesses.

Fear and terrible images of a child taken, tortured, possibly killed—especially in Walkers Corner—swept away all thoughts, except for what she needed to do next. She might not be able to undo the past, but this time she would do everything she could to help save the child.

It would definitely blow a hole in the camping trip, though, her first with the delectable Pete Harris in his eight-year-old RV. Damn. She liked the way he traveled, the way his mind worked, the way she felt with him. His jeans and plaid shirt hugged him nicely. He moved smoothly while making sure everything was just so.

When he came over and kissed her, the fire reflected in his smiling eyes, color melting somewhere between chocolate and caramel.

Her return kiss was quick. "Sorry, something urgent's come up. Would you mind driving me back to town?" Even to her own ears her voice sounded tight and strained. "I need to go to Missouri for a few days."

"What? Now?" He stepped back, appearing concerned. "Is everything okay?"

"Yes, fine. I hate to disrupt our trip, but I need to check into something. A girl's gone missing there, outside St. Louis."

Pete tilted his head. A lock of light brown hair threaded with gray fell onto his forehead.

A bit more explanation might be called for. "There's an Amber Alert. Her name's Rose Willwood. I want to help find her. I might write about it. And follow up on another story I covered there back in the day."

Pete's brow cleared. "Want me to go with you? I have free time. We can take the RV. If we start early and both drive, we can make St. Louis by late tomorrow."

Just like that, no more questions? What an amazing guy. They'd been together for about six months, and he just kept getting better and better. Would he be like that if they lived together? She was still absorbing his suggestion last week that they do just that.

"Really? That'd be great. The place is an hour or two this side of St. Louis."

"No problem." Pete started folding the tarp he used as a tablecloth. "I'd like to see more of Missouri." He put the tarp and a lantern in one of his crates, already packing for an early departure. "How long do you think we'll be there?"

****

They left before dawn, with an hour-long detour to Vicky's house outside Denver to grab a few things and hitch up her car, which was just back from the body shop. One good thing about being unemployed—she could get up and go. Almost three months ago, the new owners of the TV station dumped her, then installed their own news director. Understandable and expected after a top-level change. Besides, the severance package gave her time to decide her next move. And now she had an opportunity to find out whether her travel writing hobby might one day turn into a paying gig. Some day.

"Make a left there, where that red car is." Vicky glanced around at what would likely soon be her former neighborhood. She didn't have much longer to decide whether to accept the out-of-state job offer. "You know you don't have to do this."

"I know. I want to." Pete made the turn. He'd bought the RV about a month before they met. He'd told Vicky his life plan had been to teach history, but his father got sick, and his mother needed help with the family furniture business. Now just turned forty, with both parents gone and the store sold, he had a spreadsheet of places he wanted to see. He wanted to stand in the actual locations where history was made, to absorb whatever was left of what had been.

"I appreciate this. There aren't any hotels near Walkers Corner, so it'll be great to have somewhere to stay."

"Like I said, this is good." Pete gave her his charming half-grin. "You okay?"

"Perfect." She blew a tiny air-kiss and straightened her jean-clad legs. She flipped down the visor, slid open the mirror, and applied tinted lip balm. She ran her fingers through her unruly brown hair. She needed a haircut. That could wait. "A bit stiff, though."

"From your accident? But you insisted on lifting things last night."

"It was just a fender bender, really." Nothing broken, just bruised. Good thing the car that T-boned her two weeks ago was a small one. "I just slept wrong."

The truth was she'd barely slept at all. Too much on her mind, starting with Pete's unexpected invitation to live together. Did she want that big a commitment? What she faced in Missouri reminded her of how badly she'd screwed up there. Could she make up for it now? Should she take the job in Dallas? Plus, the RV bed was uncomfortable. It'd be worth fixing that before they went camping again. If they did.

"I hope I can find a yoga class tomorrow. I need to work out the kinks or I'll barely be able to walk. I swear, I hit thirty-six and everything started aching. I hate to think what forty's going to feel like."

"Forty's not bad. I feel pretty good."

9

"Oh, my yes, you certainly do." Vicky mock-leered and squeezed his thigh. It was nice and taut. This might be a good time to mention the Dallas job offer, but he was now giving her the full version of the grin that tickled something in her. She didn't want to change the mood. There was already enough to think about.

He passed a small sedan. Even towing her car, they were making good time. "So other than yoga, what's the plan when we get there?"

"Depends. First, get the lay of the land. I'll sign up to help search, connect with whoever's in charge. Get a feel for the town in case I do write about it."

She took a deep breath. "When I worked in St. Louis, I covered a strange story in Walkers Corner, about a little mystery girl. A farmer found her walking alone on a levee, covered with blood, right near where Rose went missing. Middle of nowhere."

She hadn't spoken of that story, even obliquely, in nine years. What if the two cases were connected? Maybe this new little girl wouldn't be missing if Vicky had done her job right all those years ago.

"Which kid are you going to write about?"

"Depends. Maybe both. I'll focus on the places where the crimes happened and how they changed after. A true crime travel article."

The hallmark of Vicky's travel stories was a darker take on places people might like to visit. Well, it wasn't a hallmark yet, since she'd only sold one article, but it would be, once she had something to hang it on. It was still more idea than brand, but she had time, a general plan, and now, a potentially intriguing topic.

Vicky wasn't entirely proud she'd find opportunity in a kidnapping, but this was also the perfect time to follow up on the levee girl mystery and find out, once and for all, whether her actions affected whatever became of little Lisa Dee.

Pete passed an old station wagon. "I checked out Google Earth. It's mostly swamp and wild land outside town. Maybe she just got lost."

"Don't think so. She disappeared from in front of her house."

"Do you think the cops will talk to you?"

"Hope so. It'll be different not working for a news station." Vicky's voice was light, though her lips tightened, and her gut clenched. "It's been a few years, but I still know people."

"Sounds good." Pete didn't seem to notice her disquiet. He was usually attuned to her moods, one of the many things she enjoyed about him. She had never liked so many things in one man before.

Now, however, he apparently had something else on his mind. "There's not a lot to see right around Walkers Corner. I might take a couple of side trips to Civil War sites."

"Good. You should. I'll be busy." Besides, she'd rather not have anyone, not even Pete—or especially not Pete—looking over her shoulder as she poked around in the past.

Her past.

Chapter Three

Rose

Rose opened her eyes to darkness. She closed and reopened them. Still blackness. She held her breath and tried to find something familiar, anything she knew. The air, everything, was heavy. She was sinking, falling, deep into nothingness. Was this real? She screamed but didn't hear anything. Did she even make a sound? Something smelled bad. Was it her? Her arms and legs wouldn't move. She couldn't lift her head. She couldn't feel her body.

Her mind was spinning, contorting wildly but in slow motion, struggling, like wading in thick mud. Was this a bad dream? Was this real? Her insides were boiling, then freezing, about to explode, but something was pressing her chest down, down, down. The darkness was soft when she slipped back into emptiness.

When she woke again, she was on the ground, somewhere dark with one dim light. A darker shape was touching her. Who? What? Rose struggled to get up, to scream, to run, but she couldn't do anything.

Rose felt herself being lifted. A deep voice murmured, "I'm just gonna change your diaper."

Diaper? Why was she wearing a diaper? Where was she? Everything was so heavy. The nothingness welcomed her back as she stopped thinking, wondering, fearing.

Chapter Four

Thursday, November 2008

Vicky's first day in Walkers Corner turned interesting almost immediately. She tapped the screen on her fancy new phone, though she wasn't really reading as she sat alone in the town's only diner. She was too busy eavesdropping on the men in the booth behind her.

"No! That's not what she was doing." One of them had an Upper Midwest accent.

Some might call her nosy. She always considered herself curious, a crucial trait for journalists, though since she wasn't actively working, she'd cut back on tuning in to other people's business.

Mostly. Unless it was happening right behind her, and someone was loud enough to overhear. Could he be talking about the missing girl? Vicky tapped a few words under the name of the deputy who'd taken her name to become a search volunteer. It was so handy to read news and write notes right on the screen without a keyboard. Hard to believe she paid so much for this thing but it sure was a gamechanger.

She'd noticed one of the men when she walked toward him on the way to her booth. He'd leaned back and crossed heavily tattooed arms over his barrel chest. He wore a beat-up baseball cap and a scruffy denim shirt with rolled-up sleeves. When he tilted up his chin, his face was even more battered than his clothes—not from recent injury but from a life lived hard for fifty years or so. He looked tired and pissed off, and definitely didn't like what he was hearing.

Or so she'd imagined. The other guy behind her sounded young. The dividing wall was too tall to see him, but she could hear his fierce whisper. "No, that's not what I mean." Yup, a Minnesota accent. Definitely.

There was a pause. Denim Tattoo Man must be talking but she couldn't hear him. Minnesota Guy said, "No. And what would she be doing there, anyway? She was sneaking around. Acting shady."

Shady? Didn't sound like a missing ten-year-old.

"No. She didn't see me."

More likely they were talking about a neighbor, or an ex, maybe. Vicky finished her salad. She took her time, lingering over her phone and a second cup of coffee. The overworked waiter offered a refill with a wordless gesture. *"C'mon, lady, I need the table."*

Time to leave. Vicky slid from the booth, figuring she'd see Suspicious Minnesota Guy on her way back from the restroom. She straightened her clothes and scratched briefly at the spot on her pants she'd noticed earlier in yoga class.

There was a line for the restroom. By the time she returned, the men were gone, their table cleared, and several sheriff's deputies had settled into the booth. Vicky gave them a small nod on her way out, but no one responded. They appeared exhausted and dead serious. No doubt they'd been searching for the missing Rose, gone four full days now.

Vicky paused to hold the front door open for two sweet, very slow old ladies, who said, "Hello" and

"Thank you, dear." Vicky had plenty of time to re-read the *WHERE'S ROSE?* posters in the window as she returned their greetings.

Outside, she surveyed the street before going around to the side parking lot. No sign of the two men. They hadn't been talking about the missing girl, anyway. Still, it was always interesting to learn why someone would sneak around.

She headed toward her dusty car. No point washing it now. It would just get dirty again when she got to the campground.

She took a quick drive around Walkers Corner. She'd been here only one time nine years ago, and she hadn't stayed long enough to get a good feel for the place. There wasn't much on the surface to make it stand out from other nice little rural towns in the rolling hills of central Missouri. Vicky noted the location of the fire station so she could work that into her walking route. Firefighters usually had a handle on what was going on. She drove by the library. She had high hopes for the chatty librarian she'd met at yoga.

Pete stood near the grill when Vicky arrived at the campground. He'd opened the RV canopy, put a sunshade over the picnic table, and set up chairs around the fire pit. He was in his element traveling by RV and obviously wanted her to like it, too.

He opened his arms, battered outdoor saucepan in one hand, barbeque fork in the other. "Hey. How'd it go?"

Vicky stepped in for a hug and a very welcoming kiss. "Mm. Hi. Great." She gave him a squeeze as he turned toward the grill. "I drove over to the sheriff substation—it's about twenty miles from here—and signed up to help with the search. Scoped out where the girl disappeared. Went to yoga—man, I needed that. Had a salad. How was your day?"

"It was good. I spent most of it setting up camp and getting groceries. So you're not hungry?"

"Not right now, but it wasn't a big salad, so I will be soon. What're you making?"

"Chicken. It'll keep." He set about briskly preparing his starter chimney with paper and charcoal. He once said he used to be a gas grill guy, but now preferred wood or charcoal. He clearly enjoyed the extra time, tools, and attention required to create and care for a fire. The man knew how to take his time and do things right.

Pete happily embraced the tasks built into traveling by RV. He wasn't particularly mechanically inclined—in fact, shortly after they met, he'd joked about missing the fix-it chromosome. He wasn't the guy to rebuild an engine or even change the oil, but he clearly liked planning, organizing, and setting up camp.

Vicky was happy to leave him to it. It was his RV. Besides, she'd done enough planning and organizing to last a lifetime. She had other priorities now.

****

That evening, Vicky glanced around after a few bites of grilled teriyaki chicken and vegetables. "This is really nice. You've been busy."

"I figured we'll be here a few days." He pointed his fork at the *Campground Manager* sign posted in front of a permanent-looking RV at the end of their row. "I met the managers, the Wagners. Beth and Tom. They seem like good people. They sure like to talk."

"I'm glad you picked this place. It's pretty." Only four of the two dozen or so spots were occupied. "I bet it's gorgeous in the spring, when everything's green." The fall color was fading and some of the trees were almost bare. The air was damp and chilly.

She pointed at a giant oak limb looming over a nearby RV. "Seems like a bad idea to park right under that old branch."

"It does," he agreed. "So, are you set with your friend?"

"Kerry James. Yes, we're on for dinner tomorrow."

The two women went way back. They'd been reporters at competing TV stations before they advanced to news management jobs—Kerry in St. Louis, Vicky in other cities.

"You worked together here?"

"In St. Louis. We never worked at the same station at the same time, but we'd see each other on stories and got to be friends. She's from Missouri." Vicky put down her fork. "People stay here. I met more locals in this state than anywhere else I've lived. Once, I asked a gal if she was from here, and she said, 'Oh, gosh, no. I'm from Belleville!' Belleville's just across the river."

"That's normal. You've just moved around more than most people."

"I guess."

Pete picked up his plate and stood. "Are you planning to spend the whole day in St. Louis?"

"Yeah, I'm going to do some research at the downtown courthouse before I meet her."

"How about I drop you there? Then I'll take the car and do some exploring. You can text when you're done with dinner, and I'll pick you up."

"Great, then you can meet Kerry. And on the way, I'll show you where I used to live."

Where she'd lived when everything in her life jumped tracks. Again.

Chapter Five

Kerry James
Friday November 2008

On the hour-plus drive to downtown St. Louis Friday morning, between giving directions and running commentary, Vicky texted and called contacts to set up and confirm her plans for the day.

"Take the next exit." She took them on a detour through Forest Park, site of the 1904 World's Fair, so she could point out The Muny, the outdoor theatre. "It's in the city charter that, quote, 'the last two rows are reserved for those who cannot afford to or are disinclined to pay.' End quote. I love that phrase, and the thinking behind it."

They drove past the TV station where she'd worked, and the sites of a couple of interesting news stories. They got stuck in morning traffic near her old apartment.

"Wasn't this crowded when I lived here."

"It sounds like you liked St. Louis."

"Yes, but I never planned to stay long. I wanted to get back to California."

Pete glanced at her. "So, it was just a step along the way to somewhere else."

Uh-oh. This conversation could too easily swerve to the topic of living together. Not a good time to go there. They'd been seeing each other for months—exclusively, enthusiastically, energetically. Still, she was surprised last week when he floated the prospect of getting a place together. They'd agreed to talk about it later. The ball was in her court, but it wasn't the only one. And she wasn't ready to play.

"Pretty much. That's how it worked out." Vicky gazed out the window. She'd had many second thoughts as she packed her apartment, three floors up in a beautifully restored brick building in the Central West End. Back then, she liked the physical process of moving from one place to another. She enjoyed deciding what to take, what to leave, deploying boxes and bags until she had a separate pile to go in the car, the essential things she wanted to keep right with her.

She'd had a notion once, that shedding non-essentials was like a body protecting itself from freezing, like blood retreating from limbs to protect the core functions, the lungs and brain and heart. She'd rolled her eyes at her contrived analogy.

The famous Gateway Arch framed their route to the courthouse. Vicky pointed out an arrangement of massive, rusted walls of steel. "That's the Serra sculpture. The first time I saw it, I assumed Serra referred to the California missionary. I didn't get what slabs of metal had to do with him or what he had to do with Missouri. Turns out it's the name of the artist."

"Sure. Richard Serra." Pete pulled over at a bus stop. "This okay? Let's call or text later."

They kissed, Vicky hopped out, and Pete headed off to see Smallpox Island, a speck on the Mississippi River where Confederate soldiers with the disease had been taken to die. It was one of the sites on his to-see list. Abraham Lincoln was challenged to a duel there, but the other man backed down when Abe chose the weapons. Sabers. Abe's reach was clearly superior to his much shorter opponent's.

At the courthouse, Vicky met a chatty old friend in the sheriff's department, just to visit and get the inside scoop on the Rose Willwood investigation. Background info. Theories. The cops didn't have much to go on. There were rumors about the aunt who was supposed to be babysitting when the kid disappeared from in front of her house.

Later, Vicky dropped in on a couple of hearings and an attempted murder trial to see who was working. She chatted up a bailiff and a court clerk, pals from her days as a reporter, then headed off to research property records, to find out who owned what near Rose's house. Her stomach burned at how close that was to where the levee girl turned up. One girl lost where another was found. Less than two miles and nine years apart.

****

That evening, Vicky was already seated when her friend walked into the restaurant. Kerry looked great—sharp and confident in a charcoal gray dress, bold belt, and high-heeled boots. Her dark hair was cut short, with bangs falling gracefully to one side. Vicky's disobedient mane would never cooperate like that.

They hugged and exchanged compliments before they slid into the booth. Vicky was glad she'd decided to wear black pants and her dressy sweater instead of her usual hoodie and jeans or yoga pants. These days, she never dressed like she was going to a meeting because, of course, she wasn't.

Vicky tipped her glass. "I'm having chardonnay. Wasn't sure how much time you have so I ordered some spring rolls."

"That sounds great. I'm good for dinner." Kerry caught the waiter's eye and pointed to Vicky's glass, then herself. They dipped into the peanut sauce as they caught up. They hadn't talked in person since before Vicky's divorce three years ago.

Kerry leaned forward. "Tell me all about this guy you're with."

"Pete Harris. I've never liked so much about a man before. He's smart, he's funny, he's even a good listener." Vicky lightly bit her lower lip and raised an eyebrow. "Plus, he has the most beautiful back. I love the way his shoulder blades move."

"Oh, my." Kerry picked up her napkin and mock-fanned herself.

"Exactly. And he's a great cook. He's tidier than me, so I've upped my game there, which I needed to do. Traveling by RV, you have to put things away."

"How long's this trip you're on?"

"Depends. I saw the Amber Alert about the little girl missing in Walkers Corner, and since we were camping anyway, decided to come to Missouri."

"Rose Willwood." Kerry slumped slightly. "She's been missing five days now. We've done a lot— Amber Alerts, stories every newscast, even a live phone bank with the sheriff."

"I'll volunteer if you do another one. I signed up at the sheriff's department to help with the search. The deputy said they'd call, but right now they have all the help they can use."

"Yes, they are well-organized. FBI, helicopters, dogs, tons of ground searchers. They've covered miles around, as far as she could have walked and then some.

They're running out of places to search."

"Heartbreaking. Her poor mom."

Vicky had never had a child, but she'd interviewed enough distraught and grieving parents to feel some of the agony that slashed their lives. She could barely remember her own parents, but whenever she heard about a missing kid, her baby sister's face filled her mind. She tamped down the wave of emotions she always felt about that loss before it could take hold.

"Rose's friend was right there when it happened?" Vicky asked.

"Aaron Dankin. They were riding bikes. He says he got to the end of the block, looked back, but Rose wasn't there. Her bike was on the ground in the cul-de-sac."

"And Rose's aunt was on the porch? Watching her?"

Kerry pursed her lips. "So she says."

"What, you don't believe her? Do the cops?"

"She claims it was just a couple of minutes between when she last saw the kids and when she heard Aaron calling Rose's name. The cops tell me this Sara Willwood is not terribly reliable. Drugs."

"No chance it's a custody thing?"

Kerry shook her head. "Probably not. The birth father hasn't been around since before Rose was born. They weren't married, or at least she uses her maiden name, Willwood. She works at the local diner. They moved to Walkers Corner about a year ago."

"I've seen reports by our friend Rick Carr. He's gotta have good connections, being an ex-cop."

"He hasn't gotten much either."

"Are you glad you hired him?"

Kerry shrugged. "He's a decent reporter and good on air."

"He learned from the best. He sure liked hanging around with us news people." Vicky paused. "I always thought he'd really be something if he'd just tone himself down fifteen or twenty percent. And his clothes? I swear he made detective so he wouldn't have to wear a uniform every day. Remember how he'd strut around with that fancy leather bag?"

"He still carries it." Kerry tilted her head. "I wish I could give him more time to work on Rose, but we need him on other stories, too. We're always understaffed these days."

"We're lucky we were reporters when we were."

They spent a few minutes reminiscing about the days when they could focus on one story at a time. When they didn't worry about budgets and ratings. When pressure from the general manager and corporate were someone else's problem. That's what bosses were for. The good old days, before they became bosses, and the pressure fell on them.

Vicky took a sip and a slow breath. Time to dive into the real reason she'd come back here after all this time. "Rose went missing close to where that other little girl was found on the levee, right?"

"Lisa Dee. Yes, Rose's house is just a couple of miles from the levee."

"Little Lisa Dee. I still think about her."

Nine years before, in 1999, a farmer found a little girl walking out in the middle of nowhere, covered in blood and crying her heart out. At the hospital she couldn't, or wouldn't, say a word. A nurse talked with her, trying out names. The girl just stared at the floor until the nurse said Lisa. The girl looked up for a dazed moment before her eyes glazed over again.

At first, the cops and reporters called her Lisa Doe instead of Jane Doe. Then someone pointed out that while Jane and John Does were unidentified, they were usually dead. That sounded awful for a live little girl, so they changed it to Lisa Dee.

Vicky took another sip. "No one figured out who she was?"

"No. And we never learned anything about where she came from."

"Lisa on the Levee." Vicky used the old newsroom nickname for the story. "Last I heard, she was in a hospital in Chicago."

"As far as I know, she grew up there, in hospitals and foster homes."

Vicky put down her glass. "That story stuck with me. We all just move on when there's nothing new to report. It was just left hanging."

"There's always something new pushing the old stuff back," Kerry agreed. "There's never enough time. But Lisa definitely sticks out."

"I like that about my life now. Having time."

"I bet. It's hard to imagine. So how is it, travel writing? Sorry, I haven't read your stuff yet."

"True crime travel writing. I just started. A magazine published an article I wrote a couple of months ago. The editor said to submit what I write next, and she'll consider it."

"Oh, you're freelancing."

The faint hint of judgment in her voice made Vicky chuckle. "Good thing I don't have to make a living at it."

"I bet it's nothing like TV news."

"That it is not." Vicky loved writing for TV, even under pressure, maybe especially then, when time was measured in seconds and every word counted. "Have you ever written non-news?"

"No. Not really." Kerry paused. "Well, maybe a bit of fiction, a few times, in monthly reports to my boss."

They clinked their glasses. Over their second glass of wine, they got a little gleeful talking about a former news boss they'd both worked for, at different times and stations. His creepy behavior had finally caught up with him.

"Remember how he'd always say, 'fake it 'til you make it'?" Vicky pretended to barf. "And stand too close when you're sitting at your desk?"

Her friend mock-shuddered in disgust. "What an ass. Though I don't think 'fake it 'til you make it' is total BS. It's just the way he said it."

"Exactly. It's not bad to plan how to act. Did I ever tell you about the last time he said it to me?"

"Tell me."

"This was just before I left St. Louis. I tried out for the weekend anchor spot. Did you hear about this?"

"Not from you."

"Uh-oh. I had to talk him into letting me audition. He finally agreed, but it was last-minute, and he acted like he was doing me a big favor. So, I'm heading to the restroom to get ready, and he calls me into his office, supposedly for a pep talk. He starts talking about himself and keeps going on and on. The crew already has barely enough time to fit me in before they have to get ready for the newscast. Guys came by twice saying we needed to get started, but he kept talking and talking and talking, and I was dying to pee."

Kerry chuckled.

"Yeah, and so by the time I got on set, it was starting

to feel fairly urgent." Vicky demonstrated, twisting and fidgeting. "And then there was only like ten minutes left until they had to get to work on the newscast."

Vicky covered her eyes in mock embarrassment. "I don't think I got through a single sentence without messing up. Thank God there's no tape." A friend in editing had erased the only recording of Vicky's awful audition.

"Umm."

"What?"

Kerry chuckled. "You probably shouldn't have called him names."

"I'm trying to read on-camera and he keeps whispering in my earpiece, 'Just fake it and you'll make it.' You saw tape? No way. Tell me you're lying."

"You said he was an effin' faker, and not even good at that."

"Ha! There's no tape. I wasn't wearing a mic then."

Kerry's phone buzzed. "I have to get this." She left the table to take the call.

Vicky finished her wine. Thank God she could end her audition story on a chuckle. It was the most profoundly embarrassing humiliation of her professional life and yeah, she'd been furious and let loose at her boss. It still burned.

"Work. Nothing major." Kerry slid back into the booth. "Hey. I remembered something, after you said that about Rick strutting around with that bag."

"He could be insufferable."

"He wasn't so bad. Don't forget, I hired him. I thought you two might have had a thing going for a while…"

Vicky did her Mona Lisa gaze.

"Anyway. Remember when everyone was staked out near the farmer's place? The one who found Lisa? I forget his name."

"Williams? Wilson?" Vicky frowned slightly. She prided herself on her recall. "He wouldn't let us on his property."

"Wilton? I can't remember." Kerry shrugged. "I got a message on my pager. This was before we all got cell phones. We still used those pagers where you typed out messages—"

"Willets. He found Lisa in May 1999."

"Right. Anyhoo, it was more like garbled notes than a whole message. I thought Rick might have sent it by accident, though he'd never paged info before, just his number. Anyway. I don't remember details…it was like…kitchen… yeah, kitchen. And a name, a woman's name."

"What name?"

"I can't remember now, but I tracked her down at the time. She lived near the levee."

"Did you talk to her?"

"Yes. I tried to find out if that message meant something, but I didn't have much to work with. I asked if she'd seen anything odd, did something happen in her kitchen? She claimed she didn't know what I was talking about, she hadn't reported anything. She was pissed I even knew her name."

"That's it?"

"She finally said a cop was there, asking about the levee girl, and she might have said something out loud without thinking. But it was nothing, just talking to herself."

"Did you ask Rick about it?"

29

"No. It seemed like a dead end. And if he sent it by mistake maybe he'd do it again. I forgot all about it until now."

"Sooo…" Vicky stretched out the syllable. "I don't get it. What's the connection?"

Kerry made a just a sec motion. "This's been bugging me since your snide comment about Rick's bag—"

"Not many guys carried them back then. Especially not cops. We used to call them man-bags, remember? His was reddish leather." Vicky liked detail and had reason to remember what Rick carried. "The handle was carved bone or—"

"I'd forgotten all about this. One just like Rick's was on the porch floor. At first, I thought it was his. Then I got paged someone found Lisa's shoe and took off."

"Really? Could you see what was in it?" A low-level vibration thrummed deep inside as Vicky pictured Rick, his kitchen, his bag. The day her life had changed so completely. If it had something to do with the levee girl…

Kerry shook her head. "No. But it made me think of Rick. And it didn't seem to belong. It was a humble place. The bag was upscale, like his."

They discussed possible explanations for its presence on the porch. Vicky favored the idea it was Rick's, and he had something going on with the neighbor lady. Kerry dismissed that, saying it was a woman's tote, brand new but dirty.

They paused while the waiter delivered two pots of herbal tea and a single fruit torte with two forks.

"By the way, Vick, you didn't answer me about whether you had a thing with him."

30

"You didn't put it in the form of a question." Vicky shook her finger in a mock scold. "I wouldn't call it a thing." She poured a taste of tea to see if it was ready, then put the pot down. "Talking about his bag reminds me. I should tell you something about Rick, from back then, but it doesn't feel entirely right, since he works for you."

"He didn't work for me then. He wasn't even in news."

"Still. I would have told you this before you hired him, but I'd already left Missouri." Vicky briefly reexamined her motive for telling his boss now. Surely it wasn't because he had humiliated Vicky so thoroughly. No. It could be relevant now.

Kerry's gaze was direct and serious.

Vicky picked up her teacup. "It might have been important."

"Just tell me."

"Okay. His bag." Vicky swirled her tea before she continued. "This was when he lived in town, out by me. It was the same evening, right after my nightmare of an audition. I was pretty upset. I stopped at a liquor store on my way home."

She went on a brief tangent to grouse about Missouri's blue laws back then, when you couldn't buy anything but wine and beer in grocery stores, and not even that on Sundays until after noon. You had to stock up on trips to the liquor store. Sometimes it looked bad.

She described the encounter nine years ago. Rick wore jeans and a sweatshirt. His shoulders were slumped. "You know how shopping's a good time to think because it's okay to stand and stare? But he stood there longer than usual, not picking anything up."

Kerry listened intently, not moving. Vicky paused, wanting to be careful. It could be wearying, remembering and deciding what to share.

"I said, 'Hi, Rick,' and he jumped. He looked awful, like he'd been doing some serious drinking."

"What'd he say?"

"You know him, he always wants to make a good impression. He was friendly, acted normal. But he was sad. It sounds like an old country western song, but he had to put his dog down that afternoon. Long story short, we went to his place, had drinks, and talked for hours."

"About what?"

"His dog. The area. Our histories."

"And?"

"Bear with me, I'm getting to his bag. We sat on his porch drinking whiskey. He was drinking hard. I was sipping."

It was a painful memory, the kind she could recall with clarity but usually chose not to. They'd sat on Rick's front porch on two shabby wood chairs placed side by side, facing a crate used as a table and footstool. Rick cracked open the bottle and took a deep swig. "Ahhh. Like they say, 'Smooth as Silk.'" He passed the whiskey to Vicky, who sipped a small taste and shuddered slightly.

"I'm more the white wine type, but I remember it left a nice little burn. I think it was the last time I drank straight from the bottle." Vicky was stalling. And this was the easy part.

"His new bottle was half gone by the time he told me about when he first got his dog, back when he was in high school. She was a new puppy. Margie? Maggie, I think. Anyway, he'd just gotten her. He was out with his dad, who was seriously pissed off about something."

"Was he sheriff then?"

"Yes. Rick said they were at someone's cabin, a shack really. Rick let Maggie run around while the sheriff was inside. He could hear him yelling. Then he stormed out and hauled off and kicked Maggie like a football. She hit a tree. Broke her leg."

"How awful."

"She limped her whole life. I said it must have been hard, having her put to sleep. He said he shot the old dog to put her out of her misery."

They both shuddered slightly.

"Rick said"—Vicky made her voice gruff— "'Pa never said sorry for nothing.' But he had that bag when he came out and gave it to Rick when they got home. He said it's the only thing his father gave him that he's kept."

"That's a weird story. Why worry about telling it to me?"

"There's more. I'm trying to remember this exactly. It was a long time ago. Rick said he'd been at the cabin before, when he was a kid. He was pretty well smashed when he told me this. He was with his father and…I want to say the caretaker maybe… anyway, a man and his son. Yeah, caretaker. The son was older, a teenager. The men drove off and left the boys.

"The older kid took off into the woods and Rick followed him. I remember he said the guy was like a ghost. He could barely keep up. They stopped at a clearing where his dad's SUV was parked next to a cargo truck. Rick was scared because there were men with rifles or shotguns, long guns, like guards. People were carrying things from the truck into a big house."

Kerry sipped her tea, watching Vicky intently.

"Anyway, I asked what he thought was going on, but Rick changed the subject and got up. We went inside to get a drink of water. I happened to see a document next to his bag. A state grand jury subpoena for a case involving his father."

"Happened to see?"

"Hey, it was out on the table. Had to do with illegal distribution. I didn't see of what. Anyway, Rick was pissed." Vicky skipped over the humiliating part about how he rejected her.

"What'd you find out about it?"

"That's the thing. Nothing. I should have, but I didn't follow up." Vicky paused. The familiar surge of guilt tapped from under the surface. She might have been the only one—besides Rick—who knew about both the cargo truck and the grand jury investigation. And she was certainly the only one who also saw what she saw two nights later, in the bed of a pickup in front of his house.

"It was right before I left for Texas. We all know an investigation can stall out and die if no one cooperates and no one's reporting on it. Or maybe there was nothing to it. I don't know. But Rick knew the state was investigating the sheriff. His dad."

"Did you ask him about it?"

"A couple days later but only briefly. He wouldn't talk about it."

"So you're saying he knew his dad was into something dirty."

"He had to suspect it. He had the subpoena, and he remembered the cargo truck from when he was a kid. I think he didn't want to know too much that might touch on his old man."

Vicky paused to let that sink in. "Which is something I would want to know about my lead reporter, when his father was sheriff for thirty years."

With both hands on her teacup, Kerry leaned forward, her voice serious and very intense. "What are you thinking?"

Vicky would be equally concerned if she learned this about a key news employee. Was it right for her to talk about this? Was it ethical? Well, it was true. Was she violating his privacy? No. He'd told her the stories, and she saw what she saw. Would this hurt him with his boss, professionally? Maybe. But a child is missing. Everything's on the table.

"I'm thinking Rose was kidnapped close to where Lisa was found on the levee. I know it's a stretch, but they might be related. And it sounds like there was some crooked shit going on, at least at one time. And I think Rick knows something about it, or at least suspects."

Vicky clenched her fists. "Don't you want to know what the sheriff was up to? Grand jury documents were secret. I should have followed up. At least passed the tip along. The state probably didn't find enough and dropped the whole thing. Did anyone check out that property when Lisa turned up on the levee? Where the boys spied on their dads. That sure sounded suspicious."

Chapter Six

Walkers Corner, May 1999

The girl woke up in darkness, to the sound of water running. Mama must be getting ready to take a bath. Then everything in her screamed, "No!" The air was wrong, thick with cold and terrifying smells. Where was she? She couldn't move.

"Mama? Mama?" she whispered.

She opened her eyes wide but there was only blackness. Not even a hint of light. Her arms and legs wouldn't move. The only sound was her heart pounding, banging like a crazy drummer. She was so thirsty.

What happened? How did she get to this strange place? She tried to remember where she was before. When she and Mama were together. She couldn't think. Her mind was empty except for shadows of fear and terror.

She called out loud, "Mama?"

It was so, so dark. She struggled to sit up, to twist to one side, then the other. Her body wouldn't move. Nothing. Something held her arms tight against her body. Her legs were stuck together. She couldn't feel her feet.

"Mama! Mama? Where are you?" She screamed with all her might. "Mama! Help me!"

She paused to listen but heard only the echo of her terror and the pounding of her heart. She shivered, sobbing. She wanted her mama and the steam in the bathroom, and all the good smells in the kitchen and the familiar things in her room.

"Help! Help me. Is anyone there?" She shrieked until her throat felt coated with broken glass. She could barely breathe. "Mama. Please. Mama," she whispered before she surrendered to the darkness.

Chapter Seven

Walkers Corner, Saturday, November 2008

While Pete drove away from the campground, Vicky relaxed in the passenger seat, enjoying the Saturday morning sunshine and scenery.

"Pete, if you come across anything I might want for my article, let me know, okay?"

He took one hand off the wheel to gently touch her thigh. "Sure, I'd be happy to, if you'll take notes about any good fishing spots."

That was fair, and the end of their little bargain. Pete's plan for the day was to see the Cahokia Mounds, just across the Mississippi in Illinois. He'd told her about the ancient settlement. Archeologists believe that about a thousand years ago, in the 1100s, it was home to as many as twenty thousand people, more than the population of London at the time. When Europeans showed up in the 1600s, they named it after the Cahokia people who lived in the area.

Vicky planned to spend the day finding talkative, knowledgeable locals. She would work her way into the community so she could help find Rose. That, and follow up on the levee girl. Then write about it, maybe.

She pointed toward an intersection. "There's good."

Pete pulled over next to the road that led to Main Street, Walkers Corner. They agreed where to meet later, exchanged a quick kiss, and she set off walking.

She enjoyed the brisk autumn air as she checked out yards and houses and the occasional business. She liked seeing how people lived and worked. So far, Walkers Corner appeared to be a perfectly nice little midwestern town.

A few blocks from downtown, she paused to admire the library, which graced a large corner lot. The brick building stood on a slight rise, with low wide steps inviting visitors to enter. On one of several benches strategically placed under nearly bare trees, two children and a woman huddled together with a book. Behind them was a small playground. A library playground. What a great idea. How long have they been doing that?

Inside, a large *WHERE'S ROSE?* poster dominated the entryway bulletin board, featuring what looked like her school photo. She wore a big, mischievous grin and a flowery blouse that picked up the bright green of her eyes. Her dark hair fell below her shoulders. The poster was a sad addition to the typical schedules and announcements. There was also a photo gallery of dozens of people at library events. Nice touch. Vicky tucked that away in case she ever wrote about this place.

She immediately spotted the librarian, her new yoga buddy, standing across a counter from a bearded young man with a phone to his ear. "Hi, Liz Ann, right? I'm Vicky. We met at yoga? You said you could help with my research?"

Liz Ann squeezed her shoulder. "Of course I know who you are. Welcome! This is George. He's the one who really runs the place."

George smiled and rolled his eyes at his boss as he pointed to the phone. Vicky mouthed "nice to meet you."

Liz Ann tugged at her. "Let me show you around. I'm so glad you came."

She took Vicky on a tour of the library. She chatted about upcoming events as she zipped around, greeting patrons by name. She was a petite powerhouse in a gorgeous emerald-green sweater, black leggings, and boots, graying black hair cut stylishly short. Glasses hung from a sparkly chain tangled around a bold black pendant on a leather cord. She talked fast, but with a distinct southern accent.

"Oh, one sec, darlin'." Liz Ann went to a woman dressed in a traditional Catholic nun's habit—long robe, headpiece, the works. When she returned, Liz Ann said, "She's from a convent school near here. It's about a hundred years old. We work with the kids."

"It's been a while since I've seen a nun in full regalia." Vicky touched Liz Ann's arm. "By the way, I love your sweater. That shade of green is so pretty. Are you from here?"

"Oh, dear, no. I'm from Savannah, Georgia. I've been here almost twelve years now." She launched into a rapid-fire account of how she'd come to be head librarian in Walkers Corner, Missouri. "I love it here. The people are terrific, though unfortunately, my dear, there just aren't very many interesting single men."

"Lucky for me I'm not in the market at the moment." Vicky chuckled. "I hope you don't mind me saying I have never heard a southern accent spoken so fast."

"Oh, mah child." Liz Ann drawled it out to seven long, soft syllables. "I just always have so much to say. This is my office."

The small room was filled with artwork, plants, and neat shelves of books. It smelled faintly of something fresh and clean, maybe jasmine. Liz Ann led the way past her desk to two armchairs angled at a large window, next to a small table on which sat a low vase containing chrysanthemums.

Vicky stood at the window. "This is so pretty. My gosh, nice view." Even readied for winter the landscaping was beautiful.

"It's lovely, isn't it? That's all George. He and the garden club do it all. So how can I help you?"

"If you have time, I have a few questions about the area. History, industry, that sort of thing…"

Liz Ann was already nodding.

"And maybe some juicy gossip?"

"My specialty." Liz Ann arched an eyebrow. "It's fine. I'd love to help."

****

By the time Vicky left the library, she had a pretty good idea of the town layout, history, government, and what people did for a living. Liz Ann was a wellspring of local information. The whole community was traumatized by Rose's disappearance. Liz Ann said she, like everyone, was terrified someone could just come along and snatch a child. Such a bright little girl. She and her mom have been here about a year now. They come to the library every week and were big fans of magician stories.

Vicky slowed to read a sign on a snaggle-toothed fence fronting a small house. *Ted's Tackle 'n Tie*. It appeared Ted's fishing gear business took him away from yard and house maintenance. Weeds grew high around a dented aluminum boat perched upside down on blocks near the porch.

The sign reminded Vicky of Pete talking about bass

fishing on the trip out here. She'd found it endearing he got so animated on the subject of lures. He'd gone into considerable detail about how a good lure looked natural and believable.

"Bass are predators. You want your lure to be their prey."

He drove mostly with one hand while he used the other to describe lures shaped like insects or crawfish or smaller fish. Vicky didn't know much about fishing. She'd always assumed it took more patience than she normally had, but Pete made it sound strategic and kind of exciting.

"If you know what the fish are chasing, you can pick a lure that resembles something already on the menu. You can fit your lure to the fish's attitude. Is it hungry? Aggressive? Then a faster, noisier lure might work. When they're passive, you might try something quieter." He'd paused and glanced at her. "Is this boring?"

"No, not at all. It's like figuring out how to get someone to tell you something." It made complete sense. Bait mattered for both fish and people. Same principle. Vicky's mind had bounced around, wondering what might motivate people in Walkers Corner to talk.

Pete had fallen silent and kept driving, probably thinking about fishing.

****

A few blocks from the library, Vicky approached the Walkers Corner Volunteer Fire Department. Under the sign's faded red letters, the big vehicle door stood open. A man sat out front, his chair tipped back against the brick wall. Perfect. As Vicky swerved toward him, he dropped the front legs down.

"Morning!" Vicky was at her cheerful best.

"Morning." He leaned forward to get up.

"Oh, please, don't get up on my account." Vicky waved him back down, but he stood up anyway. He wore jeans, heavy boots, and a battered camo jacket, which bulked up his already sizeable frame. He took off his cap to reveal frizzled gray hair, a crinkled face, and scruffy beard. He had to be in his seventies. He didn't appear to be the fittest of firemen, but then, this was a volunteer station.

She put out her hand. "Hello. My name's Vicky Robeson. I'm staying at the Wagners' RV park."

"Don Winters." He took her hand and gave it a good shake. "How're you?"

"Just great, thanks. Do you have a minute? I have a quick question."

"Yes, ma'am."

"Do you happen to know what kind of tree that is?" She pointed across the road at a tree with vivid red leaves.

"That there's a sassafras tree. People used to make tea from the bark. Maybe some still do. Supposed to be good for all kinds of things, but it's poisonous if you take too much."

Awesome. A talker. Vicky liked talkative people, assuming they were interesting and knowledgeable. One of the best things about working in television news was access to experts and good reasons to ask questions.

They stood side by side in front of the station gazing at the sassafras tree. Vicky put her hands in her back pockets. "Well, it sure is pretty. Doesn't look dangerous."

"People used to grind up the bark to thicken soups, too."

"That's interesting." Vicky meant it. She gestured at the station. "Do you work here?"

"Well, I used to, but with my bad knees I cain't do much anymore, just a few chores around the station. Keep an eye on things."

"That's got to be a big help. Are you from here?"

"Born and raised and expect to die here."

Vicky chuckled with him. "Then I bet you know as much as anyone about the area."

"Likely more than most."

"Great. I'm working on an article for a travel magazine."

"Is that a fact? What about?"

"It's a work in progress." No need to telegraph her plans without reason. "Would you have a few minutes to help me with a little background?"

"I'd be right happy to try. Here, let me get you a chair. Would you like some coffee?"

"Absolutely." Vicky followed him into the station. There was just room enough for one small fire truck and a pickup. Equipment, coats, and helmets hung neatly on the walls.

Don led the way to a small kitchen and seating area. He poured two cups of coffee and handed one to Vicky, then picked up a chair, carried it outside, and set it down next to his.

They settled in for a nice chat, beginning with the usual comments about the weather. Don appeared to be one of those natural talkers who didn't often have anyone who wanted to listen. Vicky used one of her favorite starters. "What can you tell me about Walkers Corner? How was the town started?"

Don grinned. "I don't go back that far."

Vicky grinned back. "I checked the archives at the county building and library. I couldn't find much on Walker, other than a death notice in a ledger from the 1880s."

"Why'd you do that?"

"I like looking at original records."

"People back then were too busy getting by to write much down. Mebbe notes in a bible."

"Everyone I've met so far seems nice."

"There's no reason not to be. It's a fine place to live."

"I see a lot of people volunteering to search for the little girl who's missing."

"Most all of us know each other. The girl and her mama been here, must be ten, twelve months now. Rita works at the diner."

They spent several minutes speculating about the disappearance of little Rose Willwood. Don was of the opinion it had something to do with family. "I reckon her daddy took her. How long you in town for?"

"A few days. It's so terrible, not knowing what happened to her."

"That it is. Well, plenty of good things going on round here, too." Don spoke enthusiastically about this year's soybean crop, then proceeded to tell a few stories about the ups and downs of his hometown, how it never quite got over the textile mill and glass factory shutting down, the starts and stops of other businesses.

"Does the news cover any of that?"

"No, we're not big enough." He paused. "But 'bout nine, ten years ago, a strange thing, we had a little girl turn up, walking out in the middle of nowhere, no idea where she came from. News people were here for that."

Perfect. "On the levee? I was one of them. Lisa Dee. I was a reporter at a TV station in St. Louis."

"You don't say?" Don briefly re-examined her, then asked which station she'd worked for. He said the fella who did the weather there did the best job. Some of those kids on the other stations didn't even know how to pronounce names right.

"There's one reporter, used to be a deputy. He grew up around here. I worked some with his pa, the old sheriff."

"You mean Rick Carr? I know him. He worked on the Lisa case."

"That's him. Rick does a good job. One of the few TV people anymore who knows what he's talking about. You friends with him?"

"Haven't seen him in almost ten years. Where do you think little Lisa came from?"

"Nobody knows. Mebbe someone just dropped her off, like some people dump a dog they don't want no more. No one ever showed up looking for her. Never heard who she was."

"You don't think she could have been a local? Someone's kid nobody knew about?"

"It's possible, I suppose." Don sounded skeptical. "But a bunch of us was talking when TV was showing her picture. She didn't look like nobody 'round here."

Vicky's insides froze. In that picture, Lisa Dee had looked exactly like Vicky's lost little sister. Same curly jet-black hair, cute little chin, and big, scared eyes. She could never think of one without thinking of the other. The photo was everywhere back then, and it stabbed her heart every single time she saw it.

Not a good time to dwell on that.

"Did you help search for her family?" Vicky made her voice sound casual, though she'd always wondered how thorough the search had been. It wasn't like a lost child. Lisa was a *found* child.

"Sure, we all helped." Don sat up a little straighter. "We searched everywhere but never found any sign of where she come from, other than her shoe near the levee. Or might've been her sweater. Sad thing, that little girl. Why're you so interested?"

"I've always wondered what happened. So strange. What's out there now, where she was found?"

"The Willets place? Not much has changed. Joe runs about eight hundred acres of soybeans. Does all right with it. It's not all his land, most he rents from a couple of neighbors. Not much out there 'cept fields and the levee, a creek, couple houses."

"Someone was telling me there used to be a lot of moonshining around here during Prohibition."

"Oh? What'd they have to say about that?" There was a hint of wariness in Don's voice.

"Just that. An old guy at the courthouse told me it was big all over Missouri."

Don seemed reassured. "There might've been some home cooking."

"Bootlegging?"

"Oh, yes, ma'am." Don sounded wistful. "My daddy had some wild stories to tell."

They paused to watch a car slowly pass the sassafras tree. The driver, an old guy like Don, looked at the two of them sitting side by side in front of the station. He lifted his hand at Don, who returned the greeting, as did Vicky. Don was no doubt already eager to tell his buddy all about his visitor. She could imagine them speculating about what she was up to.

"Where'd you say you're from?" he asked.

"I live in Colorado." For now. "Different kind of landscape. I remember there being a lot of wild land out by the levee."

"Yes, ma'am, still is, but it's mostly off-limits now. Feds claim it's theirs. Used to be, people come from all over to hunt. Even had a nice place they could stay. Good business. That's done with now, some damn guv'mint wildlife thing."

Before that train of thought gathered steam, Vicky jumped in. "What was it, like a hotel? Is it abandoned?"

"Hunting lodge. Not abandoned, just not used anymore. There's a fella keeps an eye on things." Don's lips pursed. "Anyway, those days are gone."

Hunting lodge. Caretaker? Hadn't Rick mentioned following the caretaker's son? "Where Lisa was found, out by the levee, that's not far from where Rose went missing, is it?"

"'Bout two miles, I'd say." Don launched into a rambling road map of what was between the two locations. There wasn't much, but he milked it for several sentences.

"Anyone still live there, who was around when Lisa showed up?"

"They're all still there. Willets, Becks, the old Miller place." Conveniently, Don seemed happy to think out loud as he ran through who'd lived where and for how long, where somebody's daddy used to make moonshine, who used to work where.

"What kind of work did your daddy do?" he asked.

"Oh, various things." Vicky didn't know and didn't want to talk about herself. She needed to write down her mental notes. "Well, I've taken up enough of your time." But another quarter hour flew by before Vicky shook his hand goodbye.

She resumed her walk. Old people with time on their hands could be regular fountains of information. As she strode along the edge of the road, she reviewed her chat with Volunteer Firefighter Don. He was interesting enough to get a title in her short-term memory filing system.

****

Vicky had timed her day so it was mid-afternoon when she arrived for her second visit to Sam's Corner Table Café. That tended to be a productive time to go to restaurants. The food was sometimes tired, and the staff almost certainly was, but people often had more time and more inclination to talk.

Two SUVs bearing the logos of the local county sheriff's department drove out of the parking lot as she entered the diner. Sam's could hold several dozen diners, but the only customers sat at a table near the window— a nicely dressed older couple who might be having afternoon pie.

A young woman with spiky, dyed-blonde hair was carrying a tray of dishes toward the kitchen. Tall and wiry, she wore an apron over jeans. Her sleeveless top revealed an elaborate floral tattoo on a well-toned right bicep. "Hi, have a seat." She gestured with her elbow toward the area near the couple. "I'll be right with you."

Vicky smiled at the couple as she passed them. They sat on the same side of the table and were indeed eating pie. She chose a stool at the end of the counter where she could turn to face the room. The menu was computer-printed, one two-sided page slipped into a plastic sleeve.

She pulled it from its niche between the hot sauce and napkin holder and studied it.

A moment later, the woman returned with a coffee pot. She stopped by the couple's table. They chatted a moment before she headed toward Vicky.

"Hi. Coffee?" She appeared even younger up close.

"Yes, please. And some water."

"You got it. I'll be right back. By the way, we're out of the soup special."

Vicky took her time fixing her coffee and reading the menu. The couple stood up slowly. They held onto each other as they walked to the door. The woman was tiny and looked frail, so Vicky didn't expect her to holler in a surprisingly robust voice. "Bye, Sam! We'll see you next time."

Ah. Vicky gave herself a mental scold for assuming a man owned the place.

"Great, see you soon." Sam waved to them on her way back to Vicky. She set down a glass of water. "What can I get you?"

Vicky ordered a turkey sandwich with a side salad. As she waited, she read a brief history about the café on the back of the menu. A couple from Springfield, Illinois, Phil and Jennie Hanford, opened it back in the sixties, using her mother's favorite recipes. Sam Dumain took over the café in 2006, and still prepares many of the original dishes.

If she did include the restaurant in a travel story, Vicky would describe it as a traditional rural Missouri diner, with homemade biscuits and chicken fried steak on the menu. Some of the furniture might be original. Style had not been the builder's priority, which was probably a good thing. Some styles hold up better than others. This style was sturdy.

Someone had poured a lot of heart into the café, without spending much money. Talent and determination came to mind as part of a description. The colors were strong—interesting combinations of soft mauve and golden orange, bold red and muted sage, set against black accents. The mismatched wooden chairs were made comfortable with simple cushions. Nothing overdone.

The corner table that gave Sam's diner its name made Vicky wish she knew seven people here to share a meal with.

Sam bumped through the swinging door, cleared a large table on the other side of the diner, and carried the trayful of dishes into the kitchen. The door had barely stopped moving when she was back with Vicky's order.

"Thanks. I heard her call you Sam." Vicky picked up her fork. "This is your place?"

"Yes. For almost two years now."

"Did you do the design? I like the window treatments."

Sam exuded a slight air of 'Damn right, I did.' "Thanks. It was a lot of work. I'm glad you like it."

"Nice. Nothing fussy. Contemporary comfort." Vicky waited a beat. "You seem young to own a restaurant."

Sam shrugged. Early twenties at most, no makeup on her pale, unlined face. Below unplucked brows, her clear brown eyes were intelligent and sharp. A shadow of dark roots showed under her short, white-blonde spikes.

But she acted efficient and confident, and seemed older. Vicky used to be like that. Behave like you're knowledgeable, responsible, and in charge, and people automatically add a few years.

Vicky added, "I like the name. Sam's Corner Table Café. A little play on the town name?"

"Hm."

"Walkers Corner. Corner Table."

"Hmm. Can I get you anything else?"

"No, thanks. But can I ask you something?"

Sam tilted back on her heels. "Go ahead."

Vicky launched into her spiel. "My name's Vicky Robeson. I write for a travel magazine about interesting places, off the beaten path."

"Around here?"

"Mmhm. Just trying to find a few things to say about the area. Any ideas?"

"Sure. It's off the beaten path and not very interesting."

Vicky chuckled. "That's funny. I might've heard that before."

Sam smiled and pivoted away. "I'll think about it. Be right back." She cleared and wiped the old couple's table, then bumped the kitchen door open with her hip, moving smoothly with the fluidity of repetition, no motion wasted. She didn't have her tray when she returned. She poured herself a cup of coffee and leaned against the counter, facing Vicky.

"I asked the cook. We have a few caves near here, but nothing famous. There're better ones to the south. There's one near Bonne Terre where people go to scuba dive."

"Any famous battles take place here? Discoveries? Outlaw hideouts?"

"Not that I know of." Sam shrugged. "Not much

happens around here."

"I heard about that little girl gone missing. Anything new on that?"

Sam's eyes closed tightly, briefly. "No."

Vicky waited in hopes Sam would mention the girl's mother worked for her. She didn't. Vicky said, "A couple of sheriff's cars were leaving when I got here. Do you also have a police department?"

"No, the county sheriff handles things." Whatever warmth Sam had reluctantly revealed before dissipated.

Time for a detour. "This must be so hard for everyone. I was just wondering, is Walkers Corner an actual town?"

Sam's gaze didn't change, but Vicky could almost feel her thinking, 'You idiot? Haven't you heard of the Internet?' She was right. Waste of a question chip. Vicky sometimes felt a bit foolish asking basic questions, but she liked hearing the range of responses. People were often eager to educate the outsider. It was interesting when she already knew an answer and a local gave a different one.

Sam took a sip of coffee. "Technically, we're a township."

Vicky scanned her memory for details about Missouri's many forms of local government. "I was just wondering, since it's small but there's a library and post office."

Vicky had already thoroughly cased out downtown. It had the makings of a good spot for drivers to stretch their legs, pop into a shop, or have a cup of coffee. Some of the businesses on the main drag were either trying too hard to be appealing or had given up completely. Walkers Corner had its charms, though with a subtle tinge of desperation around the edges.

"You have a nice downtown. And I love your café." Vicky asked about the local economy. She inquired about agriculture, even though she knew darn well those were soybeans being harvested. And no, Sam couldn't think of any particularly interesting craftspeople.

Sam's laconic responses made it clear that, while the Lisa-found and Rose-lost stories might make Walkers Corner interesting from the true crime standpoint, it could be a challenge to appeal to readers mostly interested in travel. But every place had a story to be told. She just had to find it.

Maybe she could write something about small downtowns over-folksifying to appeal to tourists. Cute can be charming. Trying too hard can be a little sad.

A woman entered the diner. She wore sunglasses, old jeans, and a sweatshirt. Her shoulders slumped, brown hair drooped. She walked toward them.

"Rita! I didn't expect to see you today." Sam opened her arms and hugged the woman, who slowly returned the embrace.

Rita. This had to be the missing girl's mother.

"Hi, Sam. I'm sorry." Rita spoke softly, her voice hoarse. "Thanks for the check, but I'm not ready to come back to work. Not while Rose is still missing."

"Of course not, Rita. You stay out as long as you need to."

"I'll quit if you want."

"Hush. No. You come back when Rose is home safe and sound." Sam's voice cracked. "She'll be back soon, I just know it."

Vicky sat two feet from the sobbing women. Her heart swelled with agony for them.

They stepped apart, and Sam reached past Vicky to get napkins. She handed one to Rita before she dried her own eyes. "Vicky, this is Rita Willwood. Vicky's here writing a travel article."

"I'm so sorry about your daughter."

"Travel? Here? There's nothing to write about." Rita dried her eyes without removing her sunglasses. "Good luck. Nice to meet you. Sam, I'll be in touch, okay?"

They hugged again before Rita left. On her way to the kitchen Sam waved to Vicky. "I've got to get back to work. Good talking with you."

****

That evening, Pete and Vicky sat across their fire pit from Tom and Beth Wagner. It was Vicky's idea to invite the campground managers to dinner, to get to know them a little better, thank them for all the recommendations, and follow up on a few things Kerry had mentioned the night before. Vicky made the sides and Pete grilled the delectable pork chops.

Tom had been caught behind an accident that afternoon when a truck rolled and spilled its load. "There were chickens squawking all over the place. The road was covered with feathers and guts and dead birds."

"He took that curve too fast." Beth sounded certain. She and her husband were the kind of couple who, after thirty or so years together, appeared designed as one unit, to fit together comfortably in sweatshirts and jeans, beers in hand.

"Or the truck might not have been loaded right," Pete added, "and the load shifted."

They spent a few minutes discussing other interesting accidents. Vicky said, "When I was a rookie news manager, a TV engineer and I were talking about a plane crash, somewhere in North Carolina, I think." She outlined the preliminary findings: foggy morning, wrong runway, new lighting system.

"Anyway, I said, 'If the runway guy had been on time it wouldn't have happened.' And the engineer says, 'Yeah, or if someone told the pilot they changed the lights, or the regular pilot was flying. It'll be in the accident chain report.' He could tell I didn't know the term. He explained how investigators methodically examine all possible factors—weather, mechanical systems, people—and trace back to where the accident started, where something happened, or someone could have intervened."

"It's a clear way of thinking, done right," said Pete.

"I started trying to think that way, about why things started to happen, not just what happened when they did."

It certainly wasn't an original concept, that one needs to know the past to understand the present. But for years, Vicky had kept herself too busy to think much about her personal history. But here, now, she had a chance to learn whether she was a link in the chain of events that led to Rose Willwood's disappearance.

"Can I get anyone a cold one?" Pete's offer of another round of beers was unanimously accepted.

After he resettled in his chair, Vicky said, "I knew a nun once who would have been great at that job."

"Wait." Beth held up her hand. "What job?"

"Ha. Sorry, I sometimes forget people aren't jumping around in my head with me. Accident chains. This one nun I had as a teacher, she could find out what happened with anything. She wasn't mean, but she could get almost anyone to spill everything."

"Almost?" Beth drew out the word to make it sound suggestive.

"Not me. I didn't get in much trouble." Vicky paused a beat. "At the time. But they didn't know what I was thinking."

Beth laughed and leaned over to tap bottles with Vicky.

"Sister—I can't remember her name—she was good at explaining things." Vicky paused. "There was another nun who was just the opposite. Once I asked in her class why people yawn. She said, 'because they're sleepy,' like I didn't know. She got irritated when I asked the follow up, why that particular action. It was obvious she didn't know."

"Wait." Pete leaned forward. "You went to Catholic school?"

"Just for a couple of years. Long enough to learn a lot of rules." Vicky chuckled. "Once, a kid who was up at the chalkboard thumbtacked that nun's headpiece to her chair. It almost came off when she stood up. It was hilarious. Who's ready for some ice cream?"

****

After dessert, with everyone suitably loosened up, Vicky got to her main goal for the evening. After Kerry said the bag on the porch was just like Rick Carr's, Vicky had decided to track down its owner. Between property records she'd noted at the courthouse and the names Firefighter Don mentioned, it wasn't hard to identify where Kerry had seen it. There only a few properties anywhere near where Lisa was found on the levee, and they hadn't changed hands in decades.

"Beth, do you happen to know someone named Joan

Beck?"

"Joan Beck." Beth folded her arms across her ancient blue sweatshirt as she tilted her head and gave Tom a significant look. "Joan Beck. We know her. Or knew her, anyway."

"Hmm. I take it you don't particularly like her?"

Beth picked up her beer. "Maybe she wasn't all bad." She settled back and lifted her bottle. "But her family! What a mess. I felt sorry for her."

Tom spoke up. "Who're we talking about? Bill's sister?"

"Yeah, Joan. She was a couple years behind us." Beth said they'd gone all through school with the Becks, or their sibs or cousins had, but it was hard to keep everyone straight sometimes, thirty-odd years later, even if you'd lived near them all your lives.

One story led to another. Beth's brother used to run around with Joan's older brother, Bill Junior, until Bill left with that gal who moved back to Colorado. Bill got himself killed driving drunk a few years back. He was a lousy driver even when he was sober, which wasn't often.

"Bill and his pa and their bunch were always drinking or fighting or stealing something," said Tom.

"And drugs. Dealing and doing drugs. There was bad history in the Beck family." Beth sounded indignant. "Her dad drowned a puppy because it peed on his shoe. Remember?"

Tom scowled. "I saw him do it, right in front of us kids. With his bare hands, in a bucket. He was an asshole."

He told the rest of the story, with Beth throwing in color commentary and occasional corrections. Joan

Beck's father was, by all accounts—or at least according to Tom and Beth—a vile drunk who abused everyone in his family, a mean man who never held a regular-paying job as far as anyone knew. Joan's mother worked at the diner and took in laundry to make ends meet.

When Joan was still in high school, her father took off. Up and left her and Harriet, her mom, without a word about where he was going. He left his pickup the next town over. Most everyone figured good riddance.

After several minutes of Beck family stories and rumors, Beth asked, "Why are you asking about her, anyway?"

Vicky waved her hand vaguely. "I had dinner with a friend who mentioned something about a woman who lived out by the levee." No need to mention the bag on the porch. "I did a little research and found her name. So, what was Joan like?"

"She was a loner," Beth said. "Not friendly at all. Smart, but no one expected her to turn out any different than the rest of her family. I'm not sure she even graduated, did she?"

Tom drank his beer. "Don't remember."

Beth shook her head. "That whole family was a train wreck. Her poor mom died of cancer. Such a hard life. Joan's practically a hermit, still living in the old house, out by Miller Creek. I think she's the only Beck left."

"And that's a good thing." Tom tilted back to finish his beer. "By the way, yawning's got something to do with your brain needing oxygen." He opened his mouth in exaggerated drowsiness. "Right now, mine needs some sleep."

****

After dinner cleanup, Pete and Vicky settled in to

watch a movie. Vicky was comfy in pajamas, under the blankets. Pete shuffled through a stack of DVDs while Vicky recapped the day.

"Interesting what the Wagners had to say about the Becks. Don, the firefighter, mentioned them, too. He's a talker. I loved the guy. He said his pa used to tell stories about running moonshine."

"I bet there was a lot of that around here."

"Supposedly he and his buddies ran booze to half the state, they had a regular distribution system set up."

"Hmm."

"I asked what happened to the setup after Prohibition was over, and he grins at me kinda sideways and says, 'There's always something needs moving.' Then he gets all coy and won't say anymore. It was like he was enjoying a bad-boy moment. Or maybe he was just BS-ing me."

"Hmm."

"And earlier, he said he used to work for some guys, made good money, mostly hauling stuff. So, I wonder whether he was part of the distribution system."

"Mmhmm."

"Seems possible, doesn't it?"

"Maybe. How about this?" Pete held up the box. Action movie. She gave a thumbs up. He slid the disc in before settling back against the pillows. "Sounds like he had some interesting stories to tell."

"And some might've even been true." Vicky had seen our hero kick ass in this movie before, so she had time to think about the day's events. When there was a lull in the action, she said, "What's the word George Bush made up? Mis-underestimate? I might have mis-underestimated Don. He's a talker, but I got the feeling he was working me for information."

They stopped talking to watch the scene where the assassin smashes through the hall window trying to kill the amnesiac hero. When the long car chase started, Vicky opened her laptop to make a few notes and do some research. As a journalist, she loved that so many records were available on the web. But personally, more and more, she thought there was way too much private info available to anyone with Internet access.

Darn. No wi-fi, again. Well, official records were good, but only told part of the story. Even with documentation it was often hard to know what really happened. And people surely found it easier to choose how—or whether—to tell a story that was recorded only in human memory.

Chapter Eight

November 2008

Rose didn't move when she awoke. She wasn't sure if her eyes were open. Everything was so dark. She was deep in a fuzzy black tube that smelled like dirt. Its sides moved in and out like an accordion. Her whole body throbbed. A metal box shrank and squeezed her head until her skull almost burst. Her arms and shoulders burned. She tried to lift her hands but giant rubber bands or something held them down. Her legs wouldn't move.

She returned to the darkness.

Sometime later, she felt something hard pressed against her mouth. A voice said, "It's okay. Open up."

Rose froze. Who said that? Where was she? She wanted to be home. Now she was on the ground sitting against a wall. Something covered most of her eyes, but she could see a dim glow at the bottom. She tried to focus but a black cloud floated in and blocked the light.

Rose knew she should be terrified, and she was. She'd never been so scared. She couldn't move. She was too soft and heavy and slow. Was she going to die? Where was she? Her mind floated and bobbed in hazy circles. How did she get to this strange dark place? Mom must be wondering where she was.

"Open your mouth." The voice was low and sounded far away. "It's okay. Drink."

Oh, her mouth was so dry. Her throat burned. She was so, so thirsty.

Something hard pushed against Rose's mouth, again and again. "It's just water, take a drink."

She parted her lips and gulped hungrily. She had never been so thirsty. She gagged, spewing liquid.

"Goddammit, you got me wet," the voice growled, then made a sound that might have been a laugh. "Oh, well, it's just water. You need to take it slow."

"Where am I?" Rose choked out the words. "What are you doing?"

"Now, don't you worry. Relax. You can go back to sleep after you have something to eat." A spoonful of something mushy was pushed into her mouth, followed by another, and another. Rose was so tired she could only swallow while the voice kept talking, talking, talking...

"We'll live in fancy hotels and eat whatever we want. You'll have lots of pretty clothes, anything you want—"

"I want to go home."

"Home is with me, now. Don't you worry. I'll take good care of you." A hand brushed Rose's hair away from her face, then stroked her cheek. "You're so pretty. Just relax. Have you ever seen a redwood tree? We'll go to California and see them. They're hundreds of feet tall. Can you imagine? There's one wide enough you can drive a car through..."

Chapter Nine

Sunday, November 2008

On Sunday morning, Vicky drove the twenty miles to the nearest rental car lot and parked. Pete nuzzled her neck, caressed her back, and murmured, "All right then. Are you sure?"

"Absolutely." She kissed him nicely, with just a hint of tease. "Go. I'll be busy here." Pete enjoyed going off on his own, and seemed to like that she did, too. It made their time together very agreeable.

They kissed the kind of kiss that might have gone somewhere if they weren't in a hybrid vehicle parked next to a gas station at eight in the morning. Pete grinned as they pulled apart. "I got a room in Louisville tonight. It's about six hours but I'm stopping along the way. I'll text when I get there."

He got out, pulled his backpack from the back seat, and walked around to her window. He leaned in to give her a slow stroke along her jaw and one more quick kiss. "Three nights then."

"We'll have plenty to catch up on." Vicky enjoyed the view as he swung his pack over one shoulder and strode toward the rental office. Mm. Okay. She had things to do.

****

A half hour later, she stood on the levee, hands in

the pockets of her warm jacket. The morning sun hadn't yet broken through the fog. Nine years ago, she'd been one of many journalists camped out here after a farmer spotted little Lisa Dee trudging along, bloodied and wearing just one shoe.

Somehow, the landscape seemed prettier back then. Maybe it was the mood—everyone was eager to find out why an unidentified little girl would be alone, miles from a paved road. What led up to that? Where was her family? How'd they get separated? Vicky had hoped to cover a joyful reunion.

Maybe the place seemed prettier then because Vicki was younger, had great friends, and was always around interesting people. She loved, loved, everything about being a reporter for a big market TV station. Getting to talk to people, ask questions, and tell stories. Reporting.

But not much more happened. The day after Lisa was found, searchers found her other shoe. After that, nothing. The search for her family was scaled back, and then it was almost Memorial Day and the end of May ratings. People had plans for their time off. Lisa on the Levee dropped from lead story to nothing after a couple of weeks.

It was the last story Vicky ever covered as a reporter.

Truth be told, the area probably seemed prettier back then because it was early summer. Now, autumn opened the view through the overgrown trees and bushes along the levee. To the east, a sluggish waterway lazed its way south, dark and full of rot fouling the air with the swollen smell of moist decay.

To the west lay soybean fields and the farm owned by the man who had found Lisa on the levee. Vicky would go down that road later, after she made a couple other stops. First, the neighbor lady.

Vicky scuffed her way down the levee back to her car, double-checked directions, and drove on the paved county road until she turned onto one made of gravel and dirt. She slowed so she wouldn't raise too much dust as she drove through farm fields. Maybe no one cared, but no reason to risk making anyone mad.

She pulled into a wide spot in front of the Beck house. So far, it was much as Google Earth had suggested—a half-mile dirt road leading to a decrepit house and two outbuildings in the middle of open farmland. Flat, with just a few sad-looking trees near the house, and a line of vegetation in the distant back, where the creek must be.

There were no vehicles in sight. She rolled her window down part way, stuck her hand out, and waved as she gently tapped the horn, just in case any mean dogs lived here. She'd never been comfortable around dogs she didn't know.

She grabbed her tote, got out, and stood inside her open car door, visualizing Kerry's story about the leather bag on the porch. It was a lonely spot. The house sagged, the paint peeled, and one of three front steps missed a board. A satellite dish sat in the yard. Interesting feature.

The only sounds were rustling leaves and the ticking of Vicky's car. She'd once asked a mechanic why cars did that. He'd eagerly explained about different materials cooling at different rates. She liked people who could explain how things worked. Connections and consequences.

No one appeared. Vicky leaned in and tapped the horn again.

Nothing.

She slammed the car door, then walked up the steps. The two beat-up wooden chairs on the porch hadn't been sat in for a long, long time. She turned to contemplate the dirt yard and soybean field. Dust still traced the path of her car.

Vicky knocked. "Ms. Beck? Hello, Ms. Beck?" She knocked again, and again, and again. "Ms. Beck?"

Silence. Dark curtains blocked any view through the lone front window.

"Ms. Beck? Don't worry, I'm no one official."

"Ms. Beck, I'm going to go around the house, okay? Just in case you're out back."

"Who are you?" A woman's clear voice from behind the door. She sounded sharp and suspicious.

"Oh, hello, Ms. Beck. Thanks for answering. My name's Vicky Robeson. Can we chat for a few minutes?"

"About what?"

"I'm talking with people about local history for a travel article."

Silence. Then, "Why me?"

"Someone mentioned that you've lived here for a long time and might be good to talk with. Just for a few minutes."

"Who mentioned me?"

"You remember Tom and Beth Wagner? Well, I don't know what Beth's name was before they got married. They went to high school with you. I'm staying at their RV park. They said to say hello."

An even longer silence followed. "This door doesn't open. Go around back."

Vicky strolled along the driveway leading to a derelict-looking detached garage. Its doors were closed. An old blue pickup was parked behind the house. A plastic Adirondack chair sat near the steps next to a big wooden spool used as a table.

Vicky stepped up to the small back porch. The door was cracked open an inch. "Hello. I just have a few general questions."

The floor inside creaked. The gap grew another inch, through which appeared one bright blue eye under straight white bangs. "Who'd you say you are?"

"My name is Vicky Robeson."

"Are you a reporter?"

"No. Well, I used to be. Now I'm just doing research for a travel article."

"Travel? Here?"

"Yes, it's a pretty place, and has an interesting history."

The door opened wider to show Joan's skeptical face. "No, it doesn't. Nothing ever happens here."

"No? Has your family lived here long?" The Beck name was on property records going back to the forties.

"Since the sixties."

Interesting discrepancy. Joan did not appear to be a loquacious individual. This was going to take some work.

"Oh, back in the sixties, a lot of this area was swamp, before it was drained for farming, right? Can you tell me about that?"

"You just said everything there is to say about it."

"Ha." Vicky put on her most non-threatening look. "There was also that little girl found on the levee nine years ago."

"That didn't have anything to do with me."

"Oh, I know. I'm trying to find a woman who was in the area about the same time."

Kerry's mention of a high-end woman's bag on the porch was enough reason to assume a woman left it there. Now, seeing the place, it seemed even less likely the bag belonged here. So, whose was it? Enough material to bluff. She had nothing else to go on anyway. Yet.

Joan frowned. "A woman in the area? What?"

"She had a really unusual leather tote bag."

Aha. A flicker of interest. Finally. The door opened enough for Joan Beck to step outside. Short white hair, faded sweatshirt, jeans, boots. She was lean and fit, a good head taller than Vicky. Weathered and outdoorsy. Capable. Wary.

"What woman?"

"That's what I'm trying to figure out."

"What's that got to do with travel? And why are you asking me?"

"She was seen around here."

"A woman seen nine years ago? How's anyone supposed to remember that?"

"I know. It's a long shot."

"Well, I'm busy."

"Just real quick—can I get a drink of water? I forgot my bottle." Vicky made no movement to leave. "Also, the bag was made of dark reddish leather, with a carved bone handle." At least, that's how Vicky remembered Rick's.

Joan paused, then said over her shoulder, "Oh, come on in. Just for a few minutes."

Vicky followed, grinning inside. Joan no doubt wanted to know what Vicky knew as much as Vicky wanted to know what Joan knew. Still, it was good to get invited in.

An enormous Rottweiler stood just inside the door, every muscle taut and focused on Vicky.

"Oh." She froze and stifled a gasp. "I didn't know you have a dog."

"This's Ruby." Joan touched the animal's back. "Ruby's a good girl."

Vicky stayed next to the door. "I didn't hear her bark."

"No. We don't believe in warnings, do we, Ruby?" Joan rubbed the dog's head. "Come on in, she's not going to hurt you. Unless I tell her to. Have a seat."

"Sure, yes. Thanks." Vicky edged her way to the wooden chair nearest the door and sat, her tote bag on her lap.

Joan opened a brown curtain above the sink, letting in the morning light. That seemed to be a signal. Ruby's nails clacked as she walked to the table and lay underneath it. Vicky tucked her feet back.

"I just made coffee. You want some or do you really want water?"

"Coffee'd be great."

Joan took two good-sized mugs from a white cabinet above the Formica counter and filled them from an ancient percolator. The room was clean, painted pale yellow. It'd been decades since anyone had updated the stove, counters, and cabinets, though the refrigerator was modern and the flatscreen television mounted above the table was high-end. A current model.

"I like your kitchen. It's homey."

Joan didn't answer. She handed one cup to Vicky and used her foot to pull out the only other chair. She sat. She didn't offer cream or sugar.

"As long as we're having coffee…" Vicky opened

her tote bag and took out a small white paper box. "The Wagners mentioned when you were in high school, there was a bakery that made the best cookies. Howard's Bakery. I stopped by on the way here."

Vicky savored the aroma of the amazing oatmeal cookies as she slid the parcel across the table. She knew they were amazing because she'd eaten one on the way over.

Joan opened the box and took out a cookie. "I haven't had one of these in years." She took a bite. "Mmm. The best."

They sat sipping coffee and chewing cookies in silence for a few moments before Joan took an exaggerated, pointed look at the wall clock above the stove. "Okay. I have things to do. What's this all about, really?"

"I'm trying to find the woman with the bag." Where there was a woman's bag there was, or had been, a woman. Presumably.

"So you said. Why?"

"Okay. A friend told me about a woman who was here the same time as the levee girl. I'd never heard about her, and I don't think the cops did either. I thought I'd ask around."

"What's that got to do with me?"

"My friend talked with you."

Joan tilted her head. "You're going to have to give me more than that."

"Direct. I like it." No reason not to play it straight. "She saw the bag on your front porch. Like I said, I'm doing research for a travel article. I'm building it around Lisa Dee, the mystery girl on the levee."

Silence.

Okay, so give a little more. "I was working in St. Louis at the time. I was a TV reporter."

"I thought I recognized you."

"Is that why you're giving me such a hard time? I get it. But her story haunts me, y'know? How's it possible no one knew that little girl?"

Joan was silent, but she might be starting to thaw. Her face was slightly softer.

"The case has never been officially closed, but after all this time? I want to talk to people who didn't necessarily want to talk to anyone official. Who didn't say anything back then or didn't realize until later what might've been connected. Like the girl and the woman." As Vicky sat back, she put extra friendliness in her eyes. "Or who maybe had very good reason not to talk."

"And?"

"And I want to talk with the bag's owner."

"Fine. Good luck."

"Do you know where she is?"

"I have no idea who she is or where she is."

"But she was here." That much was clear already. "How long did she stay with you?"

"Why do you want to find her, whoever she is?"

"I'd rather explain to her." Vicky raised her last bite of cookie and deadpanned, "Damn fine cookie" and popped it into her mouth.

Joan rolled her eyes and gave a hint of a smile. She squinted at the wall clock. Maybe she had something to get to, but it appeared to be more of a message than a time check.

Vicky followed her glance. "If you'd rather not talk about her, I completely understand. It's up to you."

"I don't want to talk about any of this."

"I understand. It's fine either way. I did just show up without any warning." Vicky leaned forward. "Look. I get it's hard to talk about this, especially with someone who just appears out of the blue. But it's been nine years, so whatever was going to happen already has. What difference could it make now if you tell me about her?"

Vicky fiddled with her mug to give Joan time to think. It didn't surprise her when someone was reluctant to share something private. She was more often surprised by how much people did tell her, frequently far more than she'd be willing to share. She was one-sided that way. Not secretive, necessarily—just keenly aware that once something was shared, the sharer has no way to control how it's received or what the recipient might do with it.

Joan sat, unmoving, offering no clues to her thinking. She had the brightest blue eyes Vicky had ever seen, and a strong face, framed by a lot of living, that didn't need words to say, "don't mess with me."

Vicky leaned back into her chair. "I get it. I really do. I bet I'd feel the same way if someone asked me."

"Well, I'm asking. What's this all about? You tell me why you're really here, and I'll think about it."

Vicky held Joan's eyes for a long moment. Joan was hard to read. People sometimes said that about Vicky, though she considered herself reasonably expressive, unless she didn't want people to know what she was thinking. Like right now, as she chewed over what level of truth to share. "I told you. I covered the story of Lisa."

Joan crossed her arms. "It's not going to be that easy. Tell me why you're so interested. And I don't believe this crap about a travel story."

"I really am working on a travel article. But I also

knew someone involved with the case."

"You're talking about Rick Carr."

"Oh, you know Rick? How'd you know I meant him?"

"How do you think?" Joan's voice was even.

When in doubt, don't commit. "I'm not sure." There. Brilliant response.

"Why do you think I brought him up?" Joan's eyes probed.

"Because he has the same kind of bag. Do you know where he got it?"

"How well do you know him?" Joan's voice was low and clear, neutral.

"He was a cop and I was a reporter. We'd see each other on stories."

Joan raised an eyebrow. Clearly, Vicky had to share more to get her to talk. "Mostly from work. Then I ran into him one day. Funny, I just told my friend this story. This was right around when they found Lisa, the little levee girl."

Vicky recapped the liquor store encounter.

Joan gestured "get on with it" with her coffee cup. "And? You're sitting on Rick's porch getting a little loose…"

"Not really loose. I wasn't, anyway. He told me about putting down his dog. We talked about work."

Vicky paused and sipped her coffee. They had gone inside. She'd leaned against the doorway, next to his bag and paperwork on the table. His face reflected in the window when he filled a glass from the tap. He looked beat down. She knew exactly what that was like, to let yourself sink deep into how bad you feel.

"So were you seeing each other?"

"No. The closest we ever got to anything personal was when we hugged—once." Vicky tried not to think about two sad people in need of human comfort. Then her shock at what followed. No reason to say any more about The Rick Bag Incident.

"Anyway, he had the same kind of bag as this mystery woman. Do you know who makes them?"

"That's it? You hugged?"

"With our jobs it wasn't a good idea to get involved."

"Did he say that, or did you?"

"Ha. We agreed." Vicky liked drawing information out from people, but it was uncomfortable being on the other end. Enough. Joan clearly wanted to know something specific about Rick. She was older than him, but they were from the same rural area. Were they friends or foes or lovers, or insignificant to each other? Interesting.

"Why are you asking about Rick?" Vicky raised her eyebrows and tilted her chin in light challenge.

"Why are you asking about this woman?" Joan set down her coffee cup. "This is my life here. I need to know what you're after. You didn't really tell me what happened with Rick. Don't forget I know him, too."

Why does she care about what might have happened with Rick? "This is more about the woman. It could be coincidence that she and Rick had the same bag. But she was here, right here, at the same time as Lisa."

Joan gazed at Vicky before she gave one sharp nod. "Okay. A woman was here. Why do you want to talk to her?"

Vicky exhaled softly. Inside, she did somersaults. Her hunch about the bag had paid off. "She and Lisa must have been connected. Had to be, two people showing up way out here, at almost exactly the same time. Did the cops ever even know about her?"

"Let me see some recent work."

"Sure." Vicky pulled out her phone. A single bar. "It might take a minute."

She finished tapping and set it down. "While we're waiting, I'll just tell you. I'm planning to write about the mystery of Lisa. I'm putting a travel spin on—"

"Did it come up yet?"

Vicky checked her screen. "No. It's just one article, but it'll give you the idea."

"I'll get my computer." Ruby got up from under the table, followed Joan to the doorway, and sat just outside the kitchen.

Joan murmured something to the dog when she returned. She placed a sleek laptop on the table, flipped it open, and spelled, "R-O-B...?"

Nice laptop. "E-S-O-N. Vicky Robeson."

Joan clicked keys and scanned the screen. Vicky assumed she was Googling her and regretted not updating her online presence lately. She wanted to ask for Joan's wi-fi password but that might be pushing it.

After tapping and reading for several minutes, Joan closed her laptop. "All right. But I still don't get why a travel magazine would care about this."

"The way I—"

Joan put her hand up. "I already decided, okay? You're right. It was a long time ago."

Vicky leaned forward, barely breathing.

"Okay. Your mystery woman. I've never told a soul a word of this." Joan glanced at the clock and took a sip of coffee before continuing. "It was late. I'd just finished supper."

Joan explained she was working in town at the time, as a cashier at the grocery store. That was before she got a job transcribing legal notes at home. She was a certified paralegal now. Vicky got the distinct impression Joan didn't particularly like being around people and handling legal paperwork fit her solitary nature better than selling bread and milk and cigarettes.

"I didn't have a dog then. There was a noise at my back door and when I opened it, a woman stood there. Her face was bruised and swollen, like she'd been beat up."

Vicky didn't move or take her eyes off Joan.

"I asked if she was okay, and she no more than opened her mouth than she fainted right there on the back porch."

"And you took her in?"

"I put her on the couch. She woke up when I dabbed at the blood on her forehead, checking to see how hurt she was."

"You didn't take her to the doctor? Call for help?"

"It'd take too long. And she wasn't so bad off. Cuts and bruises, but nothing broken, as far as I could tell." Joan shrugged. "She wouldn't say what happened."

"How old was she?"

"She looked young, late teens, early twenties. She had the bag strapped across her body."

"How long was she here?"

"Just that night."

"Hmm. What else did she say?"

"Just what I told you. I cleaned and bandaged her up a bit. She wouldn't get out of her clothes to take a bath. She had some soup. I fixed her a bed on the couch. We watched some TV before bed."

"That's it? She didn't say anything else?"

Joan picked up her mug. "In the morning, we had coffee on the front porch. I was getting refills when she ran into the kitchen, half-yelling, half-whispering that someone was coming. She begged me not to tell anyone about her. She took off toward the creek, limping but moving fast. A few minutes later your friend knocked on my door. Guess she told you about that, so you know the rest."

"She didn't say anything about a little girl?"

"Nope."

"Did you tell the cops about her?"

Joan crossed her arms. "No."

She seemed to be daring Vicky to ask why not, so she did. "Why not?"

"She begged me not to."

"What about the cop who was here? You told my friend he might've overheard you say something."

Joan shrugged. "That was separate. He came around asking about the little girl before the woman ever showed up at my door. I was about to make him coffee when I noticed my best knife was missing."

"Why didn't you tell him?"

"I didn't know who took it, or why. I wasn't sure what was going on, so I kept quiet." Joan paused. "I've had my differences with cops. I don't talk with them if I don't have to."

Sure would like to know more about that. Maybe later. "After the woman ran off, did you think about telling the cops? You know they'd have wanted to talk to her."

"She begged me not to. She didn't want anyone to

find her." Joan dropped her voice to almost a whisper. "And when we were watching the late news, there was a story about the little girl being found. And she kinda squeezed her hands together like she was praying, and said, 'Thank God.' I figured if she'd wanted to come forward, she would've. She knew the girl was safe."

"I can see that." Though not entirely. A person would have to have a very good reason to sit on this info all this time. And to tell it now. "I wish we had her name, so we didn't have to call her 'the woman.' "

"There's more I didn't tell you."

Of course there was. "There is?"

"She had blood on her. It wasn't all the way dried."

"Was she stabbed?"

"More beat-up than cut, but she wouldn't let me check her. I don't think the blood was from her."

"She fought back."

"And she might have won. She got away, anyway."

"You said the last you saw she was running out your back door?"

"Her name was Alisa. She didn't say her last name."

"The last time you saw Alisa, she was running out back?"

"I told her to wait for me at the creek, that I had to go to work but I'd take her somewhere safe later. It was dark by the time I looked for her."

"She wasn't there?"

Joan shrugged.

"What was in her bag?"

Joan pursed her lips.

"Come on, Joan."

"Back off."

"Okay, how'd you know Rick had the same kind of

bag?"

"He had it with him, sitting right there where you are."

"Rick was the cop in your kitchen?"

Joan got up and went to the percolator. "What's it matter?"

"Just curious. What'd he say?"

"He said a girl was found walking up by the Willets place."

Joan took a long time with the coffee refill, her back to Vicky. "He asked for coffee. I was about to make it and noticed my knife was missing. I might've said something then."

"About the knife?"

"Maybe more like 'what the hell.' Who knows." Joan returned to the table and sat down. Ruby returned to her spot under the table. "I told him I didn't know anything about a little girl. And I didn't. Don't."

"You knew Alisa and Rick had the same kind of bag."

"Not until later. Alisa showed up hours after he left." Joan made a little hmph sound. "He sat there, all polished up and acting official. I started thinking about how much I hated his pa. I told him to leave, that we're not going to have coffee and act like friends, 'cause we're not. His daddy dragged Mama and me back here, the one time we had a real chance of getting away. Our one chance to have a normal life."

There was a faint quiver in Joan's voice. Vicky willed herself not to speak, not to move, to just listen.

Joan's jaw tightened. "His pa stood right there in his sheriff uniform telling Mama she needed to stay home. Said Bill Beck was a decent guy and he'd be more careful about his drinking. What a sick joke. Anyway, Rick left, and later that evening Alisa showed up."

"Wow. I can understand why you'd be mad. How old were you when you and your mama tried to run away?"

"Twelve."

"That must have been incredibly hard." No wonder Joan didn't go to the cops. She probably identified with Alisa.

"So." Vicky acted as though something had just occurred to her. "When Alisa ran off, she left the bag on the porch. Where my friend saw it."

Joan dipped her chin once, fast, more of a jerk than a nod. "I forgot about it until it was too late."

"And you still have it. Can I see it?"

Joan eyeballed Vicky, then stood and left the room, saying only, "Wait here." Ruby returned to the doorway and stared at Vicky, who didn't move from her seat.

Several minutes went by before Joan returned, carrying a box wrapped in a plastic garbage bag. "I've kept it ever since that day."

Vicky barely breathed.

Joan picked up a dishtowel and brushed off dust. She opened the bag and removed a cardboard box. "I hid it away in case she ever comes back."

She opened its flaps and took out a package wrapped in brown paper, about the size of a mostly full ten-pound sack of potatoes, but not as heavy.

Joan carefully undid the wrapping. "I've wondered if this could ever be evidence against me somehow."

Inside was a tote bag, made of a rich dark leather, deep brown with the slightest hint of crimson. Its flap was held in place by a two-inch long toggle hooked into an intricately carved, ingeniously simple handle. It was gorgeous.

"Against you for what?" The clasp resembled old Chinese ivory carvings. The bag did remind her of Rick's, as she remembered it, though this one was not quite finished. The flap had a raw edge, and one side of the strap wasn't knotted like the other.

"I don't know. I kept it anyway." Joan undid the clasp and opened the flap. She tilted the bag so Vicky could see what was in it, then used the dishtowel to take out each item and place it on the table.

There wasn't much: a wood-handled kitchen knife, covered with what looked pretty much exactly like old, dried blood; something that resembled a desiccated potato; and a silver hair clasp tarnished nearly black.

"That's my knife," Joan said unnecessarily. She picked up the hair clip. "I think she was filing down this end, maybe to make a weapon."

"She used your knife, instead."

"That's what it looks like."

"How'd she get it? She was in your kitchen before she stabbed someone?"

"Hell if I know. It doesn't make sense."

"Do you think she and the girl were together?"

Joan started packing up the bag and its contents. "Probably." Her movements were abrupt. "Okay, that's enough. I have things to do." She stood up.

"That's a lot. I think I can understand why you kept it to yourself." Not entirely, though. Keeping the bag might bolster the mystery woman story, sure, but there's got to be more to it. "I can't imagine how anyone could hold it against you for helping her. Do you know who makes these bags?"

"There's no reason for you to repeat any of this."

Vicky tilted her head. She'd made no promises. "I'm glad you decided to talk with me." Though she still wondered why she had. "I'm going to keep trying to find Alisa. If you think of anything else, will you call me?"

When Joan didn't reply, Vicky put her card on the table and stood up. "Well, guess I better get going. Thanks for everything. I'll keep you posted if I do end up writing anything."

Chapter Ten

Walkers Corner, May 1999

The girl didn't move. Her throat was raw and terribly dry. What happened? Where was she? The darkness eased away to the edges of her mind, leaving an essence of awareness, of fear and pain and confusion. She opened her eyes but there was no light. Cold dank air brushed across her face. Water trickled somewhere in the distance.

"Mama? Where are you?" she whispered. There was no strength left in her voice. "Mama?" A confusing montage of images drifted in and out of her mind—a horrible man hitting her, a strange woman holding her, dim dashboard lights, screaming for Mama.

She stretched her fingers. Oh, now she could feel under her. She was lying on something smooth but not soft. She wasn't tied up anymore. She waved her hands above her to see what was there. Nothing but another faint cold breeze, so faint she wasn't sure it was real. She struggled to sit up. She froze when her hand touched something.

"Mama? Is that you?" She ran her hands over the motionless form. Mama's puffy jacket. She got to her knees to gently shake her. "Mama? Mama? Please wake up."

Chapter Eleven

Joan Beck
Walkers Corner, Sunday November 2008

Joan and Ruby stood next to the house, watching Vicky expertly back up and out the narrow driveway, leaving a light plume of dust in her wake. Well, that was certainly interesting. The dog nudged Joan's hand, probably sensing she was still on edge.

"You're such a good girl, yes, you are." Joan scratched Ruby's head and back. Ruby had alerted her to Vicky's arrival, which was fortunate since she couldn't hear anything when she was in the basement.

She mentally replayed the conversation. Had she said too much? The nosy bitch got her to talk much more than she usually did. But then she'd also found out a few things about what Vicky was up to. Overall, it'd gone pretty well. She'd steered Vicky in the right direction. It was obvious she just ate up the story of the big bad sheriff dragging her and Mama back home. She'd seemed like the type to have a soft spot for someone who'd been through that.

Joan was certain Vicky had not revealed everything about her and Rick, which was interesting by itself. Well, it's not like she'd been completely upfront herself. Still, she wondered if showing the bag had been a good idea. But that went all right. She could almost see Vicky picking up the scent, preparing to track it.

She walked toward the back of the house. She sure as hell hadn't wanted a bunch of cops searching her property back then. And definitely not now. She wasn't going to let anything mess up the deal. She paused and looked toward the creek, thinking back to when she was seventeen.

****

Joan had bookmarked her homework page with a pencil. "I'll do it, Mama, you just sit." She stood up from her seat at the small kitchen table.

Big Bill Beck was on his usual tear. "And get me a goddam beer!"

Jerk. What's he expect? He shows up late, and no one even knows whether he's coming. It's better when he doesn't come home at all. It was best when he was gone for days. Those were nice times, when Joan and her mama, Harriet, could cook good meals, sit quietly and read, or sew and watch a little TV.

This wasn't one of those times. He stank of booze and cigarettes layered over his unwashed body. His boots had tracked dirt all over their nice clean floor.

He shoved her as she passed. Her ma caught her eye with a gentle look. Joan put the beer can down slightly out of his reach instead of crushing it into his face.

He always made them sit with him while he ate, so they had to listen while he wolfed his food and chugged his beer. Joan worked on her geometry homework. She funneled her rage into drawing sharp angles. When her pencil lead snapped, The Bastard ridiculed her, saying she was dumb, even dumber than her mother, and school wasn't going to help, considering what little she was good for.

The usual.

Joan couldn't remember ever calling her father Papa or Daddy. She might have when she was a toddler, but from the earliest she could remember, he came with bad things. As her vocabulary advanced, she didn't call him Dad or Pa. If she had to refer to him, she just said 'he' or 'him' and everyone knew who she meant.

In her teenaged mind, he was The Fucking Bastard. Once, Joan let that slip out loud to her ma, who got upset and made her promise not to call him that. Out of respect to Mama, she dropped the F word, but not the sentiment.

Now, almost done with high school, Joan had started letting her hostility show. He didn't even care his wife was so, so sick.

Joan clenched one fist under the table, sneaking peeks at her ma. She was frighteningly thin. Her wrinkled skin was stretched tight, almost translucent enough to see her skull. She was shrinking. She'd barely tasted her own good stew, the stew that The Bastard was stuffing into his hateful mouth. Mama wouldn't last much longer. It would be horrible to be left all alone with him.

Finally, finally, he shoved his bowl across the table, crumpling Joan's paper. He heaved his chair back and got to his feet. "I'm going out," he announced. Joan smoothed out her homework, her face a mask, as he stomped out of the room. He always swaggered like he wanted to fight.

As usual, he slammed the front door. When minutes passed and the truck didn't start up, Joan said, "I'm going to see what he's doing." He didn't take the truck, so he was going across the creek.

"No, no. Honey, just leave it."

"I'm going, Mama. He never walks anywhere. He's being sneaky. I want to know what he's up to."

Joan was sick of him, sick of everything, and she was going to do something about it, even if she didn't know how or what, or when.

She slipped out the back door and paused, listening. Yep, there he went, down the back path. It wasn't hard to track him. He clomped around like a restless bull. Anyone could follow him.

Joan crept soundlessly in his wake. She had roamed outside all her life, ever since she was big enough to get out of the house by herself when the yelling and fighting and hating got to be too much. After dark was the best. There were so many ways to hide.

Clouds skittered past the half moon, which gave off enough light for Joan to easily follow the overgrown path. The crunching of her father's passage helped, too. He was either going to the lodge or the cabin. She'd know after he crossed the creek. Follow the path all the way to the lodge or take the turnoff for the back way to the caretaker cabin.

Before she stepped onto the first rock of the footpath across the creek, Joan glanced back at the house. The glow from the kitchen was the only light, other than the moon.

Joan hurried to catch up. He was quieter now. She didn't want to lose track of him. He took the uphill path to the lodge. The path was overgrown and barely visible, with trees and bushes overlapping it. The ground was dry, branches and twigs brittle underfoot.

She had to move like a hunter. Joan had spent a lot of time in the woods with her big brother Bill Junior, back when he was still a good guy. He'd hunted ever since he could carry a rifle. Bill taught her how to track and shoot and get around in the woods and swamp. She missed him.

As she drew close to the lodge clearing, she heard men's voices, but couldn't make out what they were saying. She hunched behind a bush. The Bastard was nowhere in sight.

Silently she drew herself up to move closer. An arm snaked around her neck and cut off her breath.

"You little shit. You think I don't know you're sneaking around after me?" The Bastard's horrible breath burned her ear as he tightened his grip.

Joan thrust herself up as hard and fast as she could, throwing him off balance. She kicked back at his knee. He staggered backward, cursing under his breath. The instant his hold loosened, Joan ran toward home, wheezing, furious that she'd let him catch her.

She could hear him behind her, running full tilt, breaking branches. He was catching up. He caught her hair and yanked her down just before the creek. He kicked her again and again. She rolled and scrambled, trying to escape him. She struggled to get back on her feet. He slammed his ham of a fist into her jaw.

She thudded down on the rocky ground, fighting the void at the edge of her mind. He dropped his knee into her belly, his big hands at her throat. He was breathing heavily but was otherwise silent, almost calm, as he throttled her. Joan struggled and twisted. She was going to die. His ugly face and the moon over his shoulder were the last things she would ever see.

The moon was fading away to darkness when The Bastard collapsed half on top of her, his hands still grasping her throat, but softening. Joan screamed silently, as she had learned to do as a child, and squirmed out from under him.

And there stood her mama, Harriet, holding a rock that was surely covered with her husband's blood. The moonglow shone behind her, haloing her messy hair and tiny body in its nightgown and robe. It was so like Mama to place the rock on the ground instead of dropping it. She looked sadly at Joan and sank gently to the dirt.

"Oh, Mama, are you okay? Omigod. He was going to kill me!"

Joan picked up the rock and made sure The Bastard was good and dead, then crawled to her mother. They huddled together in the shadows, staring at the body, twisted on its side in the dim moonlight. A pool of blood spread around his head, a dark and fitting crown.

Joan shivered. "Goddamn, the fucker was going to kill me! You saved me, Mama."

Harriet sighed. "I should have done that a long time ago."

Joan closed her eyes, wishing it all away. After several minutes, or maybe it was longer, she shuddered awake. Everything was still there—The Bastard, bloody rock, blood on the ground. Where had her trembling, frail little mother found the strength?

"Come on, Mama, we need to get you back to the house."

They stood, both quivering.

"We need to get rid of him." Harriet's voice was barely a whisper.

"I'll take care of everything. Let's get cleaned up. I'll come back."

Harriett didn't argue. She could barely stand, much less help move him, but she had never appeared stronger.

She had suffered more from the disease that was her husband than from the cancer within her.

The house appeared unchanged, but it would never be the same. Joan took charge. She started a washer load of their blood-splattered clothing, helped her mom bathe, and put her to bed before she jumped into the shower. She dressed in rough clothing and heavy boots.

"I'm going, Mama. I'll be back as soon as I can."

"What are you going to do, honey? You can't lift him."

"I'll drag him. I know a place. First, I'm going to get rid of the truck. If anyone comes looking for him we'll say he was here but left right after supper."

Joan didn't see anyone on the way to the bus station, twelve miles away by road. She left the truck parked at the station, which like everything else was closed up tight. She made the return trip on foot, taking the shortcut through the woods and the edge of the swamp.

More than three hours after she left the truck, as the sky began to lighten, Joan arrived back at the creek.

There was no pool of blood, no sign of what happened. The Bastard was gone.

Chapter Twelve

Sunday Afternoon

Vicky drove straight to the diner from Joan's house. She needed lunch and wi-fi. The midday rush had eased, but several tables were still occupied, including the booth where Vicky had eavesdropped her first time here. She smiled at Volunteer Firefighter Don, who was sitting with a group of men. He grinned, waved, and said something to his table mates, who turned to look at her.

Vicky pretended not to notice. She headed toward a table, nodding to Sam, who again wore jeans, a sleeveless T-shirt, and no makeup. She'd colored her hair even blonder, the spiky tips almost white.

Vicky opened her laptop and got busy searching. Sam poured coffee. "Hi, how are you, Sam? Anything new?"

"No." Sam gestured toward Don's table. "The guys there with Don were out all night. No one's talking about giving up the search, but Rose's been missing for a week. People are getting pretty discouraged."

"It seems worse that it happened in front of her house, doesn't it? With two other people right there." Presumably. There had to be more to it. "Feels like nowhere is safe."

"Yeah. So, what can I get you?" Sam clearly wanted to change the subject. No doubt she'd had similar conversations with customers all day, every day. Her cafe was the best place in town to get caught up on whatever was happening.

Vicky was already a regular here. A temporary regular. She ordered tomato soup and half a turkey sandwich with avocado on toasted sourdough, mayo, no mustard.

By the time Sam returned with her order, Vicky's online search had turned up four local vendors of handcrafted leather goods.

"Looks great," Vicky said. "Sam, you are absolutely right. There aren't a lot of scenic attractions here. I might need to focus more on the interesting people. Speaking of which, a couple of days ago, I noticed someone who looked familiar. I've been trying to place him. Older guy, tattoos on both arms? Wears a cap?"

"That could be half the guys in the county."

"Ha. I was hoping he was one of your regulars. He was in that booth." She pointed with her chin. "Talking with a younger guy who sounded like he's from Minnesota."

Sam shrugged, apparently uninterested in discussing other customers. She looked toward the door as Liz Ann, the librarian, entered and made a beeline toward Sam and Vicky.

"Hi, Liz Ann," said Sam. "Your sandwich order's almost ready."

"Great, I'll just sit a minute. Okay if I join you?" Liz Ann sat without waiting.

"Hi, of course. I was just telling Sam she's right, it's hard to find much to write about to appeal to tourists. Though the library is beautiful."

"Why, thank you, darlin'. It does get a lot of love.

What've you been up to?"

"I took Pete to get a rental car. He's gone to Kentucky for a few days." Vicky mentioned strolling along the levee that morning. Her visit with Joan Beck didn't come up.

Sam lingered, standing with coffeepot in hand. "Vicky, the search teams said thanks for the food you had sent out to them last night."

"Oh, good, glad they liked it. And thank you for making it. I'm sure it was delicious."

Don walked over to stand next to Sam. "Hello, ladies." He lifted his arm as though to put it around Sam, but at the last minute had enough sense not to. "And what are y'all up to?"

"Just talking." Vicky didn't want to encourage him.

"Hello, Don." Liz Ann shook his hand.

Don launched into a description of the weather and how it was likely to change, then waited until it was clear they weren't going to invite him to join them. "Well, I best move along. But first, I have a question, Sam. Should Walkers Corner have an apostrophe?"

"Not when I write it."

"What do you ladies think?"

"It depends," Vicky and Liz Ann said in unison.

"Walkers? No." Sam refilled their mugs. "It wasn't named for someone named Walker. It was a meeting place. For walkers."

Vicky smiled. "I bet that joke's been around as long as this place has had the name."

Don managed to chuckle while glaring at Sam, apparently for stealing his line. He'd probably said it so many times it was considered public property. After he left, saying he had to get back to his table to help plan the search, Liz Ann said, "It does change how you think of the place, though, doesn't it?"

After Liz Ann left with a tray of sandwiches for the Friends of the Library party, Vicky got to work on her laptop.

****

When Sara Willwood walked in, Vicky immediately recognized her because she'd seen her on television, the distraught aunt of the missing girl.

Plus, Sam greeted her with, "Hi, Sara. Anywhere's fine."

Sara glanced around, her eyes sliding slowly past Vicky. She appeared tough, like she could handle herself, and probably others, too. Tall, early thirties. A low-cut red T-shirt and a beat-up tan leather jacket topped worn jeans and boots. Clothes that might have once fit snugly now hung on her lanky frame. Straight hair fell halfway down her back, a shade between light brown and dark blonde. What some people used to call dirty blonde, and maybe still did. That always struck Vicky as mean, and she immediately regretted that the term had even occurred to her.

Sara didn't appear to respond when Sam poured coffee and squeezed her shoulder.

The circumstances might not be ideal, but Vicky might as well do some poking. No telling when she'd have another chance to talk to one of the witnesses to Rose's disappearance. Maybe she would say something she hadn't mentioned to the cops. It was possible. She stood up and approached Sara's table, slowly so she would notice her coming.

"Hi, excuse me, sorry to interrupt. Do you have just a minute?"

Sara just looked at Vicky. Great, another one who clearly did not want to talk.

"I'm a travel writer, just chatting with people about the area. My name's Vicky Robeson. Can I ask you a question?"

Up close, Sara's skin was grayish, her eyes and nose red and runny. "I don't have a minute." She clearly had no interest whatsoever in speaking to the bozo in front of her.

Caught in the awkward position of preparing to sit down, Vicki straightened her posture. "Okay, sure, sorry to bother you. I'm sitting right over there if you change your mind. I just have a couple of general questions."

Sara ignored her.

Don paused by Sara's table on his way out, but they didn't speak. Vicky studiously avoided his glance and tapped at her laptop. She took her sweet time finishing her lunch and another cup of coffee. If she tilted her head ever so slightly, she had a straight-on view of Sara, but she made a point of not looking. That seemed like the right strategy when, after several minutes, Sara got up and walked toward Vicky.

But Sara did not appear the least bit friendly. Her jaw clenched and unclenched as she approached. Vicky got the immediate impression Sara really wanted to hit her or do something equally aggressive and pain-inducing. Vicky sighed inside and smiled. "Oh, hi, great, please sit down."

Sara stood a little too close and too tall for comfort. "You need to mind your own business and leave us alone."

"Who's 'us'?" Vicky made sure she sounded curious, not aggressive or defensive.

Sam materialized with a lifted coffeepot. "Refill?"

Vicky nudged her mug forward. "Yes, please."

"Is everything all right?" asked Sam.

Sara had to move to make room for the coffee refill. "I mean it. Leave us alone."

Vicky put out her hand. "Nice meeting you. Let me know if you change your mind and would like to chat."

Sara spun on her bootheel and left.

Vicky dropped her hand. "Whoa. She's intense."

Sam gave Vicky a steady look. "You know she's the missing girl's aunt."

"Yeah, I figured."

"This is a small place. Everyone talks."

"And I figured she might like to talk to me. Maybe she could use a distraction." Vicky tried to seem like someone just about anybody would want to have a conversation with.

"You ask a lot of questions." Sam made the statement calmly, just an observation.

"Yes, it's one way I do research."

"Some people don't believe you're writing a travel article." Sam's face did nothing to clarify the intent of her words.

"Well, that's a bummer, because it's true."

And it was true, though it was also true she was intentionally stirring things up, creating some movement. She was still undecided whether there was anything wrong with doing that for personal reasons. Did the classic journalism rule about avoiding conflict of interest apply if she wasn't actually working in news?

"Not everyone wants somebody writing about them." Deadpan Sam was offering either help or a warning.

"It's always like that. Anyone in particular, besides her? I'd really like to talk with her sister, Rita."

Sam didn't answer. She made a graceful pirouette with the coffeepot held high and hip-bumped her way through the door to the kitchen. Damn. Just when they were developing rapport.

When Sam returned, Vicky said, "Sam, can you take a quick break? Just for a minute." Sam paused, then sat down. Vicky continued. "I know people are hurting. I don't want to make anything worse, especially not for Rose's family. Sara made it plenty clear she doesn't want to talk to me. Okay. But I'd really like to talk with Rita, to offer support. Share some thoughts."

"About what?"

"See if I can help in some way. Talk about a few things people have told me. See what she thinks. Anyway, will you do me a big favor? I'd rather not just show up. Will you call Rita, and tell her I'd like to meet with her? Please?"

"I'll think about it."

"Thanks. Do you mind calling her now? I'd like to stop by her place in the morning."

Sam huffed exasperation but picked up her phone. "You really are a piece of work."

****

Thump.

What was that? Vicky threw back the covers, sat up, and swung her legs out of bed in one motion. She reached for her phone on her bedside table before realizing she wasn't home, she was in the RV, and Pete was gone to Kentucky on one of his historical jaunts.

Years of middle-of-the-night newsroom calls had prepared her to wake up with her mind in gear, especially when something newsworthy was imminent or already happening.

But now Vicky could barely shift out of park. She'd hardly slept. She wasn't used to so many animal noises, and she much preferred her comfortable bed to camping, even camping in a recreational vehicle.

She was rattled. Her heart pounded. She cursed her imagination, which had been her life companion and narrator, a gift and an affliction. She didn't hear anything now, but something had jump-started her awake. What was it?

Was something moving next to the RV? By now she was at the door to the hallway, holding her still-untested-in-real-life combo flashlight-stun gun. She tiptoed into the main cabin. Everything looked normal. Was she overreacting?

A scuff.

What the heck was that? When she was a kid, she would tell herself stories to explain what she saw. That man's probably mad because he's getting divorced. I bet someone threw out a cigarette and started the fire. She must be rich to live in such a big house.

Her imagination sometimes worked overtime. Her mind raced through a list of possibilities, a list built over a lifetime of news stories, thriller novels, and scary movies. She waited in silence.

Someone knocked, three firm raps on the metal door. "It's Sara Willwood, Rose's aunt."

Sara? What's she doing here? It's almost three in the morning.

"Vicky?" This time louder. "It's Sara."

Vicky leaned over the counter to lift a single slat of the blinds and peer out the window. Sara stood off to the side of the step, hands on hips, shifting from foot to foot. Their last encounter had not ended on a friendly note. Based on Sara's posture, this one was not likely to, either.

"Vicky?" Another knock, fast and insistent, and a whisper. "Come on, I know you're in there."

"What's up?" Vicky spoke in a normal tone from behind the blinds. Sara's head whipped toward the window.

"I couldn't talk to you at the diner, because of who was there."

Intriguing. "Just a sec." Vicky opened the door. She used her stun gun to gesture toward the camp chairs under the awning. Sara didn't move.

"Who are you talking about?" Vicky stayed on the step with one hand on the door handle.

"You don't know anything." Sara was taut, her hands balled into fists. She looked hostile and jittery, clenching her jaw between words. "You're poking at people and getting things stirred up that should be left alone."

"You seem a little stirred up yourself. But I get it, you must be so stressed and worried, with your little niece gone missing." Vicky opened the door wider and waved Sara in. "Come on in. We can talk about her. Or anything you like."

"You idiot. You don't know what you're doing. That old guy? Don? You need to watch out for him. I don't want him seeing me chit-chatty with you. Stay away from me."

"Wait. You woke me up at three in the morning for that?" Vicky was already talking to Sara's back. "We should talk. Come in for a minute. Have some tea."

Sara kept going. Vicky followed her around the RV toward a car parked a couple of spots away.

"Come on, Sara. You didn't come all the way out here just to tell me to leave you alone. You did that at the diner. Let's talk. What do you mean about Don? I've been wondering about him, too."

It was true. There was more to the old firefighter than he let on.

"Leave us the hell alone."

"I'm just curious about a couple of history things. I'm doing research."

Sara stopped. "What history things?" She scratched her shoulder under her jacket, then abruptly crossed her arms and glared.

Vicky paused. She hadn't planned this out, but it might be her only chance. "About when the girl was found on the levee a few years ago."

Sara was clearly jittery-high on something, hopefully nothing that would ramp up any violent tendencies. "What? I just moved here."

"Right, but you know about it, right? Your sister's ex—Bill Beck, Junior, right?" Vicky silently thanked Ramblin' Don and the chatty Wagners for the tidbit. "His family was from here, weren't they?"

By now Sara's tightened fists were back on her hips. "How do you know that? Why do you know that?"

"It's no big deal. I've been researching the area."

"He didn't live here then, either."

"Oh, yeah, I know. But he did go to high school here. Before he left for Colorado."

Sara scowled. "What does this have to do with anything?"

"Just happened to remember that. Why'd you say

that about Don?"

"He's the one you should be nosing around. Talk to him. Leave me alone."

"C'mon, Sara, relax. I want to help. You can talk to me about anything." Vicky was certain Sara had something to say and she wanted to hear it. "Come inside and let's talk."

Sara hesitated. She had an anguished look on her face. "Leave me alone."

Sara spun away and strode to the car. When she closed her car door, Vicky recognized it as the sound that had awakened her, only louder. She doubted she'd be able to go back to sleep.

Chapter Thirteen

Walkers Corner, May 1999

The girl grabbed at her mother's coat and shook her gently. "Mama! Wake up. Please, Mama, we have to get out of here."

Mama made a tiny moaning sound. She must be hurt. The girl tugged at Mama's coat. Her mother made another sound, like the end of a breath. "Mama, okay, you just rest. I'm going to get help."

The darkness was strange. And the air smelled funny. Where was she? She stood slowly, waving her hands above and around herself, trying to understand what had happened, how they'd gotten here. Her hand passed by her face. Oh, dim light in the distance. She bumped her head on the ceiling. It was rough rock, sloping down to form a wall.

She crouched and crept toward the light, her hands probing the darkness around her. She stumbled and fell. She cried out when she gashed her hands and knees on jagged rocks. She sobbed and pulled herself up. Her hands probed the shadows as she forced herself toward the hazy glow.

It was a lantern, hung from a hook in the ceiling. She stretched as tall as she could, but it was well out of her reach. She jumped and barely touched its bottom. She jumped again, and shrieked and collapsed when her ankle twisted and gave out.

The lantern swayed, casting its feeble light in a wide circle to reveal a flat, gleaming section of wall. She crawled to it.

It was colder than the rock around it. A door. She ran her fingers over it, as high as she could, and all the way to its bottom. No handle or opening.

She pounded it and screamed, "Help! Open the door! My mama needs help!" She screamed and pounded until she sank to her knees, exhausted. The shadows swallowed the sound of her sobbing. Was she going to die?

"Oh, wake up, please wake up, Mama."

Chapter Fourteen

Monday November 2008

After Sara's predawn visit, Vicky slept for a solid five hours. She often did her best sleeping in the morning. She hopped in her car, full of energy, and drove to the cul-de-sac where Rose Willwood was last seen. Or so said the aunt and friend.

Someone had chopped down an evergreen tree and bushes in the center of the turnaround, leaving the branches, trunk, and brush in low piles spilling onto the pavement. She drove past the footpath to the park before circling back around to the sidewalk in front of the missing girl's house. The neighborhood of small, modest houses felt barren and unwelcoming as she walked up to Rose's home.

She knocked, then waited on the porch until the door opened slightly. "Hi, Rita. Vicky Robeson, we met at Sam's? She called you about me?"

"Yeah, hi."

"Is this still an okay time?"

"I'm just sitting here." Rita turned, leaving the door open behind her.

Vicky followed. Rita's movements were unnaturally slow. She looked pale and shriveled, decades past her forty-some years. Her brown curls were flat and listless, and her baggy sweatshirt and jeans hung on her body.

Her eyes were tired and red, though there was fire in there, banked like embers under ash.

It had been eight days since her daughter disappeared.

"I'm so sorry. Your heart must be breaking." Vicky gently touched Rita's arm. "Is anything new?"

"No. Want some coffee?"

"Sure, if it's already made. Black's fine."

Rita motioned toward the small living room. A blanket and pillow, laptop, small flip-phone, and water bottle made it obvious the couch was Rita's nest. Vicky sat in the matching armchair, across from a small television mutely tuned to one of the twenty-four-hour news channels.

She balanced her phone on her leg and glanced around. Framed photos of Rose, and of Rose and Rita, were on every flat surface. Two vases of flowers drooped on the end table, smelling oversweetly of decay. The air was heavy and fatigued. Claustrophobic.

Rita returned carrying two mugs. She handed one to Vicky, then sat on the pillow end of the couch, retrieved a bottle from the floor, and poured a splash into her coffee cup. She tipped the bottle toward Vicky, who declined.

Rita took a light sip. "Sam said you wanted to talk to me."

"Yes, thanks for letting me come over. By the way, I see someone cut down the tree out front."

"I did that."

Vicky nodded. She could imagine doing the same under similar circumstances. A cathartic way to get some anger out.

Rita's voice sounded muffled by layers of

heaviness. "Most of the FBI guys are leaving soon, going back to St. Louis on some terrorist case they think is more important than my little girl."

Vicky searched for something positive to say about that development. "I'm sure they'll keep searching from there. And you've got the sheriff and all the volunteers. It's great to see your town all helping out."

Rita lifted then dropped a shoulder. Vicky added, "By the way, I met your sister Sara at the diner yesterday. Then she showed up at our RV at about three this morning. She told me to leave her alone, said I should be talking to Don."

"I'm not responsible for her," Rita bristled. "I'm sure not apologizing for her. Or explaining. Why should I?"

"That's not what I'm saying, not at all. What do you think she meant about Don, that's all."

"Ask her. I don't want anything to do with her. She was supposed to be watching Rose. Who knows what she was really doing."

"You don't think she was watching her?" Vicky's voice was sympathetic and supportive. If her antennae were visible, they'd be quivering.

"Rose is missing, and no one seems to know a damn thing. Including my sister."

"It must be so hard on you, not knowing."

"Especially her. She wasn't always this clueless."

"What do you mean?"

"Nothing. Sam said you might have some information about Rose. Get to that."

"Well, I wouldn't call it information actually, more like thoughts."

"What kind of thoughts?"

"I want to help find your daughter, but I'm also working on an article for a travel magazine, tied to the little girl found walking on the levee about nine years ago."

Vicky usually described her project as a true crime travel article, but considering the situation and trying to be sensitive, didn't mention crime.

"We just moved here last year." Rita sounded impatient.

"There could be a connection there."

"What, a found girl and a missing girl, nine years apart?" Rita scoffed. "I'm sure the cops would know if there was."

Yeah, sure, if the right ones had all the right information. "Two miles apart, in a remote area like this. Seems like quite a coincidence."

There was more of course—Rick's story about the cargo truck, Don's talk about a distribution ring, the investigation into the old sheriff—but that was not for this conversation.

"That's it? What makes you think so?" Rita asked.

"It's odd there'd be two incidents so close together, even if one was a while ago."

"Rose is not an *incident*."

"Sorry, that's not what I meant, not at all." Time to switch gears. Vicky took a sip of coffee and gestured toward a photo of Rita and Rose, beaming, in jeans and jackets, atop horses. "That's a wonderful photo of you two. Colorado?"

"Yes. It was her first time riding."

"You both look like naturals. You said you got here about a year ago?"

Rita made a half-shrug, half-nod movement.

Vicky paused in hopes she would say why here. She didn't.

"Colorado's beautiful. I live near Denver. Your ex was from here, right? Bill Beck, Junior."

Rita lifted a shoulder and took a sip from her mug.

"I met his sister. Joan, your ex-sister-in-law. Do you know her well?"

"Never met her. We were only married a couple of years. Biggest mistake of my life."

"I've made a couple mistakes I thought were big until I made others that were worse." Vicky could give plenty of examples, but it was enough to sound a bit sheepish.

Rita half-smiled, nodding in rueful agreement. Then her face hardened and grew shadows. "No. My worst mistake was trusting my sister to watch my daughter."

"That seems like a perfectly normal, okay thing to do—leaving your child with someone you know."

"Apparently not."

"Who would ever think this would happen?" Vicky paused to let some of her sympathy sink in. "Sounds like you two already didn't get along."

"We used to."

"That happens a lot in families." Vicky acted as though she had personal knowledge, which she didn't. "It's too bad. What happened?"

"Hmph." Rita sounded disgusted. "Drugs. She can't keep a job or handle money. Though she was supposedly getting her life together. I never should've believed her." Rita put down her mug. "But what's it to you?" She was much more talkative than her sister but apparently had her limits.

"She won't talk to me."

"And why should I?"

"Maybe I can help."

"I don't see how." Rita shook her head impatiently.

"People have told me some local history. I'm looking for connections." Vicky's phone vibrated on her thigh. She stole a glance at the screen. Ah, Rick could meet this afternoon. She had texted him to say she happened to be in town and would love to have coffee, just to catch up.

"Like what?"

"I don't know yet. That's why we talk. Maybe we'll find one." Vicky had no musical, physical or artistic ability, no performance talent whatsoever, but she could usually get people to talk. And she did have an aptitude for finding links and associations.

Rita took a drink. "What've people told you?"

"Let's start with Don. Why would Sara warn me off him?"

"No idea. The only danger with him is he'll talk you to death."

"Ha. He told me some interesting stories. He said people used to move a lot of booze and stolen property around here. Sounded like some kind of distribution ring."

"Huh. Why'd he tell you that?"

"I wonder, too." Also wonder whether those crooks had expanded into moving people. "Did your ex, Bill, ever talk about that kind of thing?"

Rita twisted her mouth. "He never talked about this place. He hated everything about it."

"That's too bad. It seems like a nice area. How do you like it?"

"It was fine until someone stole my baby."

"Gosh, sorry, of course. I thought maybe you moved here because of Bill."

"I lived here when I was in high school. It's cheaper here."

"Oh, you went to school with Bill." Damnit. She should have known that already. "Working at the diner, you must meet everyone. Had you heard about the girl on the levee?"

"Not before. I spend most of my time in the kitchen."

They spent several more minutes talking about the diner, the town, the people. Rita sighed, leaned back, and closed her eyes.

It was time to leave. "I'll let you get some rest." Vicky got to her feet, motioning Rita not to get up. "Can I help with any errands? I have some time. Do you need groceries or anything?"

Chapter Fifteen

Rick Carr
St. Louis, Monday Afternoon

Once outside Rita's house, Vicky sat in her car to text Rick. Coffee at three would be perfect. He replied with the location. She mapped it—she still got a kick out of how easy it was on her new phone. Plenty of time to swing by the liquor store for Rita and do her own errands, too.

Hours later, Rick arrived and surveyed the busy coffee shop, a local place near Soulard Market in South St. Louis. His text had included, *"—look forward to seeing you!—"*

The unnecessary exclamation point led her to suspect his enthusiasm might be a tad artificial. Still, she warmed up a bit herself, just seeing him.

He spotted her and waved slightly, more of a nod with a faint hand movement, and strode toward her back-corner table. The past decade had eroded some of his sharp good looks, but little of his swagger. She braced herself. There was a time when her heart would have been dancing, watching him. Not now.

Rick Carr was an undeniably good-looking man. Tall, fit, tousled brown hair, jeans, forest green shirtsleeves rolled up; he moved gracefully but looked like the kind of guy who could knock down doors. Which he had done, back when he was a cop. Glances rippled in his wake.

He kept his eyes in her direction, but she knew darn well he was indexing the room. He was good at not letting people know what he noticed. As was Vicky. It was handy, the ability to take mental notes without being obvious.

"Hey, you."

"Great to see you."

They pulled each other into a quarter-hug, trading complimentary comments. She caught a faint whiff of something clean and slightly woodsy as they quickly separated.

"I'm going to order." Rick gestured at her mug. "Need anything?"

"Nah. I'm good."

Vicky had invited Rick to coffee the day after she started work at the TV station in St. Louis. A detective, he sometimes served as the public information officer for the sheriff's department, so she was bound to interact with him. She liked to meet key people outside of crisis hours, though meeting in the middle of one was often more memorable.

There had always been tension between them—a pleasant electrical hum that held promise of perhaps leading somewhere interesting. But the last time they were together, the tension wasn't pleasant anymore and never would be again.

When he returned with his coffee, he had a to-go cup instead of one of the heavy mugs.

They spent a few minutes carefully recapping the last near-decade. Both divorced, no kids. His marriage was doomed before it even started six years back. It just took a while to finish. Once hers started ending, it was over immediately. Openly ending, anyway.

They were both factual, sharing little of the flavor of those developments. With minimal description, he said he was seeing someone. He said a few nice things about his boss, Kerry, which he no doubt expected Vicky to pass along. She told him about Pete and his RV, about being unemployed. No, she wasn't sure what her next move would be. No reason to mention the Dallas offer.

"How was it for you," she asked, "switching from cop to reporter?"

"No regrets."

Rick said he'd stayed long enough to earn a police pension, and TV work was always interesting, though it sure didn't pay like people assumed. He got the weekend anchor gig two years ago and was in line to get the big job—the main anchor slot. He'd better be first in line, he joked, with all he brought to the station. But the current guy showed no signs of getting ready to retire.

"But yeah, sure, sometimes I miss carrying a badge and gun."

They chatted briefly about the current state of the news business, their wary love of social media, and the wonderful and terrifying connectiveness of the Internet in general. They exchanged a few updates about people they knew.

Vicky asked about the missing girl. If anyone had the inside track, it was Rick. "What do you think happened to Rose Willwood?"

He shook his head. "It's tough. No one saw anything, or if they did, they're not talking. Might have been a random snatch and grab."

"I thought you didn't believe in random."

"I don't. But everyone says the same thing. She was there in front of her house and then she wasn't."

They speculated about the possibilities for a while before Vicky asked, "Remember Lisa on the Levee? Well, I know you do, you worked the case. It's bizarre no one ever figured out who she was or where she came from."

"She went through something bad, that's for sure."

"It must have been hard, having it still unsolved when you left the sheriff's department."

"There hadn't been any leads in years." Rick shook his head. "We checked out every tip, every missing persons report even remotely close to her description. Nada."

"No matches on the blood? DNA?"

"No," he said. "We never found anyone belonging to all that blood on her."

"I know you spent a lot of time working it. Any tips you got really excited about?"

"Nothing that led anywhere. Why do you ask?"

"I'm working on an article for the tenth anniversary of the case." She explained her idea about how to make the story appealing to fans of crime stories as well as travel buffs. "Kind of a true crime travel article. If there was a crime."

He waited, clearly skeptical.

"Well, if you think of anything, will you let me know?" She hoped she didn't sound needy.

"Not likely, but sure."

"Good enough," said Vicky. "By the way, I noticed something different about you when you walked in."

"What, that I look ten years older?"

"Don't fish. No, you used to carry a leather bag

everywhere."

"I still do. But I didn't think I'd need anything to have coffee."

"I remember it was sharp-looking. Not many guys carried bags back then. Do you remember where you got it?"

"A guy I used to know made it."

"Cool. Does he sell them?"

"No idea."

"Hm. Who is he?"

Rick cocked his head to one side. "You wouldn't know him."

"I'd like to get one like it."

"Huh." Rick exuded skepticism, just as she would have if given that lame reason. He picked up his cup. "Well, I better get going…"

"Rick, wait, remember when I was at your place the first time—"

"If it's about anything personal between us, there's nothing to talk about."

"It's not personal, it's about your father—"

Rick scowled. "He's dead and gone. There's nothing to talk about." He stood abruptly. "I gotta go, I have a meeting. Good luck with the article."

He took his coffee to go, as another wave of glances rippled in his wake.

****

Vicky finished her coffee while she kicked herself for not getting straight to the subpoena she'd seen in his kitchen. She'd stalled. She'd enjoyed chatting with him, enjoyed the pull and presence of the man. Years ago, she'd been sure the magnetism was mutual. It was a relief to let go of any lingering illusions.

116

She wasn't surprised their meeting had ended abruptly, and with such finality. It would have ended sooner if she'd gotten right to it. Rick certainly hadn't become any more trusting in the last decade. Should she have told him she'd talked to his boss about him?

He sure grew cold when she mentioned the bag. Maybe it reminded him of how much he'd talked that night on his porch, and the document she'd seen in his kitchen.

****

As she drove away back to Walkers Corner, Vicky reviewed what she'd told Kerry at dinner two nights ago—highly condensed versions of what Rick had revealed a near-decade ago—about his dog, the caretaker's son, and the two boys spying on their fathers.

She had a nice long drive ahead of her. Perfect time to talk.

Kerry answered with, "Hi, I only have a minute. How was coffee with Rick?"

It'd been months since Vicky ran a newsroom, but she remembered well what it was like, always in semi-triage, deciding what needed attention and what could wait. Limited time for anything not immediate.

Kerry was clearly busy. The short version would have to do. "Mostly good, until he suddenly had a meeting to get to, right after I asked him about the bag. I told him I wanted to get one like it."

"I'm sure he didn't believe that."

"Not even a little." Vicky slowed down behind an old car going at the exact speed limit. She often found herself driving faster when she talked. "He didn't like it, either, when I brought up his father."

"I bet."

"I was wondering if you're going to talk to him about what I told you. About the subpoena? I didn't have a chance to. Well, to be honest, I stalled 'til it was too late. Then he was out the door."

"I'm still thinking about it." They spent a minute talking about that before Kerry interrupted herself. "I'll call you later. Gotta go."

After her abbreviated call with Kerry, Vicky passed the slowpoke station wagon, then let her mind drift to the second-to-last time she was with Rick, the night they'd drunk whiskey on his porch.

In his kitchen, when he handed her the glass of water, she'd taken it without breaking eye contact, then set it on the table without taking a drink. They had reached for each other at the same time. Or maybe she reached first.

As she drove on, a small surge tingled from her head to her foot on the gas pedal as she remembered that embrace, her arms around Rick's lean waist, her head resting on his chest. His shirt was still cool from sitting outside, but she could feel his warmth radiating through it. He smelled of whiskey and outdoors. His chin rested on her head. His arms wrapped around her back. It felt good. All kinds of good.

Vicky could still remember what ran through her head, through her whole being. *He's a cop, you can't do this. Oh, he feels so good. You can't do this, it's not professional. You can't get involved. Oh, man, I want to kiss him, is he going to kiss me? I hope not, I hope so. I'm about to move away, I don't even know where. Come on, this is no time to start up with someone. Don't do this. But why not? I'm going to move away, anyway...*

Vicky glanced at the speedometer. Oops.
She let up on the gas.

Chapter Sixteen

May 1999

Every part of her body ached when she woke again. The girl kept her eyes closed, listening. She carefully straightened her legs and stretched. Sharp rocks dug into her back. She opened her eyes and gazed at the lantern above the metal door.

She had to do something. Mama always said you don't get anything done just sitting around. Mama worked so hard, even after she got sick. And now she's hurt.

First thing, see if there's another way out of here. She sat up so fast she got dizzy, then waited, listening. She listened for the sound of running water. She didn't hear it now. She started on one side of the door and worked her way along the wall of the cave. That's what it was. A cave. She'd been in one before, just a little way, on a field trip. This smelled the same.

She stood on tiptoe to assess how high the uneven wall was, then squatted to gauge where it turned to floor. Don't think about being underground. How could anyone ever find them? She explored cautiously, feeling sharp rocks jutting from ceiling and walls, jagged holes in other places. She peered into the darkness. The lantern was far away. It was all she could see. How big was this place? How long had she been exploring? It seemed as big as her classroom, but she couldn't tell if she'd already covered this section. She wanted to be back in school. But she wouldn't be there anyway, now, since she and Mama had to leave home. They'd been together on the bus, Mama talking in her sweet soft voice. Then something happened. Something bad. A man hit her.

The floor sloped sharply where the wall and ceiling met. She had to crawl to continue. She paused to listen. There. Running water, just a trickle. And air, fresh air. She lay down and reached under a rock ledge.

Chapter Seventeen

Tuesday November 2008

By her sixth day in Walkers Corner, Vicky had made herself something of a fixture at Sam's café, and not only because of its good wi-fi and great coffee. She was staked out at a two-top table near the window, where she had a perfect view of the post office. Autumn afternoon shadows and gray skies darkened the street.

A dusty white pickup pulled into one of the diagonal spots across the street, right in front of the post office. She finished typing but let her field of vision widen enough to watch the driver. He got out of the truck and carried something into the building.

She put her laptop in her tote bag and left money on the table, including another sizeable tip. It was like renting a workspace that came with food. She called out, "See you later, Sam!" She didn't cross the street until after she passed the truck, so she could note the license plate in case this approach didn't work.

The driver was leaving the post office as she neared his truck. She figured him for close to sixty. He wore a jacket, jeans, work boots, and cap. He held a small piece of paper in his hand. He caught the door for her, then let go when she waved him off.

"Thanks. Oh, hi, aren't you the one who makes those cool leather bags?"

He gave a slight nod.

Impressive he showed so little reaction to the question. She put out her hand. "Hi. My name's Vicky."

He took it and shook it twice, just long enough for her to feel how hard and callused his hand was. It was like a roughly padded glove, one intended for use with hot sharp objects that required dexterity when handling. He smelled lightly of work and the outdoors, not unpleasantly.

He said, "Mike."

Vicky stepped toward his truck so they wouldn't block the sidewalk. "It's great to meet you. I ordered one of your bags. You have a good website."

Mike tilted his head back.

Ah. A thrill of recognition surged through her. It was Tattooed Diner Guy, whose friend she'd overheard in the diner her first day here, talking about someone sneaking around.

"The tote bag," she added. "Full-grain leather, vegetable dyed."

No response.

"With the carved bone handle."

It'd been a few days since a razor last touched his still-handsome face. His expression was neutral, at rest. He seemed like a man who didn't give a rat's ass about anyone's opinion of him.

Vicky beamed. "I paid extra for guaranteed five-day delivery."

Not even a barely raised eyebrow. This one was no talker.

"I'm supposed to get it early next week."

He wore a denim shirt, open one button, over a graying T-shirt, under a well-worn field jacket, its brown and green pattern fading toward beige.

"I have a friend who's had a bag like it for at least twenty years and still uses it. I searched for one like it and found your website."

She was talking too much and too fast. He was so still it was unsettling. His hat hooded vivid green eyes. He exuded nothing but stillness as he waited for her to go on.

"You do beautiful work. The carved handle is so unusual."

Still no reaction. Better ramp it up a bit. "How funny. Maybe you just dropped off one to send to me."

Did his eyes change? Was that a yes? Maybe? Good Lord, how can anyone be so motionless? He didn't shift his weight or nod or change his expression, just gazed right at her with those disconcertingly calm green eyes.

"It's so nice to meet you."

He nodded once and reached toward the truck door handle.

Shit. She couldn't let him leave. Might as well go for broke. "I'd like to talk with you sometime, about a woman who had one of your bags. She was here the same time the little girl showed up on the levee."

Mike's head tipped a fraction to one side. Good, he was interested.

"Can we have a quick cup of coffee?" Vicky motioned toward the diner, which would close in twenty minutes. She hoped Sam would waive her usual closing time if by some miracle this guy was willing to talk that long.

He lifted his chin, just barely.

The diner was almost empty. Vicky glanced at Sam and gestured 'two' before she walked straight back to the corner booth and took the side facing the room. Mike slid onto the bench across from her. Sam followed with a coffeepot. She looked at them like she wanted to say something, then poured, turned, and left without a word.

On the short walk from his truck to the booth, Vicky had rehearsed how she would start the discussion. Two could play the game of strategic silence. Though he might not be playing anything. Maybe he simply didn't talk much.

"Thanks for talking with me." Vicky silently snickered at herself. So far, he had spoken exactly one word. Mike. "My name is Vicky Robeson. I'm writing a travel article."

Nothing.

"I'm interested in learning about local products and crafts. Like your bags."

He didn't say a word or change his expression but somehow projected disbelief.

"Have you been making them long?"

Impatience joined the disbelief. "A while."

He took a sip of his coffee, without taking his eyes away from hers.

Vicky held out for a good twenty seconds. "I'm tying my article to how the area's changed in the years since the little girl on the levee. Kind of a true crime travel story. If there was a crime."

Nothing. This was getting tiresome. The man was doing absolutely nothing to hold up his end of the conversation. Perhaps a more direct approach. "I bet you see a lot of what goes on around here. Did you ever see the levee girl?"

"No."

"Who do you think she was?"

"No idea."

"Such unusual circumstances. Where do you think she came from?"

"Don't know. What do my bags have to do with anything?"

Aha! An actual sentence. His voice was strangely compelling; low and measured, clear but with a growly undertone.

Vicky took a slow sip of coffee. Good. He's interested. "A woman showed up with one of your bags at the exact same time the girl was found."

"Showed up where?"

Great, she had info he wanted to know. Maybe they could do some trading. "Where'd you meet her?" she asked.

"What makes you think I did?"

"She was hurt and filthy, but her bag was brand new. She hadn't had it long."

"I've sold a lot of them."

"And they are not cheap. Did you sell her one? Give her one?"

"I don't know who you're talking about."

"Sure you do, or we wouldn't be sitting here." Vicky sat back. Clearly, he wasn't going to volunteer anything. Annoyed to hear the plea in her voice, she pressed. "Come on. Talk to me. Were you trying to help her?"

Mike slid out of the booth and stood. "Who do you think you are, questioning me?"

"I'm trying to set something right."

"Set what right?"

"It'll take a few minutes. I'll tell you about her and your bag. It's important."

Mike's eyes narrowed as he appeared to weigh his

options. "Some other time. I have things to do." He headed to the door.

Vicky followed. "Just say where and when."

"The library. Ten tomorrow."

"I'll be there."

Chapter Eighteen

Tuesday Afternoon

Vicky watched Mike walk to his truck, his gait smooth and fluid. She held the door open for several people as they left the diner, saying, "Thanks again, Sam," and "We'll see you next time."

Sam stood inside holding an empty tray. "Thanks, y'all. Good luck out there." She beckoned Vicky in, flipped the sign to CLOSED, and locked the door. They were the only ones in the diner. "I see you met Mike."

"Hi, Sam. Yeah. He's not much of a talker. Are those volunteer searchers who just left?"

"Yes. That group's been out every day, what is it? Nine days now. Everyone's exhausted."

"I signed up to help but no one's called me."

Sam glided to a table and stacked dishes. "You have to know your way around. They're searching some rough country."

Vicky piled plates at an adjoining table. "Let me help. I used to wait tables."

Sam chuckled. "You couldn't have been very good at it."

"I was terrible! I didn't last three days."

Sam briskly scraped and restacked the dishes, then paused, holding a handful of cutlery. "So. Mike. He's an interesting guy. What did you two talk about?"

Vicky picked up a plate. "I ordered one of his bags. He doesn't talk much."

Sam arched her eyebrows in mock surprise. "He doesn't?"

"Barely at all." Better wait before saying much about him. Besides, the volunteers had sparked an idea. "Sam, I was thinking about the volunteers. I want to find a way to help out, to support them. More than buying sandwiches. What do you think about doing something for them? As a thank you."

Sam appeared skeptical.

Ah, an opportunity to convince someone of something, one of Vicky's favorite activities. She started winging it, thinking out loud. "Or a fundraiser, to cover gas and food for the volunteers. Or to raise money for a reward."

Sam frowned.

Vicky was warming up, feeling inspired. "It'll boost morale." She waved the plate. "We could invite the sheriff, and FBI if they're still around. Maybe get some new leads. We could have it here, at the diner."

"What?" Sam looked almost horrified. "I'm not set up for that."

"We'll keep it simple."

"The place isn't big enough to make it worthwhile."

"We could use the parking lot. Move tables and chairs outside. What's the weather supposed to be? We'll ask for donations. It's for a good cause. People can sign up to help search."

"I don't know—"

"It'll even be good for business."

Vicky was being presumptuous, perhaps even pushy, but hey, it was a good idea. It'd help the volunteers, be something positive for the town. Plus, she could shake things up, get close to key players, put certain people together.

Sam's quizzical expression held a glimmer of interest.

Vicky put down the plate, the better to gesture. "Do you know any musicians? We could sell soft drinks and coffee, maybe cookies—or your cinnamon rolls! No, that'd probably be too much work."

"I don't know…"

Vicky pressed. She needed to get something going, to give her reason to talk with people. The travel article explanation—while true—only went so far. "We'll need to start right away, get on social media, print some posters. Notify the St. Louis news people, they're crying for a new angle to the Missing Rose story. People will help get the word out."

"I've never done anything like this."

"I've organized lots of things." Vicky waved both hands in a gesture that said it was no big deal. "We'll make it an event. It'll give the news people something new to talk about. They'll be all over it."

"Maybe…" Sam was definitely starting to sound interested, which fueled Vicky's enthusiasm.

"Actually, maybe we do sell your cinnamon rolls, for an extra donation, I mean. They smell so good. I'd donate ten bucks for one. You'd have to make a lot of them. I'll help you."

"People around here don't spend money like that. They don't have it."

Vicky resumed collecting dishes. "We can drop the price. The donation. But we want to raise money. You could give away your rolls if you want to, but believe me, people will donate extra once they smell them."

"I would need to know how many, to get supplies."

Good. Sam was estimating expenses. Most likely then, she was in. "What's the most you could make, if you had plenty of help?"

"I'll figure that out." Sam bumped open the door to the kitchen and took her tray to the dishwasher. "How many do you think we could sell?"

Vicky followed with a stack of dishes. "A lot. What do you say we plan for midday Sunday? That gives us four days. Plenty of time. We'll get people to help."

"I need to think about it."

"Sure. Sooner we start thinking the better. Let's just loosely work it out. How many rolls do you usually make in a day?"

"Four dozen. And I need to get started on tomorrow's batch. It's the last thing I do before I go home. My kitchen's not big enough to make rolls and breakfast at the same time."

"And they sell out every morning."

"They do. We would have to be organized." Sam uncovered a large bowl. "See, I made the dough earlier. It's ready to roll out for tomorrow."

She began punching it down. Sam's hands smoothly massaged and flattened the dough as she talked about the choreography necessary to maximize the number of rolls she could produce in her small space.

She popped the lid off a container, scooped out a spreader-full of creamy light brown filling, plopped it on the dough, and slathered it neatly and evenly all the way to the edges.

Vicky inhaled deeply. "Mmm. What's in that butter besides cinnamon and sugar? I smell something else.

Something delicious."

"Oh, it's just an old recipe. So, I roll this up and slice it." Sam formed the dough into a long tube and cut it into sections, placing the pinwheels side by side on a pan. "We take them out to rise again in the morning. We bake a dozen at a time so they're always warm and fresh."

Sam took the first full pan, covered it, put it in the fridge, and closed the door. "Thirty dozen. We can make thirty, for sure. More, with enough help. I'd have to get foil pans."

"Wow. You figured that out in your head? There's a lot of steps."

"Someone taught me a formula for baking different large quantities when I was a kid." Sam started on another batch.

Interesting. Vicky admired competence in all forms. "That's really something. Okay, let's say our goal is thirty dozen. We'll invite reporters out to do a preview story on you making the rolls to raise money for the search. They'll want to cover that."

"I'm not talking to any reporters."

"Two of the St. Louis stations do Sunday morning news. I bet they'll want to do live shots. Maybe we get one of their anchors to emcee. Do you think Rita might be up to making rolls? That's part of her regular job, isn't it?"

"Yes, but—"

"The missing girl's mom, back at work to support the searchers and say thank you to the community. It'll probably be good for her to get out of the house."

"Hm. I'll ask her, but I doubt it."

"It's worth asking. I hope she wants to. We had a good visit. Thanks for calling ahead."

"Yeah." Sam put the last pan in the refrigerator, then started on the dirty dishes.

"Lot of work, running a diner," Vicky observed. "How'd you learn?"

"I worked here for a year before it was mine."

Vicky had read the café story on the menu, but asked, "Who owned it before?"

"The Hanfords. Phil and Jennie. They died in a car wreck. A drunk driver plowed into them."

"Terrible. Too damn many drunks. Then you bought it?"

"Actually, they left it to me in their will."

"Wow. They didn't have family?"

"They had a daughter, but apparently, they had a fight and she left decades ago. They never heard from her again. Broke their hearts."

"That's sad." A familiar hum ran through Vicky as she briefly figured timelines and made a mental note to research a few things. Interesting. "Do you have family around here?"

"No. But the Hanfords practically adopted me after I started working here. They let me live in their daughter's old room." Sam's pause seemed wistful before she resumed her cleanup. "They were wonderful people."

"Must have been hard to lose them. Did you know them growing up?"

"No."

"Oh. I was just wondering if they were the ones who taught you how to bake in large quantities." There were only so many places a kid would learn big-batch baking. A family restaurant or bakery, maybe a group home. Or an institution, like Vicky had lived in.

Sam didn't answer. Vicky gestured with her phone. "I started a list of what we need to do. Is there a good local band?"

By way of answer, Sam started the dishwasher and motioned Vicky toward the front of the diner. "Okay, that's it for me. I'll think some more about the fundraiser."

"Great. I want to help, to pitch in somehow to help find Rose. This is something I can do. If you'll take charge of the baking, I promise I can get everything else done." Vicky handed her phone to Sam. "Here, put in your info. I stay up late."

Sam rolled her eyes but took it and tapped.

"Do you think the sheriff will want to speak?"

"He hates public speaking."

"Oh, are you friends? What do —"

"I didn't say we're friends. I know him. Everyone knows him."

"Okay, but he'd do it, right? Why wouldn't he? He could talk to a lot of people at once, pick up some good info."

By now Sam was holding the swinging kitchen door open and gesturing toward the front entrance.

Vicky stalled. "I need to meet him. I left messages but never heard back. I want to see if we can trade ideas."

"The sheriff usually comes in for breakfast around eight."

There was a firm knock on the back door, followed by three quick taps and another knock. Vicky raised her eyebrows at Sam, who grinned. "None of your business. Now scoot."

Vicky took her time retrieving her bag. Sam unlocked and opened the front door.

Vicky paused in the doorway. "We could hang a big thank-you banner right here over the front door." She looked toward the sidewalk. "Oh, hi, Sheriff. Linden, right? We were just talking about you."

The man said, "No one answered the back door."

Sam opened the door wide, rolling her eyes. "Oh, for God's sake. Vicky, meet Sheriff Hal Linden. Sheriff, meet Vicky. She wants to ask you something."

Linden touched the brim of his ranger-style hat, like a movie cowboy greeting the new lady in town. "Heard about you."

He was tall, bigger than average, mid-thirties, and not the pampered kind of thirties. Dark bags under his eyes weighed down his deeply creased face. He needed a shave. His brown uniform looked like he'd slept in it.

"Uh-oh." Vicky smiled. "Good to meet you. We're planning a fundraiser, Sam and I, on Sunday to help with Rose—"

Sam raised her hands in a slow-down gesture. "We're only talking about—"

"Yes, but we need a few commitments before we can push 'go.' There's a lot to do." Vicky focused on the sheriff. "Here we just met and I'm asking a favor. I know you're swamped with the search and investigation, but we're hoping you can say a few words?"

Linden raised one eyebrow.

Vicky barely gave him a chance to answer in case he was going to say no. "Sunday at ten or eleven. It'll probably be on TV. We'll have a stage, hopefully music, sell Sam's rolls. We're still working out details, but we'd want you to talk about the investigation. You can thank all the volunteers in person. We'll be raising money for them, or to add to the reward if you think that'd be better.

Hopefully both."

Linden dipped his head slightly, enough to indicate understanding without committing to anything. "Depends."

"We'll get news people out to cover it. I know it's hard to plan ahead when you're working hard to find Rose. But it'll be a great chance for you to talk to people. We'll be talking to people, too. We could trade notes after. Like a volunteer task force."

"Thanks. We already have a task force. I'll think about Sunday. Sam, I'm here for those sandwiches."

There was an awkward moment as Vicky shifted aside to let him enter the diner. "Great, thanks." She made her voice upbeat, like he'd agreed to something. "Maybe not a task force, more like junior deputies. Kidding. Consultants. I'll look for you tomorrow. Pleasure meeting you, Sheriff. See ya, Sam."

Vicky waved as she left the diner to take a walk before heading back to the campground. It would do her good. She had things to think about. Other than Volunteer Firefighter Don, people around here didn't freely give away information. A fundraiser was a great idea. She could get in on the action and help the family and searchers. It'd be an ideal way to talk with people, dig around, stir up a few things. Plus, it'd be the perfect way to volunteer. And she'd have good reason to talk with the sheriff. He said he had his team, but he struck her as a reasonable man. He'd talk with her. At least listen. Maybe Sam could help convince him.

Interesting. They have a special door knock.

Vicky strode along, visualizing information and details she'd collected over the last few days. She liked history, macro and micro. What people's parents did, how they lived. What else was going on at the same time or place. Never know when it might come in handy to know something about something.

When the sidewalk ran out, Vicky crossed the road to walk facing oncoming traffic. She played one of the imaginary games she used when she had a lot on her mind. She pictured blocks filled with information—people, places, events, and memories. Blocks of facts, emotions, motivations, of different sizes and shapes, tumbling into stacks, forming columns of varying importance.

The columns holding her personal past and potential future were filling up fast. Ah, hell. She had to decide about the Dallas job. It was a great offer. And she needed to answer Pete about living together. She couldn't have both. Or could she? Would he want to move? She didn't have a great track record with full-time relationships.

She texted to see how his trip was going. He was about to check in wherever he was spending the night. She said everything was great, she missed him, and had a lot to tell him. Should she mention Dallas? The station had called again, wanting an answer—but that wasn't a texting type of conversation. Later.

Even with her jacket, knit hat, and quick pace, it was cold. A vehicle loomed over the rise. She automatically stepped farther onto the narrow shoulder. The large vehicle veered sharply at her, filling her vision with grillwork. She flung herself out of the way. Almost out of the way. Something grazed her foot as the truck sped past.

"Whoa." Vicky wrestled herself up from the dry bushes she'd landed on, her heart pounding, her breath hard to find. "Shit." She wasn't used to falling, much less jumping out of the way of fast-moving vehicles. It took effort to get out of the brush and onto her feet.

"Jesus! Was that on purpose?" she asked out loud. She took inventory: shoulder and hip were going to hurt, a few scratches, numb foot. She flashed to something she'd read once. The writer described being hit by a minivan while he was walking. The driver was distracted by his dog, wasn't it? The specific, vividly gruesome account of the impact and the writer's injuries and recovery were etched in her memory. Thank God this wasn't anything like that.

This was probably an accident too. Not even. A near-accident, really. She was so focused on thinking she might not have paid enough attention to traffic. Maybe she was closer to the road than she realized. Maybe the truck didn't actually swerve. She hadn't seen the driver or noticed anything about the vehicle, other than it was coming at her. She was pretty sure it was gray. A pickup. Or maybe a SUV. Maybe light blue.

Maybe she should report this. But what would she say? Nah. No point in adding to her embarrassment.

Chapter Nineteen

Early Wednesday November 2008

Vicky deliberately arrived in town well before her ten o'clock meeting with Mike The Bag Guy so she'd have time for a brisk walk. She needed to loosen up her banged-up hip and shoulder. Then she'd go to the diner to 'bump into' the sheriff. And maybe have one of Sam's cinnamon rolls, with the secret ingredient Sam declined to disclose. She hadn't tried one yet. It was time.

The library wasn't supposed to open for more than an hour, but the lights were on. Vicky peered in. Liz Ann was talking with someone.

What the heck? Was that Mike? Laughing?

Liz Ann spotted her, waved her forward, and opened the door. "Vicky! Hi! I'd like you to meet someone."

Mike had the remnants of a grin on his face. He held a small plant half-wrapped in brown paper.

"Vicky, this is Mike, Mike Miller."

"Hello, again. Yes, we've met. I ordered one of his bags."

Liz Ann and Mike were already moving toward the back of the library. Liz Ann glanced back. "Oh, you did? They're beautiful, aren't they? Are you here for the garden club meeting? We're about to start."

Vicky followed them. "Yes, I am, if it's okay with everyone…" She could catch up with the sheriff later.

Everyone consisted of five people in an alcove, sitting at a large library table covered with newspaper. Several small plants were placed in the middle, roots wrapped. Mike put his plant with the others and sat down.

Liz Ann made quick introductions. Vicky was so pleased to meet sisters Barb and Susan, both retired schoolteachers, and yes, she remembered George, the assistant librarian. "We almost met at the library. You were on the phone. Nice to actually meet you."

"Sure. How ya doing?"

Ah. The Minnesota accent was unmistakable. George was the Younger Suspicious Guy from her first time at Sam's Café. She'd pictured someone more like a movie Viking—big and muscular, with flowing blond hair. George was in his thirties, tall and skinny. He wore glasses, a short, neat beard, and long dark hair in a ponytail. Well, she'd had his age about right, anyway.

"My husband, Don, told me all about you," said Susan. "Guess you could tell he loves to talk."

"Don, yes, he was very helpful."

The group quickly got down to gardening business. George ran a tight meeting.

They talked in great detail about the library garden, what needed to be done when, and who could do it. Vicky asked a couple of questions to show she was interested.

Mike added as much to the discussion as anybody. No more Silent Swamp Guy. Maybe he didn't like strangers.

Toward the end of their hour, the members traded plants and small talk before the meeting broke up. Time to open the library.

Vicky dawdled until Liz Ann said, "Well, I need to get to work. So glad you came." She headed to the front desk, leaving Vicky standing with Mike.

"I'll see you at ten." Mike turned toward the row of public computers.

"Want to talk now?"

"Ten's better."

"Sure. Perfect." She'd have time for a cup of coffee. She needed the caffeine. The sheriff might still be at the diner, and maybe a cinnamon roll with her name on it.

Barb and Susan from the garden club were at the corner table when Vicky arrived. They waved. "Vicky, come sit with us."

"Thanks. I can only stay a few minutes."

Barb asked, "What's the big rush?" just as Susan asked, "So what'd you think of our meeting? You almost fell asleep when we were talking about the vines."

"Sorry, I hadn't had any coffee. And I'm not great with plants."

Once they were in dirt and getting water, Vicky expected them to take care of themselves. These people were serious about vegetation. Something called bindweed had invaded the garden. Battling it sounded more like slow-motion warfare than gardening. Vicky's mind had wandered away, until something caught her ear. What was that? Something about a cabin? She'd wanted to ask, but the club was already back on topic.

After she got her coffee, Vicky asked, "So how long have you all been with the club?" She didn't quite say 'y'all' but came close. The soft pronunciation was contagious.

The sisters talked over each other. They'd been helping out for ten years, or was it twelve? But George

141

started at the library, must be six years now, he's the one who really got them organized. Liz Ann didn't even garden before he came. Mike had been there the longest. He did a lot of work but hardly ever attended meetings.

Vicky was tempted to talk about the fundraiser but decided it'd be better to wait until a few things were nailed down. She drank most of the refill. "Well, I have to get going."

On her way out, Vicky checked in with Sam, who said she couldn't talk now, but was okay going ahead with the fundraiser. And the sheriff had agreed to speak.

When Vicky got back to the library, Mike was coming out the front door. She pulled out her phone and checked the time. "You're leaving? It's only five 'til."

"Let's talk out here." Mike gestured toward a bench.

Vicky followed. "I saw Barb and Susan at the diner. It's great y'all take care of the garden."

Mike stopped at a green metal bench. "Uh-huh." He remained standing at one end.

She sat down, half-turned toward the center. "It seems like a good group."

"Yeah. What did you mean about making something right? Make what right?"

"Maybe it's more about finishing something." Should she stand? Nah, maybe he'd sit if she didn't. "I was a reporter here, a few years ago—"

"I looked you up."

"Is that what you were doing on the computer?"

"That and some business. The library has good Internet access."

"It's the nicest library I've ever been in." Vicky patted the bench. "C'mon. Sit down. Let's just talk."

Mike hesitated, then sat, facing straight ahead.

Vicky stayed where she was so she could watch him. She waited to see if he would say anything and was not surprised when he didn't.

"It's pretty quiet around here."

That was obvious, and Mike didn't reply. He was clearly not big on small talk.

"What was it like, growing up here?" she asked, using one of her fallback conversation starters.

"Quiet." Mike turned from staring at the side garden. "You're the one showed up looking for me. Why?"

"Like I said, I'm working on a travel article." And she was, but she had to know what the story was before she could write it. "It may be focused on Rose right now, but I'll definitely tie it to the little mystery girl found on the levee. Lisa. A true crime travel article. If there was a crime. It's always haunted me, that child wandering around in the middle of nowhere. How'd that happen? Whose daughter was she?"

Mike looked back at the garden without speaking.

It was clearly time for a different approach. Vicky waved her hand. "Bear with me a minute. I'll explain. You know Rick Carr, right? He has one of your bags."

His shoulder made a minor movement. Mike, Mysterious Outdoors Guy, was more talkative with her than when they first met, but only if compared to absolute silence.

"I knew Rick when I worked in St. Louis, it's been almost ten years now. One night we bumped into each other and had a few drinks. He'd just put his dog Maggie down. This was a day or two before Lisa showed up on the levee."

Vicky watched Mike directly, not pretending

otherwise. "Long story short, he was flat-drunk and told me a couple stories. One was about his father kicking Maggie into a tree when she was a pup. That same day his father gave him a leather bag he got at a caretaker's cabin. You make bags."

Now, fingers crossed that Mike was the guy Rick had followed in the woods. "The other involved you, when you were both kids and spied on the sheriff and your father."

Mike didn't show any more expression in profile than he did face-to-face.

Good. It must be him. "Rick said you saw people carry boxes from a truck into a big house. There were armed guards. It sounded suspicious. That's why I looked for you."

Something changed in Mike's face, like he alerted to a sound or a scent. "You're investigating the Carrs?" He sounded almost eager. "I was there when that son of a bitch kicked the dog, too."

Obviously, he had no love lost for the now-deceased sheriff. Great, she thought, now talk.

"I was in high school. He was at our place looking for someone. Yelled at my pa, treated him like dirt. Yeah. He threatened to kick my ass and stole a bag I made special for someone." Mike kept his eyes on the garden. "And before he left, he kicked his kid's pup into a tree."

Vicky didn't move, silently urging him to keep talking.

Mike obliged. "He had it in for me. He busted me a few times, mostly for nothing. It ruined my life, having a record. Set me on a bad path."

"Seems like you have friends here, and a pretty good business."

"Making bags, living in a swamp, is not what I planned to do with my life."

"What'd you plan to do?"

"Doesn't matter. But the old sheriff was dirty. His boy Rick might have told you what we saw at the lodge, but he didn't tell you all of it. They weren't moving boxes. They were moving women. And it wasn't only that one time."

Vicky caught her breath. "They were prisoners?"

"Appeared to be. They were in a cargo truck."

"Rick didn't mention women."

"He was a kid. Maybe he didn't pick up on it."

Unlikely, she thought. Rick was smart. "So the lodge was used for sex trafficking or something?"

"I don't know. I just know what I saw."

"Maybe the woman was one who escaped."

"What woman?"

"The one who had your bag. The girl must have been with her."

"We saw that truck when I was in high school, a long time ago. The girl on the levee was what, ten years ago?"

"Nine. In 1999. She and the mystery woman were here at the same time. Maybe there were traffickers who'd been at it all these years. It's possible, especially if the sheriff was in on it. You said he was dirty. And now maybe they got Rose."

Saying it out loud stabbed Vicky. Please don't let it be so. She couldn't forgive herself for not doing more back then. Vicky added friendly urgency to her voice. "Tell me about the woman, Mike. Maybe she escaped from there. Did you help her get away?"

Mike looked back toward the garden.

"You don't have to give me any details. Tell me

what happened. Bare bones."

Silence.

"What are you worried about? A crime? Are you worried what people'll think?"

"I'm not interested in what people think," he growled.

"Was there something illegal? Just because something's illegal doesn't necessarily mean it's wrong."

Mike stared straight ahead. She could feel it. He was going to tell her. Just wait it out. Let him talk.

Chapter Twenty

Mike Miller
Wednesday Morning

Out of the corner of his eye Mike saw Vicky lean forward on her end of the library bench. What the hell? How could she know about the woman? So, someone saw her after me. Who? After all these years, wondering if I was the last one to see her alive. The whole time expecting someone to come around asking about her—the cops, whoever beat her up, maybe a relative. But now, seriously? A travel writer? And she went to some trouble to track me down. Why?

"All right. Bare bones." He'd tell her the minimum, even though he could remember every detail. He had never told anyone, ever, about the event he'd relived in his mind for years.

"I found a woman in the woods near my cabin."

He had heard the woman before he found her, the sounds of someone unskilled in the woods, breaking branches, overturning rocks. He drew close enough to hear gasping breaths, a slow crunch of wood crackling, then silence.

She was face down in the underbrush. He scanned their surroundings, listening, before he bent over to touch her shoulder. She was small. Leaves and twigs stuck to her long, dark, tangled hair. Her torn brown sweatshirt and jeans were dirty.

"She was hurt."

He had gently rolled her over. She was young, maybe twenty. Unconscious, her face swollen and bruised. Streaked with blood. An old kitchen knife lay half-under her. It was bloody, as were her clothes. Fresh blood. He touched her neck to find a faint, uneven pulse. No large wounds. No major bones appeared to be broken.

"I carried her to my place." Mike could practically feel Vicky concentrating, extracting words from him, tugging his memory toward her as they sat outside the library. She leaned forward, watching intently.

He'd slung his gun over his shoulder, slid the knife into his bag, then bent to pick her up. He scuffed away their footprints as he carried her. He paused before leaving the woods, then hefted her limp body a little higher and headed for his back porch. She moaned but didn't wake. Mike surveyed the area before opening the door. The woods were dark and silent behind him.

"She was unconscious, but she was breathing okay. Someone'd beat her up bad."

The vibration of her deep groans pulsed against him as he carried her. He put her on his bed and covered her with his blanket. He took one more look outside before he shut the door.

"She was out for a few hours."

She had thrashed around when she woke up, got to her knees, eyes darting. She saw him and fell back, then scrabbled to the corner of his narrow bed, next to the worktable. She half-stood to reach across a stack of cut-out leather, toward his leatherworking tools. By the time her hand was there he had already pushed them aside.

"When she woke up, I gave her water and something to eat."

He'd placed the cup and plate near her, then backed away. She crouched, half-raised hands in fists. Terrified. He murmured reassurances and kept his distance. She finally picked up the cup and gulped water, her flashing dark eyes pinned on him. She picked up the sandwich and tore into it.

"She didn't say anything. I don't know whether she even understood me."

Mike glanced at Vicky, who did not move a muscle. "We heard a truck coming."

He had picked up the rest of the sandwich and put the dishes in the sink. By then she'd heard it too. She crouched lower, making small guttural sounds.

"She was terrified."

He had lifted his hands to show her, slowly, as he took her knife from his bag and put it into one he'd almost finished making. He added the bread and meat. No time for water. He took her arm and drew her to her feet. She did not resist. He tugged the bedcovers straight, then put the bag strap over her head and picked up his rifle.

"I put a few things in the bag and hid her outside."

He'd carried her several yards into the woods. He set her down gently in the underbrush, pulled branches over her, and whispered to wait there.

"It was Rick Carr. Deputy Carr." Mike glanced at Vicky. "He asked about the girl on the levee. I didn't know anything about her."

"You didn't tell him about the woman?"

"No way. I told you. I didn't trust him or his daddy. Old Sheriff Carr was mixed up in some shady deals. She might have been running from them. I don't know."

"That's what you think? Me too." Vicky sat straight, perched on the edge of the bench. "I'm glad we have the same opinion. What happened then?"

"That damn Rick took a look around my place, then I followed him to check the lodge."

Shadows had deepened the afternoon gloom to near dark when they pulled into to the lodge clearing. The old building looked like an enormous swamp creature hunched down, small window eyes staring blankly. The sagging ends of the deep porch formed a frown, with crooked teeth made of chairs covered with faded brown tarps. The surrounding trees shaded the house so completely the roof and wood plank siding were blotched with dark moss. Overgrown bushes and vines melded with the structure. Mike had always loathed the place. It was like a malignant growth on the land.

"Sheriff Carr was there, standing on the porch."

Mike had walked around the side of the building that formed the toe of the L-shaped structure. The top of the L backed up to the steep rock bluff. The dark, ragged forest formed another wall, creating a rough courtyard of bare dirt and weeds. It was empty, but two vehicles had left fresh tire tracks.

"He'd been inside. He'd walked all through the place. I didn't even know he had a key."

The place stank of years of neglect, layered with the scents of unwashed bodies and long-ago rotted food. The smell of leftover pizza was more evidence someone had been there.

Mike glanced at Vicky. "She was gone when I went back for her."

"Did you look for her?"

"Yes." Hell, yes, he'd looked for her. Wasn't for lack of trying he didn't find her. "I got sent off to search for any sign of the kid's people. Then it rained. By the time I got back she could have been anywhere."

"And you never saw her again?"

Mike shook his head and fell silent.

Chapter Twenty-One

Wednesday November 2008

Vicky waited, but after Mike finished his brief
description of his encounter with the mystery woman, he
sat on the library bench, as still as a tree or stone or
creature of the forest. It didn't take long for that act to
grow old. If only she could read his mind. She repeated,
"And you never saw her again?"

Mike shook his head no. "How did you know about
the bag?"

Fair question. Vicky had made no promises, but she
wasn't ready to tell anyone Joan's story about Alisa.

"A friend saw it when she was covering the Lisa
story. I'm not going to get into where right now."

He acknowledged that with a twitch of two of the
fingers resting on his thigh, palms down like he was
about to launch forward.

"She saw it the day after the levee girl was found.
Later that night, I stopped by to see your buddy and
mine, Rick Carr." She spoke carefully. "I'd been to his
place once before, a couple days before, when he told me
about the two of you spying on your dads."

No need to get into anything personal about either
long-ago night. She had driven past Rick's house, made
a U-turn, and parked where she could see the whole

place.

"It was after I did my live shot on Lisa for the late news."

A faint form moved behind closed curtains. Rick liked to pace and talk when he was thinking. When he had no one to talk to, he sometimes talked to himself. Two nights earlier, between whiskey sips on his porch, she'd revealed she did the same thing.

"He opened the door but said he couldn't talk."

There'd been no warmth in Rick's voice. He was in uniform, minus tie and hat. He held his landline phone in one hand, with his fingers over the mouthpiece, halfway up to his ear, like he was in the middle of talking with someone.

"I said I had a question about something he'd said at the news conference. That I didn't want anyone else to hear. He said to wait outside, he was on a call. While I was sitting on his porch a pickup truck stopped in front. I walked over to it."

It had taken a few seconds for her to realize the pickup was slowing in front of the house. She couldn't see the driver, only an impression of movement through the rear pane. Something shifted under a tarp in the open pickup bed as she approached.

"A woman's voice called out something like, 'tell Rick she's the one he talked to earlier, and he better call her back now.'"

The anonymous hand had waved, and the truck sped off into the night. Vicky returned to her perch on the steps. The engine sound faded away before Vicky realized she hadn't even glanced at the license plate. That should be instinct. Usually was. She was letting herself get distracted. She wasn't even sure what color the truck was. What was moving under the tarp?

Good thing the truck interrupted her reverie. This was no time to dwell on Rick and what might have been. She and Rick had flirted mildly, occasionally dancing a little close to the edge of something more. They'd had coffee several times, nothing unusual for a friendly cop and friendly reporter. She had no intention of getting too personal, too close to any boundaries. There'd been no suggestion of professionally inappropriate behavior. She took that kind of thing seriously.

Vicky paused her story long enough that Mike looked at her. She wasn't done. "I don't know who was in the pickup. Anyway, Rick finally opened the door. I asked if his father had organized the search. I was suspicious because of what he'd told me about the two of you watching your dads and the cargo truck, which sure sounded like some shady business. I wanted to know if they'd searched that place."

Vicky could remember everything about the encounter. She had urged Rick to set aside the fact his father was sheriff, to think about him like he would anyone else who might be up to something fishy.

"Rick basically kicked me out. I never told him about the woman in the truck. But what was weird was something was moving under a tarp in the bed of the truck. Remember, this was the day after the farmer found the levee girl."

"What was it?"

"I couldn't tell. Something big enough that I noticed. Wasn't that kind of strange?"

"Maybe. Now, where'd your friend see the bag?"

"On someone's porch."

"Whose?"

"I need to check before I say."

He scoffed. "Whatever. I need to get going." He ignored her appeal to stay for a few more minutes and left.

Vicky waited until Mike went around the corner before she got up from the library bench. She needed to think about what he'd told her, and what she hadn't told him. Her stomach had started burning the minute she mentioned Rick, remembering how she'd left his house that long-ago night—angry, hurt, embarrassed.

Or maybe it was burning because she was hungry. Breakfast was one of Vicky's favorite meals. She'd skipped today's in favor of the unexpected garden club meeting and the amazing talk with Mike. She was famished. She walked back to the diner, stoked with excitement, which made her even hungrier.

When she arrived, George was seated with Barb and Susan. Vicky joined them at the corner table, where they were all having coffee and luscious-looking berry pie. After Vicky ordered lunch, the others resumed their conversation.

"It wasn't about natural gas." George turned to Vicky. "I'm telling them about a meeting I sat in on. A company's buying up mineral rights. They've been talking to property owners all over the area." He looked back at the others. "The guy was slick. He wouldn't say what mineral, but I hear they're after something called frack sand."

Susan shook her head. "Never heard of it."

"Sand?" Barb perked up. "Remember the old glass factory south of here? They used to dig up sand."

"What was his name? Elliot? The son." Susan sounded wistful.

"Edwin." Barb sounded certain. "They left for California after the factory closed."

"Wonder what happened to him. He was one good-looking man."

After a pause to see if the sisters had more to say, George continued. "I don't know if this is the same kind of sand. They use this for mining natural gas. You know about fracking?"

Vicky was the only one who nodded. She resisted telling them all about fracking. She'd lived in Texas where it was big money.

"Fracking's how they get natural gas." George made a stirring motion. "They mix this special silica sand with chemicals and water and force it underground to break up shale rock. To fracture it. Seems we're on the lower end of a giant seam of the stuff, runs all the way up to Minnesota, near where I'm from."

George described how the Silica Sandman used a lot of big words and elaborate animated computer graphics to explain the geology and technology.

"He was kind of hypnotizing. He had this Zen-like way of putting away his electronics. He kept talking while he leaned back to unplug the power cord. Then he sits up, stops talking, and wraps up the cable with everyone watching. He puts the cable into a perfectly shaped bag, not looking at what he was doing, just straight at the audience, zips the bag closed and says, 'So you can even keep your land and make free money.'"

"He sounds like quite the salesman." Vicky's phone vibrated. She glanced at it. "Sorry to rush off, but I have to leave." She'd get her lunch to go.

"What?" Susan seemed startled. "Where are you going?"

Vicky smiled and picked up her phone and bag. "I have a few things to do."

"Wait, how's your article coming along?" Barb had her hand on Vicky's arm.

"I wish I could stay, you're all so interesting, but I really need to get going, I'll be by tomorrow."

Vicky rushed through the goodbyes. Pete was coming back tonight instead of tomorrow. She had things to do before he got back.

****

That night, Vicky sat on the bed facing Pete, legs crossed under her as she filled him in on the events of the last three days, starting with her outing to Joan's house. In dramatic voice, she said. "Then Joan stood up and said, 'I'll show you.'"

"Wow." Pete lay with his head on his pillow. It was late by the time he'd returned from his Kentucky battlefield tour. He'd already given his usual cursory trip report. Unlike Vicky, who tended to include detail and commentary, Pete's stories were spare and succinct, much like his typical routine at historical stops, which was usually quick, thorough, and never involved gift shop souvenirs. He studied up in advance.

However, this particular circuit had included a stop at the oldest continuously operating distillery in Kentucky. Before falling into bed they had enjoyed sips of the very fine bourbon he picked up there.

"I almost couldn't believe it."

"Huh." Pete stifled a yawn and pulled the covers up to his chin.

Vicky was still aching to talk. "I practically jumped up and accidently kicked the dog. Ruby. Her head was right next to my foot. But Joan said to wait. I was glad

157

because I wanted to think about what she told me."

After a long pause, Pete murmured, "Uh-huh."

Vicky chuckled. "Oh, go to sleep. I'll talk your ear off in the morning."

Chapter Twenty-Two

Walkers Corner, May 1999

The girl reached as far under the rock ledge as she could, then wiggled her shoulder to stretch farther. The sound of water flowing was louder here. There was a hint of sweet fresh air. That meant there was an opening to outside. A way out of this cave. She had to find help before those horrible people got back. Mama needed help.

She lay her face on the ground close to the opening, searching for anything that wasn't darkness. Nothing. There was rock above and around her. Her hands hurt. Her whole body hurt. Don't think about spiders and bugs and weird animals. The air smelled a little better. Go. Sharp rocks scraped her small body as she squeezed under the ledge. What if she couldn't find her way back? Don't think. Good, now there's more room. Just keep going. Go to the air. Find help for Mama.

Now there was enough room to crawl. Do snakes live in caves? Last year, in sixth grade, they'd learned about bats. There might be bats here. Bats lived in caves but flew out every night to hunt for bugs. Maybe there were bats above her. Maybe she could find where they flew out to hunt. Oh, please, please God, please help us.

Chapter Twenty-Three

Thursday November 2008

The morning after Pete returned, Vicky followed him to the rental agency to return his car before they headed to Sam's for breakfast. She kissed him when he got in her passenger seat. "Glad you're back."

"Me, too. I missed you. Guess I'm getting used to being around you…"

Uh-oh. Still not ready to talk about next steps with him. She didn't usually feel so torn about making decisions. "Me, too. I've got a lot to do for the fundraiser. I'll be out and about most of the day."

"Tell me more about that. I was exhausted last night."

"It's going to be great. Sam found a band. We put out a call for volunteers. I made a video and posted it on social media. I alerted news people. We're getting great response."

"Would you like some help? I can take care of equipment, pick up supplies, that kind of thing."

"Absolutely. Yes." Yes, yes, yes. "Can you organize people? I have lists …"

They spent the rest of the drive discussing tasks. She loved Pete's suggestion that the cinnamon roll line should first pass in front of the donation bucket and volunteer sign-up booth.

When they got to the diner, Sam gestured them toward the one open booth. Vicky waved at Firefighter Don and Garden Club Susan one table over.

"Did you hear the latest? That little shit Aaron lied." Sam filled their coffee cups. "This whole time."

Vicky pulled her cup toward her. "What? About Rose?"

Don appeared at their booth, obviously eager to tell the story.

Sam held up her hand to stop him. "I have a new waiter. Be patient, he's learning. Okay, they're all yours, Don."

He launched right in. "You know how that kid Aaron said they was together the whole time? Said they was riding bikes and he turns around and she was just gone. It turns out they went down to the school, which they ain't supposed to do. They split up there. Now he says he don't even know if she ever got back to her street."

Don said—loud enough for half the diner to hear—that Aaron had finally admitted he ditched Rose when he met his father at the schoolyard. Aaron wasn't supposed to talk to his father without his mom there, the kid probably lied to protect his father. "Mebbe he was worried his daddy did something bad. Like mebbe taking a little girl. Just a possibility."

Vicky figured Don threw out that last theory either to cause trouble or divert attention from something else.

Sam's new helper, a teenaged boy who was clearly unaccustomed to waiting tables, laboriously took their orders. After he left, Vicky leaned across the table. "Pete, can you come over to my side, so nobody hears? I want to tell you more about what I've found out. Do you remember what I told you last night?"

"Most, probably, but I was tired from the drive." Pete got up to sit next to Vicky. He kissed her as he slid in next to her. "Okay. I'm awake now. Man, I am hungry."

"I've barely touched on what Joan and I talked about." Vicky quietly recapped her visit with Joan.

Pete listened and drank coffee. Vicky assumed his attention was split between real physical hunger and his interest in what she was saying. Her priority today was to tell him about Joan and Mike, along with a few things about herself.

She paused her abbreviated recounting of Joan's story when the trainee waiter arrived with their breakfast order. He seemed momentarily confused about where to put the plates since they were now sitting side by side. Pete took a quick bite of the hash browns and asked for an extra order.

While he dug in, Vicky resumed. "And that's when she showed me the bag."

Pete looked up from his Southwestern scramble, nodded, and reached for the hot sauce. His reaction seemed somewhat understated, considering the stunning news she had seen the actual bag left by an actual mystery woman. Perhaps he needed a moment to absorb the revelation.

Pete swallowed a combo bite of eggs and hashbrowns. "I'm surprised she told you all that. Do you want to split a cinnamon roll?"

"Absolutely." She worked on her omelet while Pete caught the waiter's attention.

She put down her fork. "But now let me tell you about this guy Mike. After Joan showed me the bag, I wondered who made it. It had dirt and I think blood on it, but it was new, not even quite finished. The flap had a raw edge and one of the ties wasn't knotted like the other."

She took a sip of coffee. "The bag was just like this reporter's, Rick, who used to be a deputy. Years ago, he'd told me his dad got his at a caretaker's cabin."

She cut another piece of omelet. "I checked websites selling leather goods made in Missouri. I ordered a few bags that looked like the mystery woman's Joan had—the clasps are unique. Hand-carved antlers or bone. Then I staked out the post office—I was working on the fundraiser anyway—hoping someone would come to send out my order. And I saw him there a couple of days ago and talked to him."

She popped the bite into her mouth.

"I wouldn't have thought of doing that. That's pretty good." Pete sounded impressed.

Vicky chewed and basked for a moment. "Yup. I figured the worst that could happen was I'd end up with bags to give as gifts. If you're lucky you might even get one."

"Nice. How'd you know it was him?"

"I figured he'd be a guy a little older than Rick, who looked like a caretaker."

"What's a caretaker look like?"

"Y'know, whenever I hear the word 'caretaker,' I think 'caregiver.' I pictured an older guy, fifties or so, work clothes, dirty truck, carrying something into the post office big enough to be a leather tote bag. And that was pretty much Mike."

Vicky pointed her chin toward the volunteer firefighter. "Remember I told you about Don there, he mentioned people used to come here from all over to hunt, and they'd stay at a lodge that's closed now."

"Uh-huh."

"And later I asked him what it was like when the girl showed up by the levee. He talked about how he helped with the search for her family, how well-organized it was, how much ground they'd covered. I said wow, has anything else like that ever happened here, other than the little girl who's missing now?"

Vicky waited for Sam's helper to carefully place their cinnamon roll in front of Pete. "And he goes, 'that's different. I know they're searching hard as possible for that little girl.'"

She pulled the roll in front of her to cut it into bite-sized pieces. They each ate one and murmured, "Mmm."

"'That's different.' Doesn't that sound like they didn't look very hard for clues after they found Lisa on the levee? Like maybe they already knew how she got there."

Pete chewed and swallowed. "Lisa was found alive. And we don't know what's happened to Rose." He speared another bite.

"Well, somebody does. I don't believe for a minute she got lost. Back to Don. We know I talk a lot, but this guy really goes on and on. Like someone opened a spigot. Anyway, Don hinted about his daddy being part of a smuggling ring, long after Prohibition, said there used to be kind of a distribution hub here. I told you about that before. Then Mike told me he and Rick watched women being taken out of a cargo truck at the lodge. And Joan's story—that woman, Alisa, maybe she escaped from human traffickers. What if they're still around and took Rose?"

"Is that what you think happened?"

"Maybe. One possibility. There's a lot to think about. Okay, I need to get to work on the fundraiser. Gotta put up more posters. Want to walk off that roll with me?"

****

On Main Street, tattered *WHERE'S ROSE?* signs were posted on almost every telephone pole. The child's smiling picture had faded and looked discouraged after being in the elements for more than a week.

Vicky paused at a pole and took out her stapler. "I hope the fundraiser gets someone to come forward. Rita, Rose's mom, is going to speak. She's even going to help make rolls."

Pete placed a bright new *ROLLS FOR ROSE* benefit poster against the wood. "Besides that kid lying, what's new on the search?"

"Not much." She punched the stapler to secure the poster. "The sheriff seems like a straightforward guy. Not real talkative."

"I've been thinking about Joan. Seems odd she'd show you the bag. I wonder why."

"Same here. Maybe she finally wanted to tell someone. Or to seem like a good guy. Or to distract me. Why-ever. That's a lot to hold in for so long. And speaking of holding in..."

"Nice segue." Pete grinned, though he seemed to tense up ever so slightly.

"Yeah. I've been wanting to tell you a couple of things."

"Go for it."

"Okay. This is ancient history from when I was about to leave St. Louis."

"I like history as much as you do."

"It might be different when it's my history." She rarely spoke about her private past. Her personal thoughts and feelings formed a framework to hold onto, a buffer between her and the rest of the world. She didn't loosen her grip lightly. "But I'd like to hear what you think."

She handed another poster to Pete, who held it against a metal utility box. She exchanged her stapler for tape and taped the poster neatly. She disliked sloppy tape jobs. "This might all tie in with the levee girl Lisa. Two big things happened the same day. First…I think I've mentioned before why I stopped reporting. It was after I auditioned…"

"I remember. You joked about it being a disaster."

"It was. And I was furious with my boss, the news director. He talked in my ear the whole time I was trying to read, whispering, 'Fake it and you'll make it.' After, I went to his office and yelled at him. He said I was fired. So I went to his boss, the general manager."

She could still see herself, waving her rolled-up script, empty coffee mug in hand. "I told him that the news director said I should come to his place later, that he'd do some one-on-one coaching and teach me what he meant about faking it and *really* making it and depending on how things went, maybe he'd let me do another audition."

"He sounds like a real worm," said Pete.

They stopped to put up another poster. She punched the stapler with unnecessary force. "He was. I did say he was a fucking fake and he couldn't tell the difference between someone faking it and the real thing. Or something like that. And I threw my coffee at him. It was cold."

They resumed walking. "Anyway, right after all that, we—the GM and I—had a meeting and agreed I wouldn't sue the station for harassment, and he wouldn't fire me for insubordination. I decided too fast. I should have gotten a lawyer, but I just wanted out."

Vicky had worked two of the last five weeks of her contract. She left with a letter of recommendation and her last check—plus extra—in awe of how everything had changed so quickly.

"I left two weeks later."

She'd left for career choice number three. Options one and two were out. She had been brightly confident she would either be promoted to fill-in anchor or get the reporter job in San Francisco. Worst case, she'd assumed she would stay in her same job, which was still pretty good. She hadn't expected to be out of work in two weeks.

They taped another poster to a metal light post. "I took an investigative producing job in Dallas."

Vicky had learned in television news to make judgments—big and small—constantly and quickly. But it was one thing to decide on the fly whether video was too gory, a source was questionable, or saying something a certain way would be accurate and fair. It was something else entirely to make substantial life decisions with minimal attention to critical thinking. Like she'd done in Missouri.

"We've all done things we'd do differently if we got a do-over, right? Let's turn here. I want to see if anyone's at the fire station."

"Probably. So you stopped reporting…?"

"Yeah, but that would have happened sooner or later

anyway. It pains me to admit I wasn't great on TV."

"Come on, you had to be."

"Nope. I know talent, and I didn't have enough of it. It's fine, I'm good at other things. I'm lucky I found out early."

"Are you rationalizing?"

"Totally. I loved reporting. So, that was one thing, the audition blowup. And, you know about Lisa, the girl on the levee."

"You've mentioned her."

"And I mentioned Rick Carr, the reporter I had coffee with, who used to be a cop. He worked on the levee girl case. His father was the sheriff."

Vicky had already decided to tell Pete what happened, minus a few details. He'd get the gist. That trait of his was one of her favorites. He listened and didn't need a lot of explanation to get the point.

Still, she continued to overexplain. "That night, right after I found out I was out of a job, I ran into Rick. We had drinks. This was a day or two before the levee girl."

She pulled out another poster to give her time to compose herself. "I spilled water near some papers and grabbed them so they wouldn't get wet." Vicky gestured faintly to demonstrate the action. "One was a grand jury subpoena."

"Did you do that on purpose?"

"Whoa, that's the first thing you thought?"

"Well, apparently, yeah." Pete paused. "One of the first things. You're a reporter."

"Hmm. And what else popped into your mind?"

Pete grinned. "What was the subpoena for?"

One of the first negotiated guidelines in their

relationship was that when one of them changed the subject, the other would drop it. It was okay to return to the topic later, but enough for now. The rule was Vicky's idea, after Pete commented she changed the subject more than anyone he'd ever met.

But this she wanted to answer. "A grand jury was investigating his father. Something about distribution though I didn't see of what. Rick was furious and refused to talk about it."

She took a moment to staple a poster onto a telephone pole. "Two days later, the farmer found Lisa. I stopped by Rick's place to ask about something he'd told me when we were drinking."

Vicky summarized the story about the boys spying on their fathers. "What if—during the search—no one checked where their fathers were transporting women?"

Vicky walked faster. "Rick definitely didn't want to talk with me. I had to wait on his porch, which was fine, he was working. While I was there, a woman drove by and gave me a message for him. Long story short, I didn't tell him."

Pete slowed his stride. "That's it? You didn't pass along a message?"

"Well, there's more, but later I thought, what if she had important information about the little girl? Or Rick warned his father about me seeing the subpoena, and they covered up something. What if I somehow messed up the Lisa investigation?"

"Doesn't seem all that likely."

"Ever since I read Rose was missing, I've wondered if the cases are connected. Maybe she wouldn't be missing if they'd solved the Lisa mystery."

Pete paused and touched her arm. "Wait. That's

what this is all about? I wondered why we had to haul ass to Missouri so fast just to write a travel article."

"Well, yes. Partly." Vicky kissed his cheek. "And help search for Rose. Plus, you wanted to travel."

"Oh, right." He squeezed her butt as they resumed their walk.

She pinched his in return. "What kills me is I never reported anything about his father. I never even told anyone. I was angry and upset, and just left. Grand jury investigations are secret, so other reporters wouldn't have known about it unless they got a tip or there was an announcement."

"Hmm. I don't see how you can blame yourself for all that."

"You don't? I do." They approached the fire station. The doors were closed, no vehicles in sight. "I think a lot of storylines came together here."

Including her own.

Chapter Twenty-Four

Friday, November 2008

Friday evening, Pete and Vicky had barely gotten out of the car before Beth Wagner waved from across the campground. "Hey, y'all. Want some supper?"

Tom added, "We've got a couple extra burgers here."

"Hell, yeah." Pete grinned. "I'll bring beverages." He glanced at Vicky.

"Absolutely, let me drop my bags." She dropped her voice. "But I'd like to get to bed early tonight."

Their stop at the RV was quick. The night the two couples met, Tom had said when Beth was at the grill, you best be ready when dinner was. She was particular about serving food at its peak.

No doubt Beth and Tom were eager to talk about what-all was going on. Pete and Vicky had spent the day working on the Sunday fundraiser and had plenty to tell. Dinner was a fair exchange.

Pete handed a bottle to Tom. "Here's a little gift from Kentucky."

"Much appreciated, and I do mean that sincerely. How was the trip? You got in pretty late the other night."

"Great." Pete gave a quick outline of his route, the historic places he'd seen, where he'd had some particularly good ribs. Then everyone got busy eating.

Beth had outdone herself and the meal deserved all their attention. She accepted compliments matter-of-factly. "They were talking on the radio about that little shit Aaron. They mentioned the Rose's Rolls fundraiser."

"Yes, Rolls for Rose," Vicky said. She'd put together a quick video, news release, posters, and website to get the word out. It was all over social and news media. "I'm glad people are talking about it. Rose's mom Rita came up with the name."

Tom and Beth were fans of the band Sam had arranged to provide the music. Pete and Vicky took turns outlining the program, speakers, and equipment. The big challenge would be to make hundreds of cinnamon rolls and bake them in two small ovens on Sunday morning.

Beth half-raised her hand. "I can help bake."

"Thanks, Beth, that's so good of you," Vicky said. "I think Sam has everything planned out—her kitchen is tiny—but I'll be sure to let her know you offered."

"Well, let me know what I can do." Beth looked a tad ticked off that her obvious talents were not in demand. Tom chimed in he'd be happy to help, too.

Pete said, "We need someone to run the coffee booth—"

Tom and Beth spoke in unison. "Done."

Pete continued. "And I could use some help picking up a few things tomorrow. We'll put you to work."

Beth and Tom seemed ready to settle in for a nice long chat, but when there was a lull Vicky said, "Supper was delicious. Thank you so much. I hate to eat and run, but I have a lot to do for Sunday. And I need to get a good night's sleep."

Tom held up Pete's gift. "How 'bout a sip before

you go?"

"Ah. Okay, just a taste."

****

Back in their RV, Vicky and Pete settled at the table with their laptops to work on fundraiser tasks, occasionally exchanging information. When Pete closed his computer, Vicky got up and rinsed her mug before returning to give Pete a nice kiss. "I missed you. I'm going to get ready for bed."

Later, Pete crawled into bed, kissed her, then leaned back and grinned, elbow bent, head propped up on his hand. He looked a little ragged, but in a good way. He hadn't shaved lately, and his curly after-shower hair was messy. He leaned over and kissed her once, then again, and longer. "Seventeen long, urgent hours of RV driving to write a travel article."

"Mmhmm." He smelled pleasantly of soap and shampoo and toothpaste. She kissed him back.

He leaned toward her. "So, we're on an RV guilt trip."

"Funny. Did it take you long to come up with that?" She gave him a friendly nudge and left her hand on his shoulder. Her fingers tingled as his skin responded to her touch.

"You barely asked why I wanted to come here." Vicky combed his tousled hair with her fingers before dropping them to lightly brush his chest. "Mm. I'm so glad you did. It's good to be with you."

"An emergency travel article." Pete caressed her. "Nah. You're right. I wanted to go somewhere. With you. Mmm."

"Mmm." She caressed back. She could think later.

****

Afterward, it was barely ninety seconds before Pete was lightly snoring. Vicky lay next to him, wishing she could drop off like that—and thinking about what she might tell him if he were awake.

Starting when she was a novice in news, she had constantly run through the who-what-when-where-why checklist to make sure she didn't miss anything. The 'why' often led to her favorite answers. Some journalists insisted 'how' should be on the list of necessary newsgathering questions. Others asserted the five W's led to the how. Either way, it never hurt to ask in a different way.

Even in bed, silent in the dark, it got a little uncomfortable when she turned those questions on herself. She thought about Pete's question. How much of what she'd done was on purpose? What was an accident, or at least unplanned?

Chapter Twenty-Five

Saturday November 2008

Vicky paced around the campsite Saturday morning. "I've been thinking."

Pete glanced up from making breakfast, bowl in one hand, fork in the other.

"Like, Don, for starters," she said. "What's with him? He tells me about his pop bootlegging, and he makes it sound like, nudge-nudge, this is more than a little tale about a family business, wink-wink. Then he gets all coy."

He stirred the contents of the bowl and nodded.

"And Mike," she went on. "Jesus, he's like, Mr. Mysterious Swamp Dude. But boy, I know that guy has more to tell."

Vicky made another trip from the picnic table to the awning and back, then paused next to the camp stove. "Mike, Joan, Rita, Sam. I swear, it feels like every single person I've talked to has something to hide."

"You just met 'em. They're not going to tell you everything." Pete pointed his egg-beating fork at the skillet, where strips of bacon were close to the point of perfect crispiness. "Ten minutes."

Pete was precise. Competent. Deft, intuitive, and very, very thorough. In all ways. Everything would be delectable and ready at the same time. In ten.

"Yum." Vicky paused to kiss him. "You're growing a beard. Nice." She ran her fingers along his still-scratchy stubble. Her skin was still a bit sensitive from last night. "Do you need me to do anything?"

He shook his head.

"Okay, I'm on cleanup." She resumed pacing. Now might be a good time to talk about the Dallas job offer, but she was focused on the missing girl. "I really hope something comes out of the fundraiser tomorrow. We have to help find Rose. It breaks my heart that she's still missing."

"You are helping. This fundraiser is really coming together."

"Feels like there are connections I'm not seeing."

"What kind of connections?"

Mmm. She so loved that he asked. "For one, Joan. And her mystery woman, her bag, this human trafficking thing, which I still think makes sense…"

Pete flipped the bacon. "A woman with a hand-tooled bag and the levee girl escape from the same bunch who nine years later happen to see Rose and snatch her—it does seem a bit unlikely, doesn't it?"

Ouch. True, but ouch. "Maybe not *happened to see*. Yeah. I know, I know. It sounds lame when you say it straight up, but I'm sure something connects them. Maybe not just like that."

Vicky sat at the table. "Mmm, everything smells good. Making rolls tonight should be interesting. I'll have hours to talk with people. And we'll see who shows up at the fundraiser tomorrow."

****

That afternoon, Vicky entered the back door of the diner, toting grocery bags in both hands. "Hi, I'm back."

Sam, Rita, and Liz Ann paused their cinnamon roll-making-motions to greet her. Sam had closed early to prepare for the fundraiser which was scheduled to start at eleven o'clock sharp the next morning. One of the St. Louis TV stations—Kerry's—was going to carry it live on their Sunday morning news.

"Mmm. Smells like cinnamon heaven." Vicky opened the refrigerator to put away the groceries. "I bought up all the butter the store had. Pete'll get more when he picks up the stage equipment. He drove the RV to haul everything, should be back by nine." Along with making supply and equipment runs, Pete had organized dozens of volunteers, using his sales skills to recruit people and assign duties.

She closed the fridge. "He'll park in your lot, so we'll have a place for the speakers and performers tomorrow."

"Good idea." Sam held up a floury hand. "Oh, Mike said he can help out tonight."

"Excellent." Vicky had worked out the schedule with Sam and Pete to make sure she'd have time alone with certain people. "Don was at the store. He offered to help with the rolls." Don didn't appear anywhere on the volunteer roster. "I told him I'd tell you, but you have a system worked out and there's only room for four people to work. He didn't like it."

Vicky washed her hands next to cloth-covered mixing bowls, pans, and cinnamon rolls at various stages of production. The small kitchen was designed for turning out high-quality lunch and breakfast food, not big-batch baking. Sam had said her baking corner seemed like a big splurge of space when she redid the kitchen, but now seemed impossibly tiny.

She put on an apron. Things were coming together nicely. "I bet your regulars are grousing. You're in here making cinnamon rolls and they can't have any."

"Until tomorrow. It's good advertising," said Rita.

"Listen to you! That's the way to think about it." Vicky put on a hairnet and gloves. "All righty. What can I do?"

They talked baking logistics for a few minutes as they adjusted to the rhythm of sharing work—mixing, rolling, filling, slicing, placing. After they fell into cadence, Rita asked, "How long have you been with Pete, Vicky?"

"We met about eight months ago."

"And you live in an RV? What's that like?"

"No, no, we don't live together. Just for this trip. It's good. It's different."

"How'd you meet?"

"Furniture shopping. He sold me a couch."

Vicky had called a patterned sofa too fussy, so Salesman Pete pointed to a sleek couch that sported dark burgundy leather and sharp angles. "This would be perfect in a more contemporary setting."

She'd laughed out loud at the pivot. Pete chuckled, too. "Yeah, it doesn't exactly invite you to get nice and cozy reading on a rainy afternoon."

Since that was exactly the standard she had in mind, she'd taken another look at him. He was interesting enough to flirt with, but she was looking for a couch, not a new commitment. Then he called to see how the sofa was working out, and their relationship took off on its current highly stimulating trajectory.

"You smile a lot when you talk about him." Liz Ann sounded a bit wistful.

"Do I? He's funny, honest, smart. We feel good together." Vicky paused when her baking buddies laughed.

"It's been a long time since I talked about a guy like that," Liz Ann sighed.

"I never have," Sam said.

"Me neither," added Rita.

That led to a lively discussion about exes and endings. Rita talked about her disastrous marriage which had lasted almost thirteen months. "That's what happens when you fall for someone who peaked in high school."

Perfect. Yes, let's talk about Bill Beck, Junior. Vicky exaggerated her sigh. "I hear you. I had a boyfriend like that. You're talking about Rose's father?"

"No, thank God."

Vicky wanted to ask the obvious follow-up—Rose's birth certificate said "UNK" in the space for "father"—but Rita firmly changed the subject. "Have you ever been married, Vicky?"

"Yes, we divorced three years ago. He left me for someone he met at the gym." Her ex had completed the cliché by moving into a condo with his much younger girlfriend. Vicky didn't dwell on it. She'd focused on making her life the way she wanted it to be. It took a while to get around to upgrading the furniture.

"Hang on one second, let me get this going." Sam flipped a switch on the mixer and walked away from the resulting whirr. The women gathered near the back door. The kitchen was warm and homey, but there was nowhere to get comfortable. Rita handed Sam a cup of the tea they were all drinking, lightly flavored with lemon-infused vodka.

Vicky lifted her mug. "Pete's different. I almost hate

to say it but, if I could pick and choose features in a man, I might put together Pete."

"I know what I'd like to put together." Liz Ann purred in her sultriest librarian voice. She snickered. "I ran into an old boyfriend once, a few weeks after we broke up. And he comes up to me, all warm and sincere, to let me know he's doing fine. He said he'd thought a lot about why we broke up, and he finally understood my problems."

A pause, then they all burst out laughing.

"Yeah, he was sympathetic I had so much wrong with me. Breaking up with him was definitely the right decision."

The timer chimed. Rita joined Sam at the counter. They took dough from bowls and began kneading, their graceful motions harmonious, almost lyrical.

Vicky stayed near the door. "I think a lot about why people make the decisions they do. Whether their reasons are personal. Or financial. Or professional."

Rita added. "Or purely pissed-off."

"Or in lust." Liz Ann's whole body got into those three words. She made them count.

When Vicky stopped laughing, she said, "Exactly. We don't necessarily know why people decide something." She had wasted plenty of time on decisions that ended up being no big deal. She'd also handled complicated ones as if they were as simple as coffee/tea or heels/flats.

"It's the same with stories. People have their reasons for how and why they tell a story. Or don't tell. And people tell the same story different ways. Rub the edges off the truth to make it fit better. Plus some people flat-out lie."

"That's the truth." Rita slapped the dough for emphasis. "Like that little shit Aaron."

"Little Shit sounds like part of his name now. Yeah, that was bad." Vicky paused. "People want to edit their own history a little, I get it. One thing about reporting though—we verify facts. And consider other sides."

Rita scoffed. "Nice theory. Too bad that's all it is."

Vicky softened her voice, as she always did when she spoke with victims. She knew what it was like to be one. "Have reporters made mistakes covering Rose?"

"I guess not." Rita frowned. "Some are too dramatic. And they keep trying to talk to me."

"I'm sorry you're going through any of this. Sometimes reporters can be insensitive." An understatement. Vicky certainly could be. But she had long ago lost count of how many times she'd had this discussion. Reporting was serious business. Journalists were real-time historians, even when they were "just" reporting on local incidents, crime, heroics, politics, zoning issues. Everyday life. And death. Better get it right.

"But there aren't many stories more important than a lost child. We need to make sure people know what's going on. They might be able to help."

Rita's shoulders sagged. "I guess."

"Let's hope something good comes from tomorrow."

They worked in silence for several minutes, then Rita said, "What are you getting out of all of this, Vicky? I still don't get why you came from wherever you came from, asking so many questions, doing this fundraiser." She didn't sound antagonistic, but clearly wanted an explanation.

Sam had the same friendly-but-don't-BS-me look. "Yeah. What's your story? That travel article?"

"Yes, I'm planning to write an article. But sure, there's more to it." Time to give a little. "Did you ever catch yourself in a mirror when you aren't expecting to? When I look back at how I left here, it's like I saw myself from a different angle, and it wasn't pretty."

"Not physically, though." Vicky cocked her hip and put one wrist behind her head, posing as she smoothed her apron. "At the time that was *very* fine."

Nobody laughed, not even Vicky. "I told you I reported for one of the St. Louis stations. I don't like how I left things."

"So you're here to finish something?" asked Sam.

"At least find out what happened."

"What happened with what?" Sam was young but already had the command presence of a seasoned boss who expects real answers.

"It had to do with my job."

"You're digging into all our business, but you won't tell us yours?" Sam scoffed. "That's gotta feel at least a little hypocritical."

Gotta hand it to her. Sam didn't water down what she had to say.

"Sometimes. Yeah. But I'm here for good reasons. I want to help find Rose." And maybe, just maybe, ease a fraction of the pain in her own life.

"Uh-huh." Sam crossed her arms. "Your motives are pure, so we should spill our guts but you won't spill yours." There was a hint of humor in her voice, but just a hint.

"I am being honest. My story's not what's important."

"For heaven's sake, Vicky. Just tell us," Liz Ann said. "Why are you here?"

Vicky took an unintentional deep breath. It wouldn't hurt to hear other opinions. "Okay. This guy I knew, a cop, we'd been talking for a few hours. Honestly, I was interested and thought he was, too. We hugged, but it was just a hug."

She'd enjoyed everything until Rick shoved her away. His voice was harsh. "Hey. Back off. Now I see what you're doing, sneaking around, spying. Get the hell away from me."

She had been so shocked it sucker-punched any hint of romance out of her.

"No zing?" asked Liz Ann.

Vicky shrugged. "We weren't meant to be. When I stepped back, I spilled a glass of water. I picked up some papers so they wouldn't get wet. And he assumed I did it to read them. He accused me of trying to seduce him to get information."

"Ouch." Liz Ann pursed her lips. "That can't feel good."

"Anyway, ancient history." Though not so long ago that she didn't still wonder, a whisper of a wonder, if it was possible Rick wasn't entirely wrong. She'd seen the paperwork. Did she bump the glass on purpose? Or because he pushed her away?

Rita asked, "What's that got to do with Rose?"

"Maybe nothing. But the document had to do with an investigation into the old sheriff and illegal distribution. Of what I don't know, but this was at the same time as when the little girl turned up on the levee. I should have followed up but didn't. Your house is less than two miles from there. Way out here in the country."

183

There was that, plus the mystery woman, and what Rick and Mike saw that sure sounded like human trafficking. Not to mention Vicky's own observations at the time of Lisa's appearance.

"Surely the cops know if there was any connection." Liz Ann sounded skeptical.

Rita rubbed her face with both hands. Being a modern parent, no doubt she'd already thought plenty about sicko abusers, predators, killers—the vile cesspool of repulsive beings who would do harm to a child.

No need to add more to her nightmare. Time to move on. "You're probably right, Liz Ann." Though that's assuming some of the cops weren't bad guys themselves. "One probably has nothing to do with the other."

Vicky smiled and waved her hand around the kitchen. "My gosh, we've gotten so much done. We're going to have great turnout tomorrow."

"Yes, we are." Sam flourished a towel as she covered a large bowl. "But we still have a lot to do. We'll start the next batch after Pete gets here with supplies."

"We're doing pretty good, considering we usually do four dozen a day." Rita sounded determined to be upbeat. She had mixed, rolled, and cut dough for hours, but she looked less tired now than she had in days. Her face was rosy, perhaps from the heat of the kitchen, though her eyes held sorrow that might never go away.

"We make a great team." Liz Ann untied her apron. "But I need to get going. Good night, ladies."

"Me too. I'll be back bright and early." Rita was brisk and efficient as she prepared to leave. "Working with y'all is good therapy." She hugged Sam and Liz Ann, then gave Vicky a sad smile and warm shoulder squeeze. "See you in the morning."

"Get some rest." Sam adopted a dramatic movie voice. "Tomorrow, we bake!"

Chapter Twenty-Six

Saturday Night

After the others left, Vicky and Sam stayed in the warm kitchen, leaning side by side against the counter near the coffee pot. Vicky enjoyed the moment. This must be what it's like to be sisters in a grandma's kitchen. "I'm still impressed that you're so organized. The other day, talking about how you learned to bake big batches…"

Sam grew still.

"It made me think about when I was a kid." Vicky glanced at Sam. "I spent some time in a facility with a cook."

Sam's posture didn't change, but everything about her energy did. She radiated intensity but didn't speak or look up from her mug. If Vicky could read auras, Sam's would probably be swirling deep red. The pleasant warmth generated by the presence of Rita and Liz Ann dissipated, replaced by the heat of tension.

"It was a holding place, run by nuns for kids with nowhere else to go." Vicky stepped back from the memory of fear and guilt. Now was no time to let herself feel wounded. "The kitchen was the best place to hang out."

Sam didn't say anything, but recognition flowed between them, an understanding that they both knew pain, knew terrible loss.

"I didn't grow up with family." For one long instant, the image of her younger sister—screaming in terror, tears cutting through the smudge of smoke on her little face—obliterated Vicky's thoughts.

She faced Sam directly. "Anyway, this one nun was also a cook. We all had to help in the kitchen. She taught us to how to use math when cooking for bigger or smaller groups."

Sam frowned. "What does—"

A knock at the back door made them both jump. "Hey, Sam. It's Mike."

Damn. Terrible timing, though Vicky was eager to talk to him. What was Sam about to ask? Ah well. The mood was broken.

In short order, Mike was gloved, aproned, hair-netted, and listening to Sam's tutorial. Sam had printed out the specifics but told Vicky she liked to explain it first, so the instructions made sense. She wasn't used to anyone but Rita helping with her cinnamon rolls.

"Then you label each tray with the time and put it out in the diner next to the one before it." Sam took off her apron as she wrapped up her instructions. "We're keeping the front room cold so the rolls don't finish rising until we're ready to bake."

Vicky resisted the urge to mention that's called proofing.

"What first?" Mike looked ready to work.

"It's almost time to roll the dough. Vicky can show you. I need to run home for an hour or so."

Oh, good. It's like she reads my mind.

When Sam left, the kitchen cooled off, and not just because the door had been open. Vicky and Mike stood in silence until she said, "It was good talking with you the other day."

"Hmm."

"You probably saved that woman's life."

"Hmm." Mike leaned back against the counter. "Maybe. So, where're you going with all this? These stories you're collecting?"

He sounded curious and skeptical, not hostile, but Vicky sensed his sharp green eyes probing her mind and heart. Shields up. She shrugged lightly. "I don't know yet."

"When are you going to know?"

"When I know what happens." Vicky waved expansively to include the kitchen, Walkers Corner, everyone around here, and anything interesting in the past, present, and future.

"And you decide when that is. And you won't be around for whatever happens after."

"Come on. I'm trying to do right by this."

"And you decide what's right."

"Mike, yes, I'm asking you to trust me. Tell me what worries you."

"You're poking around in people's lives. My life."

"Some of this is my life, too."

"What part is that?"

"All right. Outside the library, I told you about the truck that stopped by Rick's. I think it was a person under the tarp."

"You saw someone?"

"It was big enough to be a person. What if it was your mystery woman? Don't you want to know what happened to her?"

"You said she left my bag on a porch. Where?"

"Haven't had a chance to see if it's okay to say. Look. I never told Rick—or anyone—about the woman in the truck. I need to know what happened."

"Why?"

"Why? Because a savagely beaten woman was running away from someone. You helped her. Maybe she and Lisa got away from human traffickers. Maybe they're still around and took Rose." She took a breath. "I know it's a long shot."

"It's a long way, too," he said. "Carr lived in St. Louis then. Hour and a half from where I found her."

"But he was from here." She paused. "The pickup driver went to his house to talk to a cop. Rick. But I was there, and she didn't meet with him."

"And you're not sure Rick was a good cop."

"I didn't say that. But yeah. There's that, too. Maybe something in all this could help find Rose."

"Let me think about it."

Vicky waited, but he was apparently going to think and not talk about it. After a minute or two she said, "Okay. Here. This batch is ready to roll out."

Vicky uncovered a bowl, took the ball of dough, set it front of him, picked up a second bowl, and did the same for herself. Music played softly, pleasantly, on Sam's speakers. She hoped Mike was listening. He seemed like the song's solitary pirate, lost out of time and, even more so, of place.

She poked down the risen dough and began kneading it. Mike did the same.

"Sprinkle on flour when it gets sticky, but not too much." Vicky demonstrated. "Sam says work it 'til it's smooth as a baby's butt."

"I wouldn't know anything about that sort of thing."

"No kids?"

"Never married. How's this?" He gestured toward the ball of dough.

"Perfect. Now pat it out a bit and start rolling."

They each rolled out a nice flat canvas of dough. They spread the pre-mixed butter-cinnamon-sugar-and-top-secret-something-else combo on top. Sam had prepared it in advance, one container per batch.

"Sam says never skimp on the good stuff."

She leaned against the counter, in apron and hairnet, dusted with flour, brown spices, and sugar, watching Mike. Either he'd done this before, or he was just good in the kitchen. His movements were quick and sure. He worked without saying a word. Vicky looked for a theme or some meaning in the dark colors of the tattoos between his gloves and rolled-up sleeves.

"Then we roll the dough nice and tight, then we'll cut slices." She pinched one edge and rolled it to form a tube. "May I make a personal observation?"

"What."

"You don't drawl like most of the locals I've met."

"Hm."

"Have you always lived here?"

Mike paused mid-stroke. "You think this place is all I know?"

"Not at all. Where else have you lived?"

"St. Louis. Chicago. Couple other places."

"Love to hear about that. I lived in St. Louis and spent a lot of time in Chicago. Great town. What'd you do there?"

Mike finished spreading and started rolling. "Wasted a few years."

"Must have been quiet here, growing up. Was it just

you and your parents?"

"Mostly grandpa and me. My dad sometimes. My mom left when I was a kid."

"That must have been hard. I never met my grandparents. What were yours like?"

"My grandmother died before I was born. Grandpa was from Chicago." Mike made a sound that might have been a chuckle. "The older he got the more he talked. I was usually the only one around to listen. Grandpa was one pissed-off old dude. He used to talk all the time about getting screwed over by his partner."

Mike paused with what might have been a fond look on his face before he came back to himself and started working the dough again. "The old man held a grudge. He was a lawyer, but he'd been disbarred. He also lost his share of the property, except to keep the cabin. He never explained that part, but decades later he was still cussing his ex-partner."

Mike's technique involved a smooth pinch, tuck, and slide along every inch of dough. "Everyone in Grandpa's family died young, and he always figured he would too. But he lasted longer than anyone expected, always talking about how he could have gotten even more even."

That raised all sorts of questions for Vicky, but she'd have to come back to that. Better let him tell this his way. It was clear when he didn't want to talk, but he was talking now, and she wanted him to keep going.

Mike had the dough formed into a nice tight long roll. "Grandpa somehow worked it so after the last partner died—which was Grandpa—all the beneficiaries had to meet, or they wouldn't inherit anything." He chuckled. "Grandpa was pissed that he couldn't be around for the meeting."

When it was clear that's all he was going to say, Vicky asked, "Who are the beneficiaries?"

He made a quick slice. "There's a trust." He picked up and held out the perfectly formed roll. "How's this??"

"Beautiful." Vicky fell silent, trying to project companionable respect and warmth. She imagined her silence flowing amiably with the smells and music and textures of the kitchen as they worked side by side.

Once his pan was full, Mike covered and labeled his batch, executing the tasks flawlessly, then tilted the pan toward Vicky in a slight bow before bumping open the door to the dining-room-turned-refrigerator. She grinned. The guy definitely had some charming attributes, now that he'd loosened up some. He was almost smiling when he returned.

A few minutes later, Sam came through the back door. "I've just got to put a few things away."

"Do you need help?" Vicky asked.

"No, got it, thanks."

Sam was quick, but not quick enough to beat the blast of chilly air that swirled through the curtain of plastic slats between the kitchen and storeroom. Store-closet, really. Vicky stretched toward the bowls of rising dough, instinctively wanting to protect them from the cold.

Sam surveyed the kitchen. "Great, you've been busy."

"Pete should be back with supplies any time now," Vicky said.

As if on cue there was a knock on the door. Sam peered out the peephole before opening the door for Pete. "Perfect. You found everything?"

"Yep." After several minutes of unloading and updating, Pete held up a bag and a bottle. "I picked up some sandwiches if anyone's hungry. And a little bottle of something to keep us warm."

"Great. Let's take a break. Who wants coffee? Tea?" Sam motioned them out of the kitchen. "Go on ahead. I'll be right there."

The others shed baking gear and picked up mugs on the way to their seats. Sam and Pete had curtained off a booth for the bake team to rest, keep their things, and nap between making rolls. It wasn't any warmer than the rest of the eating area, but there were blankets and room to sit. Vicky and Pete traded a quick kiss as they slid into one side of the booth.

A few minutes later, Sam set down a trayful of drinks. She sat next to Mike. "What'd I miss?"

"Just chatting." Vicky shrugged. "By the way, Sam, do you happen to know Joan Beck?"

Sam looked a bit puzzled. "I know who she is, but she hardly ever comes here. I hear she's practically a hermit."

"Man," Mike said. "You never stop asking questions."

Something in his voice reminded Vicky of a nature channel narrator. She chose to assume he was merely making an interested observation. "It's good to know stuff."

"If I want you to know something, I'll tell you." The challenge in Mike's voice was unmistakable. "And if I don't, I won't."

"Absolutely. I'm just bringing up a few things people might decide they want to share." Just being helpful. "Maybe there's something you want to know, too."

Mike paused before turning to Sam. "Sam, do you want to be hearing this?"

"Don't worry about me."

He didn't bother asking Pete. "You're poking at things that haven't moved in decades."

"Things were in motion before I got here," Vicky said. "We drove out here the day after I heard about Rose being missing. Ask Pete."

Pete said, "Yup. Our first weekend camping trip turned into an eight-hundred-mile road trip to Missouri."

Vicky leaned forward. "What things haven't moved?"

No one answered. Vicky strummed her mug with her fingernails. "Can I say something?"

Sam laughed. "Now you ask? What about all the other times?"

Mike and Pete tipped their cups to Sam for that little zinger.

Vicky joined their chuckles a split second late. "Yeah, I talk a lot. And I ask a lot of questions. You're right, Mike, I am collecting stories. I'm trying to figure out how things fit together."

Vicky paused to see if anyone wanted to speak up. "Let's say cops are searching for Rose from a particular angle, thinking maybe a predator took her, or maybe, divorced mom, some kind of custody dispute. Or whatever. And their search is all in that direction. But people are not giving them all the facts. Important facts. Maybe for good reason."

Dead silence followed.

"Things might fit together in ways no one realizes, because important pieces are missing. People have told me things. And by the way if anyone wants to tell more of their story, I'm always ready to listen." Vicky looked at her companions, one by one. "Sam, I've told them I think Rose being missing is connected to the girl found walking on the levee years ago. Lisa. There was a woman with Lisa, but as far as I know the cops never knew that."

Mike said, "Neither do you, for sure."

"What woman?" asked Sam.

"Not that I can prove right now, Mike. But I know it. Sam, a woman turned up close to where the farmer found the levee girl. She'd been beaten."

Sam stared at Vicky. "Are you looking for confessions or something?"

"It's good to know history."

"Then tell us yours." Sam's jaw jutted out. Her voice was challenging.

Interesting how she changed the subject away from the beaten woman.

Sam leaned across the diner booth table. "Earlier, you said you learned about cooking in big batches when you were in a *facility.*" Her tone was edged with suspicion. "Did you make that up, to try to get me talking?"

"I would never do that. Ever. But it's fair to ask. Yes, I was in a facility. My parents died when I was little. I was messed up. I spent some time in a kid psych hospital."

Pete looked up sharply, his eyebrows raised in question.

"How'd they die?" Sam's voice was blunt and unsympathetic.

It was just the kind of question Vicky would ask— though perhaps more gently—but one she didn't usually have to answer. A vise clamped her heart and lungs. When she was able to inhale, Vicky did what she always did when her emotions threatened to take over. She calmly set aside her feelings and answered as if she were reporting a story. "We lived in a tent by a river in California. There was a big wildfire."

She paused, then continued in an even tone. "We were running away. People were screaming. My dad was carrying me. A pickup truck came by, completely full, with people hanging onto the sides. They took me but there was no room for my parents."

An echo of terror surged through her. Screaming, choking in the thick smoke, holding on tight, tight as she could, holding on to everything she knew, shrieking for mommy and daddy. Then they were gone. Then everyone was gone.

"My parents died. Burned up. Their bodies were never identified. We were homeless and it seems no one was looking for us. I was six." Vicky gave a rueful half-shrug. "And evidently, I was not a very likeable kid. No one would adopt me. Though the hospital cook kind of did."

Even now, she still couldn't bring herself to tell the rest.

"You never told me that." Pete frowned. He sounded shocked, disturbed. Hurt.

Mike and Sam gazed at her across the table.

"I don't like talking about it." Vicky focused on Pete. "I did tell you I grew up in foster homes, that I ran away when I was fifteen. I would've told you more, sometime."

She refilled her mug, adding a splash from Pete's bottle. "Anyway, I was a difficult child. A bit combative.

Hence the facility."

After a few moments of silence, Sam spoke softly. "When we were baking it felt like you were talking about me."

"I understand not wanting to talk." Vicky tipped her cup to Sam. "Plenty of people would just as soon forget parts of their past."

Her words hung in uncomfortable silence. She wondered what came to mind for the others. Her head was about to split open. Everything inside her ached. She put down her mug and glanced at Pete.

He squeezed her hand. "I drove by an old courthouse today. It reminded me what you said about how there used to be only minimal records on most people, and now we're all recorded constantly."

Vicky appreciated his effort to lighten the mood. "Whether we want it or not."

"We have a right to privacy." Sam sounded defiant.

"Sure. But privacy's hard to come by, anymore." Vicky shrugged. "If the government or a hacker or some company trying to sell you something wants to, they can practically find out what song you were listening to when you got on the highway last Sunday. Or whatever."

Sam frowned. "That's not right. That's against the law."

"Technology is skipping way ahead of the law. Right or not, that's the way it is."

Pete jumped in. "Maybe we've all seen too many movies."

Sam said, "How about that DNA shit? Scary."

Vicky, ever the contrarian, cited positive points about DNA's use in reuniting families, catching bad people—and freeing innocent ones.

Pete jumped in with a quick tangent about DNA's value to historians before agreeing technology was getting to be disturbing. "Now, we leave trails everywhere we go, everywhere we look, practically everything we think."

Mike finally spoke up. "I don't know how people live like that. I grew up in the woods. I try not to leave traces."

"Do you have a phone?" Vicky asked. If he did, she needed his number.

"Nope. I don't need one and don't want one."

"How do you run your business without a phone?"

"I manage. I check my website at the library."

They chatted about privacy for several more minutes. Their shared wariness of excessive record-keeping seemed to create a bond, so Vicky teased, "Everyone's got stuff they rather keep private, right, Mike?"

Mike stared, then scoffed. "That's a hell of a question. You have some nerve." He put down his mug without taking a drink.

Vicky chuckled. "Could be anything, like who you liked in third grade. I'm not asking for any deep dark secrets, just whether you have any. I have plenty I'd like to forget. Or at least keep quiet about."

"I like quiet. And I wouldn't mind some right now." Mike seemed completely serious now.

"Ha. I walked myself right into that one. Okay. First, can we talk about a few things for tomorrow?"

"Time to get back to work." Sam slid out of the booth. "I need to measure ingredients. I'll need the whole kitchen."

"Okay, sure." Vicky assumed Sam wanted no

witnesses as she prepared her secret-ingredient filling. Was the extra spice cardamom, maybe? Or a touch of allspice? "Pete, want to go over the program for tomorrow? I have a couple ideas—"

Mike stood. "You don't need me for that. I'll be back."

Vicky and Pete spent several minutes reviewing fundraiser logistics, then she packed up her laptop. "I think we're as ready as we're going to be." She stood and tucked her phone into her back pocket. "I'm going to try to get some sleep. I'm beat. And not up to talking any more."

"I'll go with you."

"I'll be fine. The RV's right outside."

"I know. But I need your help moving a few things."

Oops. He wasn't just being overprotective. "Okay, I'll be right there."

Vicky opened the kitchen door to tell Sam she was welcome to nap in the RV instead of the booth if she wanted. Sam said thanks, she was set. As she headed to the front door, Vicky rotated a few pans and checked the thermometer. It was plenty cold enough to slow the dough.

She paused out front, then walked around to the side parking lot. The RV was at the end of the long brick wall, partly blocking the parking lot's back exit. Perfect. Pete and Mike were already at work. It didn't take long to unload the portable stage risers and some of the sound equipment. They ran an extension cord from the diner, powered up, and checked audio. Anything else could be figured out in the morning.

They stacked the risers near the RV and threw a tarp over the pile. Then they put everything else back in the

RV, leaving room to scoot sideways to get to the bedroom.

Mike said, "I'll block the entrance with my truck, so we can keep the lot clear in the morning."

Vicky air-kissed Pete as she stepped up to the open RV door. "I'm setting my alarm for five. Wake me up if you need anything."

"Hope you sleep. I'll take a nap later."

The RV felt strange; the air slightly metallic, filled with the unfamiliar smells and presence of electronics, plywood, and canvas. The mass of unfamiliar objects weighed down the RV's usual slight sway as Vicky walked to the back room. She set her phone for five, alarm on high, and put it with her shoes. She climbed under the covers fully dressed for the chilly November weather. It was no warmer in the RV than it was outside.

She closed her eyes, willing her body to relax, breathing deep yoga breaths, visualizing thoughts dissolving, floating away from her mind. She wasn't going to sleep, but she needed to rest. It was good to let go, soft and warm in the dark, the aromas of baking preparations on her clothing gently replacing all other smells.

Chapter Twenty-Seven

Mike Miller

After Mike left the diner, he drew a deep breath, stunned. For an instant, he'd come close to telling Vicky what had flashed through his mind. He'd already told her more about himself than he'd told anyone in his whole life. She was like a friendly vampire, sucking out people's life stories before they realized what was happening. He shook his head as he headed to his pickup. *Hell no*. There was no good reason to say a thing. No way. He had simply taken care of a problem. There was no way to tell what would come of it if anybody else knew. Or knew he knew.

****

One night thirty-odd years ago, when Mike was still a teen, he'd been spying—as he often did—on his pa and several other men behind the lodge. It was obvious they weren't there to go hunting or have a barbeque. A box-truck drove in. No headlights.

The driver killed the engine. Mike heard, then saw, movement at the edge of his vision, on the far side of the lodge. The men at the truck didn't react. Most of the building was between them and the disturbance.

Mike followed the sounds of a struggle—branches breaking, angry human sounds with no words, then running footsteps thudding through the woods.

Heavy breathing and grunts grew louder as he neared the creek. He crept close enough to peer through the underbrush. The moon shone a bluish spotlight on two forms grappling and struggling in a clearing thirty feet in front of him.

Mike froze, trying to comprehend what he saw. A man straddled a woman, his hands at her throat. Her legs kicked frantically. The man was twice her size. Neither made a sound.

He recognized the man. Joan's father, that lowlife Bill Beck, who sometimes did jobs with his pa. He was strangling some poor woman. Mike was about to stand when he saw, near the creek, a pale movement. A tiny wraith in a flowing long gown, arms upstretched, wafted up behind Beck.

Mrs. Beck. Harriet.

Joan's tiny mother lifted a large rock with both hands over her head, then slammed it down on her husband's head. He slumped to one side with a loud grunt.

Wow. She bashed his head in. That little old lady.

The woman—girl—on the ground struggled out from under Beck. She got to her feet, stumbling, swaying, gulping deep breaths. It was Joan Beck. He used to see Joan roaming the woods when they were kids. She'd seemed as at home in the wild as he was. She always pretended not to see him.

Joan picked up the bloody rock her mother had set down. She knelt next to her father and stared at him a moment. She lifted the rock overhead and smashed it full force into his face. Mike could hear the dull thump of cracking skull and soft tissue. She said, "You." She raised it and bashed his face again. "Fucking." She lifted the stone a third time and slammed it into what was left of his head. "Bastard."

She let the rock fall and crawled to her mother. They embraced.

For several minutes Mike listened to the night. He could hear the hushed whisperings of the women, not well enough to know what they were saying. The creek streamed silently, slowly. Even the insects were noiseless.

Joan and her mother carefully stepped on the fallen log to cross the creek and trudge back to their house.

Damn. They whacked him. Beat his head in. That tiny old lady. And Joan. Wow. Well, he deserved it.

He waited until he could no longer hear them swishing through the dry grass. He emerged from the brush and edged toward the pile of shit that was Joan's father. Or used to be. Bill Beck was a miserable excuse of a human being. A bully. He'd threatened Mike, hit him more than a few times, and made fun of him for being serious about studying. And he wasn't even family, just did business with his pa and the sheriff.

The asshole deserved to die. Mike didn't get there in time to help finish him off, but he could do something now.

Mike kicked at the old man to make sure he was good and deceased, then put his foot against the body and shoved it onto its back. Christ, the man stank, and not only because his bowels let go when he died. He stank of filth and booze and cigarettes and just sheer meanness.

Mike pulled the bottom of Beck's T-shirt up and wrapped it tightly over the man's gruesomely distorted head to keep blood smears to a minimum. He didn't want to see that face again.

He grabbed the collar of Beck's jacket and dragged the body the few feet to the creek. He left it midstream while he cleaned up. He brushed out footprints and scuffle marks, those he could see in the moonlight. He threw dirt and leaves on the bloody spot. He carried the brain-splattered stone with him as he stepped back to the body. Dirty creek water washed away the remains of its life.

Mike studied the moonlit silence. No signs left of Harriet and Joan Beck finally ending their misery. He dragged the body behind him down the creek. He knew the perfect place.

Jesus, he was heavy. The water was knee-high when he started, which helped some with the weight. By the time the creek shallowed out and became one with the swamp, Bill Beck was dead weight. Mike chuckled to himself at the thought.

He dragged Beck behind him deeper into the swamp. It was getting close to daylight, though the sun never touched much of this place.

He arrived at the spot he had in mind as the perfect final resting place for Bill Beck. He stopped again to survey his surroundings. Moist air, mossy old trees draped with vines. Dark shades of green, water thick with the smell of rot and decay.

Mike tumbled the body into a deep pool under an ancient water tupelo tree. He found a thick branch to tuck old Bill away nice and deep. He made several trips to collect large black rocks to drop on top of Bill, to keep him in place for the turtles and fish and other denizens of the swamp. Move enough rocks around here and you could hide anything. Mike was good at covering tracks. Bill wasn't going anywhere, ever.

Satisfied, Mike looked around him as he left. The places he and Bill had touched were already slowly filling in and springing back. Swamps had welcomed and absorbed death for eons, and this one was already obliterating all trace of his actions.

Chapter Twenty-Eight

Early Sunday Morning

Vicky woke screaming, falling. Her heart hammered terror, head pounded, ears ringing. She couldn't breathe. Something stabbed her thigh, she couldn't breathe, something heavy was smothering her, trapping her. She smelled smoke.

Fire. The RV was on fire.

Shuddering waves of fear assaulted her, alerting every cell in her being to danger, to get out now. This was mortal fear. She'd seen it in other people, and certainly seen its effects, in person and on video, but this was real and now and happening to her.

Get out. Now. She untangled herself from the heavy blankets. Where was she? What was happening? She was on the floor next to the bed, but the floor was the wall and the bed stood upright. The RV was on its side, the side with the door. Find another way out. It was hot. No breath left to scream for help. The back window was near her head. She twisted around and kicked it, her leg shrieking in agony. She kicked and stomped the window. Finally. Air.

Then she was outside, looking up at the RV tipped on its side, black smoke roiling out the broken back window. She gasped for breath, sucking in deep gulps of air harsh with the stench of melted plastic and chemicals and choking fumes. Omigod. She dragged herself away by her elbows before everything went dark.

She woke to feel someone touching her. "Shit! Ow!"

"We're going to move you, Vick." Pete's voice was calm. "Away from the RV."

Vicky lifted her head to look. "Is it going to explode?"

"Just to be safe. Watch her leg." He slid his arms under hers and lifted as Sam picked up her legs.

Vicky moaned as they carried her to Mike's truck. Everything hurt.

Pete's arms tightened around her. "You okay? Besides your leg?"

She took deep breaths, trying to clear her head, to calm herself. "It burns like hell. Shit. What happened? Is everyone all right?"

"Everyone's fine. We were inside the diner." Sam lifted a knee to support Vicky's leg then unlatched and lowered the pickup gate.

Pete said, "We're gonna set you down now." They laid her gently on the truck bed.

"I'll call 9-1-1." Sam ran to the diner.

Vicky yelped. "Help me sit up. What the hell happened? Omigod, my leg!"

Pete gestured at the three-inch metal shard protruding from her mid-thigh. "Man, that's gotta hurt." He reached for it but stopped himself. "We shouldn't move it. We'll get you help here in a few minutes. Hang in there, sweets."

Sweets. He'd never called her that before. "What happened?"

Mike Miller appeared next to the truck, sooty, sweating, carrying a fire extinguisher. He set it down.

"There wasn't much fire. It practically put itself out."

"What happened?" Vicky asked again.

"Not sure yet." Pete gestured toward the RV. "Good thing the gas tanks didn't blow."

Sam arrived back at the truck. "Ambulance is ten minutes out."

An emergency siren pierced the night. They automatically looked toward the sound.

"That was fast," said Sam. "I just called."

"I need to move the truck so they can get in." Mike jumped in and drove the truck a few feet to clear the driveway.

Vicky tried not to scream when one of the tires bumped off the curb. She stared at the smoking RV. "Damn, damn, omigod. Shit."

The volunteer fire truck pulled into the parking lot and two men jumped out. The younger one yelled, "Is everyone out?"

"Everyone's out," Pete shouted.

Mike picked up the extinguisher and followed the firefighter toward the smoldering RV.

The other man was—naturally—Don, the talkative volunteer firefighter. He carried a bag to the pickup. "Everyone okay? What happened? Gas?"

"I turned off the propane before I drove to get supplies," Pete said. "I always do."

Sam frowned at Don. "You sure got here quick."

"We were at the station. We heard it blow."

"What happened?" Vicky asked again.

Don gestured at the spike of jagged metal impaled in her leg. "You're hurt." He set his emergency kit on the truck bed and opened it.

Her fingers had a death grip on the side of her thigh.

No kidding I'm hurt. "I'm fine. Is the diner okay?"

"Yeah." Pete gave her a gentle hug. "It was just the RV blew up. Damn."

"I hope it's not ruined." Vicky paused to leave some space between Pete's damaged RV and plans for tomorrow. "What about the rolls? Can we still do the fundraiser?"

Don closed his bag. "We best leave this one to the experts. We'll get you to the hospital."

"No, it's not that bad," Vicky insisted, just before she fainted.

****

The hospital smelled like all hospitals—of antiseptics and fear. People talked somewhere far away. They must have given her something. She was floating. Vicky left her eyes closed, savoring the feel of Pete's hand holding hers.

He squeezed her hand. "Hey, Vick. Cops want to talk with you."

She opened her eyes. Pete kissed her. "You okay?"

"Feeling absolutely no pain." Vicky lifted the sheet to scrutinize her bandaged thigh. She was in a hospital bed, in a curtained-off cubicle equipped with built-in oxygen, monitors, and other important-looking equipment. Only an IV line, an oxygen tube and a blood pressure cuff were connected to her, which she took as a good sign.

Two men in uniform stood at the foot of the bed. The older one stepped forward, his hat in hand, the rest of his body language forceful and serious. "Ma'am, I'm Sheriff Hal Linden."

"Of course, we met, remember?" Vicky giggled. She hated giggling. "Hello, Sheriff. Pete, this is Sheriff

Linden, he's speaking at Rose's fundraiser tomorrow."
They shook hands.

"Ma'am. This is Deputy Merrill. We need to ask you some questions."

The sheriff's voice was deep, clear, and somewhat aggressive to Vicky's ear. She braced herself, wondering why he was acting like she was a suspect. She was obviously a victim. Or a target. Jesus. What the hell happened?

"You've had a very close call. Why don't you tell us what happened."

Vicky fumbled for the remote control tied to the bedrail. She didn't speak while she pressed the button to bring her to a better sitting position. She needed time to gather her fuzzy thoughts from wherever they were hiding.

"I don't know what happened. I was sleeping and next thing I know, boom! The RV was on its side, and on fire. I was choking. I got out through the back window. That's all I know. What happened? What time is it?"

Pete spoke up. "It's morning, almost seven now. The fundraiser's today, Vick. The explosion happened around one, about an hour after you went to bed."

"Ma'am," Linden asked, "is there any reason why someone would want to hurt you?"

A smartass comment about endless lists occurred to her, but Vicky resisted. "Why? Was it on purpose?"

"We're investigating."

"Someone tried to blow up the RV," said Pete.

"We haven't determined that yet, sir."

"Oh, come on." Pete sounded incredulous. He turned back to Vicky. "They found"—he said, adding air quotes—"an improvised explosive device."

"A bomb? Shit. Omigod. I could have been killed."

Deputy Merrill said, "If it weren't for the sandbags, you might have been."

The sheriff gave him a disapproving glare.

Vicky looked at Pete. He took a deep breath. "The sandbags to brace the canopy and signs. When I loaded the RV I piled them inside, under the table. The device—it was probably a pipe bomb—was right underneath. So the sandbags were between the IED and you."

"Did you do that on purpose?" Vicky asked.

"No, it was just a good place to put them. Jesus." Pete leaned over and kissed her.

"Jesus is right. Wow." Vicky paused to appreciate her good luck. "Okay. I'm all right."

The cops kept asking the same questions and Vicky kept giving the same answers. She was sound asleep when there was a boom right under her, then she fell or was thrown upward, which must have been because the bomb blew the RV onto its side. Blankets fell on top of her and almost smothered her. She was terrified. She kicked out the back window to escape.

"We'll figure out exactly what happened," Sheriff Linden said. "I ask again, can you think of any reason someone would want to hurt you?"

"No, nothing specific."

The cops were acting like she was involved in something shady, or dangerous, or both. She suspected they were absolutely right. Her shock and fear were turning to anger, the low, slow-burn kind of fury she'd known all her life.

She channeled that into a cheerful voice. "If someone did it on purpose, I'm glad they weren't very good at it." Why the hell would someone try to blow her up? Or maybe it wasn't her, specifically. Against the fundraiser? But why? "I feel fine. I'm ready to go."

Sheriff Linden shook his head. "Ma'am, until we determine exactly what happened, it's best you stay here."

"I'm not under arrest or anything, right? The show's at eleven. You're a main speaker."

"That needs to be canceled."

"No, we can't do that. No need. Everything's scheduled. It's fine, I'm fine, I'll be with people the rest of the day, right, Pete? Really, I'm okay."

"Are you sure?" Pete patted her good leg. "Nobody's gonna blame you if we postpone it."

"What do Rita and Sam say?" Vicky asked.

"They want to go ahead."

"Good enough for me." She pressed the call button. "I need to get this IV out."

Linden frowned. "We don't know enough about what happened, and why."

Vicky pushed away the covers. "A lot of people have worked hard to make the fundraiser happen. Today. It's okay, Sheriff. And you'll be right there."

The cops backed away as she hauled herself to the side of the bed. She tugged at her open-back hospital gown, designed to be as unflattering as possible. She could almost see Young Deputy Merrill blush.

Linden said they'd wait outside and would return to the scene with her. Fine. The nurse covered Vicky's freshly bandaged wound with plastic so she could shower away some of the grit and essence of smoke, oil, and destruction.

Dark bruises and cuts covered her body. The doc

had said her leg wound was not serious. It took two dozen stitches, but the shard came out cleanly and didn't do any permanent damage.

Vicky was miffed that something so painful could be considered minor, but understood she was damn lucky. The muffled force of the explosion had sent metal and plastics flying, including the jagged piece of aluminum wall frame that stabbed her thigh. The sandbags, mattress and other padding had protected her. She didn't even seem to have a concussion, though the ringing in her ears was like a physical, vibrating barrier between her and everything around her. Every few minutes her body shuddered, reliving the terror. Jesus. She could have died.

Who wanted her dead?

Chapter Twenty-Nine

Sunday Morning

Pete followed the cops back to Walkers Corner while Vicky, injured leg stretched out on the back seat of her car, worked to draw every detail out of him. "Were you all together when it happened?"

"Sam and Mike were in the kitchen. I was snoozing in one of the booths."

She knew Pete was trying to accommodate her curiosity, but he just didn't seem to have much to say. When the RV blew, he said, they all heard the blast. It was loud and it sounded close by, and more like a deep thump than something blowing out into the air. He ran out the front door and they went out the back. Mike grabbed the fire extinguisher and put out the fire.

"You were on the ground near the back of the RV. It was on its side, the roof facing me." Pete glanced back at her. "I couldn't tell if you were moving. God, I'm glad you're okay."

He said he'd been with her since it happened, but he'd been talking to people all night. No, he didn't personally see where the bomb blew—Mike described it—but he knew exactly where he'd put the sandbags. No, no one else was hurt. Yeah, her phone was probably a goner. The laptop, too.

"You're welcome to use mine. I'm glad I had them

in the diner with me."

"Thanks," she murmured. "I have everything backed up in the cloud, so I probably haven't lost anything. I never liked doing that but looks like a good idea now." She fell silent for a moment. "Any chance this could have been an accident?"

"No." Pete eyed her in the mirror. "You really have no idea who might have done this?"

"Really, no. I'm sorry about your RV. It was probably just meant to scare me. Or you. Us."

"Well, it did that. Are you sure you're okay? We can still cancel the benefit."

"I'm fine, yeah, really." Vicky sounded perky and unconcerned. She was determined to go through with the plan for the day. "We're still on track, right?"

"We made a few changes. You'll see. Try to relax."

Relax. Right.

They smelled the aftermath of the explosion before they saw the flashing lights. Vicky was silent, looking straight ahead through the heavy morning fog that masked and muffled the small-town streets. Traffic, which currently consisted of the patrol SUV and Vicky's car, was rerouted around the diner, but the cop at the barricade shifted it and waved them through.

At the diner, a giant car dealership banner blocked the view of the parking lot. Smaller *ROLLS FOR ROSE* banners hung on it, along with balloons and streamers. A large hand-drawn sign with arrows said, *MOVED TO LIBRARY.*

"Wow! Who did all this?"

Pete grinned as he parked diagonally, two spaces past the deputies. "Everybody's helping."

"This is great." Vicky struggled to get out of the car,

but the painkiller was wearing off. She deferred to the stabbing pain and waited.

"Hold on, I'm coming around." Pete took a pair of crutches from the backseat floor before helping Vicky to her feet. Her first steps were awkward until she got the hang of moving.

If Vicky could whistle, she would have. Instead, she laughed out loud.

Liz Ann rushed out of the diner, beaming, opening her arms. Her short silver hair looked like she'd just rolled out of bed, but she was sharply dressed in a purple turtleneck and jeans, accessorized with a chunky necklace and apron. "Thank the Lord you're all right. How awful!" Liz Ann stepped in to embrace Vicky but stopped, apparently unsure of her injuries. "I can't believe someone tried to blow you up. Do they know who did it?"

"We don't know for sure anyone knew I was inside. The cops'll figure it out." Vicky leaned into a gentle shoulder hug. "It wasn't that bad. I'm fine, really, one little cut. Wow, who did all this?"

Liz Ann, who looked about to bust from the opportunity to tell Vicky everything, launched on all cylinders with Pete adding a few supportive sounds and Sheriff Linden and Deputy Merrill listening in. "It's just wonderful, y'all! We're having the fundraiser at the library. The diner's fine, except for the melted parking lot, but y'all can smell, it's just godawful and that would not be good for anyone, and certainly not fair to the rolls. Wait 'til you see! We blocked off the street in front and the garden club decorated with a bunch of real pretty plants, we set up some tables, all the volunteers did. It looks terrific. And Sam's friends with the band are a much bigger deal than she knew, and they're bringing their friends and all kinds of equipment and a stage and everything. Oh! And a pizza shop owner in the next town volunteered to let us use his ovens! Sam and Rita are there now doing test batches—his ovens are big, they can bake rolls six times faster than in Sam's. Volunteers will run rolls to the library, it's fine, only fifteen minutes away. They'll still be warm and gooey. The rolls, not the volunteers. Are you okay, hon? Are you crying?"

Vicky leaned back into Pete. "This is fantastic."

Liz Ann clasped her hands to her chest. "You bet it is. And you two can stay with me, I have a guest room. Would you like to borrow some clothes? We can stop by my place before we go to the library. It's just about three hours to show time!"

"Thanks, yes. First, I want to see the RV." Vicky took a couple long swings on her crutches to the edge of the *McKay Motors - Shop Today! Drive Away!* banner.

"Hold on, Miz Robeson, you can't go in there." The young deputy stepped in her way.

Sheriff Linden put up one hand and pulled aside the banner with the other. "It's okay. You can show us what happened."

Pete told Liz Ann they'd be just a few minutes, then followed the others behind the banner. Crime scene tape blocked off the RV end of the parking lot. Don was there with a man he introduced as an investigator with the state bomb squad.

"Thank the Lord you're all right." Don expressed his concern to Vicky while he shook hands with Sheriff Linden. They stepped aside to talk, fireman to lawman.

Vicky veered past them as she swung toward the back of the RV. She caught a snippet of Don describing

Vicky's experience, which was fine. She was already tired of talking about it. Interesting how Don's demeanor was so forceful and official, compared to his down-home way of speaking the first time they'd met, when he told her all about the sassafras tree.

Sheriff Linden and the explosives guy joined Pete and Vicky, who stared at the underside of the vehicle and the broken back window.

Pete pointed. "Looks like the device was there, and the sandbags were there, pretty much right between you and the explosion."

The bomb guy stepped forward. "Ma'am, how 'bout you explain exactly what happened."

Vicky answered every question, this time leaning sideways to indicate the RV on its side and pointing to the actual back window she'd kicked out to escape. "Now I see there's an escape hatch on the roof. I didn't know that was there or I'd have used it."

The investigator asked, "Any idea why someone would do this?"

"Hell if I know. Sorry, I'm not trying to be unhelpful. Of course I want you to catch whoever did this. But that's all I can tell you."

"Can or will?" Sheriff Linden had his hands on his hips.

"Same thing. I really don't know any more. Honest." *And enough with the third degree, okay?* "I need to sit down."

Before they left, Vicky and Pete went around to see the front of the RV. "Pete, I'm sorry about your RV," she mourned. "I hope it's not totaled."

"It probably is." Pete kissed her cheek. "It's really not what matters, sweets."

Something inside Vicky swelled and comforted her. They hugged silently, then left.

She didn't realize she was holding her breath until she shuddered and released it when they were back in the car. She didn't want to think about anything for a few minutes. Damn. I could have been killed.

Who the hell did this?

Chapter Thirty

Sunday Morning

Liz Ann adjusted Vicky's blanket and handed her a mug. "You look like you need some nice hot tea, darlin'."

"You're so sweet, thank you." Vicky was comfortably ensconced in a cushioned chair outside the library, sheltered in a cozy alcove with brick walls behind and beside her. A third half-wall allowed a good view of the stage and the cinnamon roll booth. Sheriff Linden had picked the spot, saying Deputy Merrill would be nearby at all times. Vicky mentally dubbed Merrill her Designated Deputy.

Her injured leg rested on one of the library benches. She wore a pair of Liz Ann's yoga pants, sweater, and shoes, all of which were slightly too small. Liz Ann had even given her a lipstick. Vicky always felt better with a dash of color on her face. Liz Ann provided pillows and a nice warm blanket and insisted Vicky just rest.

In her weakened, slightly dazed and giddy state, Vicky really didn't mind doing just that. Sheriff Linden stood near the street barrier next to his patrol SUV. The sun had chased away the fog as the band tested their instruments and sound equipment and volunteers bustled in all directions to complete their assigned duties. The Baking Brigade, organized by shift and currently led by

Rita, was geared up to bake, transport, and sell hundreds of rolls. The aroma of freshly baked, buttery, sweet cinnamon spirals was occasionally interrupted by whiffs of harsh fumes from the RV explosion, but the light breeze was in their favor.

Sam walked toward Vicky, passing out bite-size samples of the cinnamon rolls they would soon be selling. For donations. "Hey, Vick, Are you okay? You sure look better than last time I saw you. Mind if I sit? I need a break."

Vicky shifted her leg to make room on the bench. "Great, yes."

Holding her tray aloft and moving like an exhausted dancer, Sam lifted a folding chair, placed it next to Vicky, and sank into it. "This is so crazy. I can't believe someone blew up your RV. And in my parking lot!" She twisted to place her tray securely on the bench.

"Yeah, same here. Let's have the rest of that roll." Vicky took a sliver. "What do you put in these things? They are so good. Is that ginger, maybe?"

Sam gave her Mona Lisa Baker look.

"Come on, Sam! I trusted you with the story of my life. You can trust me with your secret ingredient."

"No. Last and final answer. This way, whenever you think of me, you'll wonder about my cinnamon rolls. And vice versa."

"That's a nice thought."

Sam inched her chair closer. "What happened to you is really upsetting. Really scary." Newly etched lines creased her young face. Her clear pale skin was smudged. Her eyes drooped, weighed down by the heavy bags below. Her normally stand-up hair was flat and a bit dirty. She was a strong, beautiful mess.

"I'm glad you're okay, Vick. I'm unbelievably angry. Things were so hard already with Rose missing, and now this. Do you think the same person did it?"

"Possibly. But I don't know for sure. Maybe I'm closer to something than I realized. Anyway, Pete said you were in the kitchen when it happened?"

They talked for a few minutes about the blast from Sam's point of view, which was the same as Pete had described. The explosion was running through Vicky's head nonstop, but in the background now because so much else was happening.

Sam leaned in, talking quickly and urgently. "I don't know if this has anything to do with what happened to you, but I want to tell you something, in case it fits in with something else, like you said last night. It might be connected."

The women were only inches apart. Vicky wasn't sure who reached out first to clutch the other's hand.

Sara approached, followed by two teenaged girls. "Sam, what can we do to help?"

Sam removed her hand from Vicky's to point. "Can you check with Rita? She's behind those baking rack towers."

Somebody must have contributed those cabinets. Good idea. Now Vicky wanted everyone to get the hell away so she and Sam could talk. Sara walked the volunteers halfway to the racks, pointed, then returned to linger nearby with a phone to her ear.

Sam said, "Ah, this isn't a good time."

Damn. Damn. "Oh, it's still early. What do you want to tell me? I'm listening."

"We should talk somewhere else. Are you up to going back to the diner?"

"Mm, I'd rather stay here. We start in a couple of hours. Let's go inside. Liz Ann said I could use her office. I'll just save these seats."

Sam helped Vicky to her feet and placed her coat across the chairs. Sara pocketed her phone and joined them.

Sam said, "Sara, if anyone needs me, we'll be in Liz Ann's office."

On the way, Sam and Vicky were waylaid by people with greetings, questions, and updates. A couple asked about the RV explosion. Sam and Vicky both downplayed the incident. No need to get people upset.

Vicky's news director friend Kerry had promised to find someone to emcee the fundraiser. That someone had turned out to be Weekend Anchor Rick. Having him emcee guaranteed TV coverage but put Vicky even more on edge. He stood on stage, an anchorman in his element, wearing boots, jeans, and sports coat, about to host a live, mostly-adlib broadcast, away from the studio, out in the field with a friendly audience. A couple of fans approached him as he looked up and half-waved to her.

Kerry hugged Vicky. "So glad to see you're up and okay." She gestured at Vicky's injured leg. "I heard it was a pipe bomb. Any word on who did it?"

"Not yet. Is the show good to go?"

"Yes. I made a few changes."

Kerry James had volunteered to manage the whole program. She didn't get many chances to produce anymore and was clearly having fun. Her station was going to broadcast the entire event, so she was invested in making it succeed. She held a clipboard with a copy of the rundown Vicky had put together, what was it, thirty-two hours ago? No doubt just to humor her. Kerry loved unscripted live events. She often said rundowns were for wimps.

Vicky chuckled. "You're in charge, which means it will be fantastic." It was amazing how much bigger the event became overnight. Exploded, even. Good thing she knew when to let others take over. When to let go. Ha.

When Sam and Vicky arrived at the library entrance, Designated Deputy Merrill trailing behind them, Sara rushed out. She held the door open for them. "Oh, hi. I was just using the restroom. I hate traveling shithouses."

"Oh God, me too." Odd that Sara had to explain.

Sam and Vicky soon settled in the head librarian's office, next to the window overlooking the garden, Vicky's foot up on a chair. "Isn't this a pretty view?"

Sam mumbled something about gardening, then fell silent.

Vicky waited an interminably long time. "You said you wanted to tell me something?"

Chapter Thirty-One

Sunday Morning

Sam started talking, like she had her thoughts all lined up and ready to go. "Everything I've told you is true. I worked at Phil and Jennie's diner. I lived in their daughter's old room."

All the drawl had gone out of Sam's rich, deep voice. "Before that, I lived in Chicago. I spent some time in a hospital for kids with problems. A psych hospital. That's where I learned to bake. I came here because I needed somewhere to be. No one knew me so I could start fresh."

Sam stared out the window, hunched forward, elbows on knees. "I've been thinking about this all night. About when you were a kid in that fire. You must have been so scared. Then having the RV blow up...it made me think about...I have these dreams or memories. Probably dreams. There's one, years ago, I dreamed or remembered something, I don't know, but I was scared. I was a kid."

Little by little, the sureness of Sam's speech faltered. "It's probably a dream. I was scared, crying, it was cold and dark, darker than deep dark in the woods at night. I was trying to get somewhere."

She glanced at Vicky, then back out the window. The morning sky had shifted to a paler shade of gray.

Vicky followed Sam's gaze toward the library garden, which gently sloped down to meet the woods about forty yards away. A few people were strolling around, volunteers or supporters here early for the show. Pete strolled by and waved at her. Someone must have told him where she was.

When it was clear that was all Sam was going to say, Vicky asked, "Do you remember if you were in the woods? Or inside?"

"Inside, but not normal inside. It smelled strange."

"Like a barn? Or garage?"

"No. Different." Sam lapsed into another long, deep silence.

Vicky waited, chastising herself for her impatience, torn between wanting to speed Sam's story along and letting her tell it her way. Vicky's mind raced and her heartrate quickened, like when she'd be reporting on a great story and the newscast was coming up and the story was still happening but she didn't have a live truck and had to hustle back to the station, scribbling her script in her notebook, talking with the photog about the sound and video and the best way to craft together the facts and soundbites and images in the little time they had, hoping nothing big happened after they left, or if it did, that lady would call, like she promised.

Vicky had loved the thrill. Oh, well. Now, a decade later, late nineties TV news seemed so last century, a long-ago era, when television news people were still among the few with cameras, microphones, and the means of communicating with multitudes of people simultaneously.

Now, anyone could instantly connect with millions with one simple personal electronic device. Simple enough for most to use, but there was nothing simple about the human changes created by the ability to communicate with many simultaneously, immediately, constantly.

That reminded her of her phone, dammit, somewhere in a pile of melted, reeking wreckage. Though now that she'd seen the RV, it didn't look as bad as she had pictured it. She'd expected to see a smoking RV skeleton, but the outside was still mostly intact. Sometimes it was good to have a little distance between a happening and when its story is told.

Speaking of which, Sam was taking an awful lot of nudging for someone who wanted to talk. The fundraiser was going to start soon.

Vicky finally spoke. "Were you alone?"

Sam could have been carved in wood, she was so still, though waves of tension vibrated from the younger woman. Sam was innately graceful and expressive, but seemed to deny those traits, to suppress those natural characteristics so she would appear tough and self-sufficient. Vicky was used to seeing Sam in her element, her café, when she was all of those—strong, confident, and elegant in jeans and apron.

But now Sam was wound up tight, like a compressed steel wire coil. When they'd entered Liz Ann's office, Sam had rearranged the chairs so they weren't facing each other. Was that a conscious action, or a habit formed by avoiding people? Or maybe it really was just so Vicky could put up her leg.

"There was a woman." Sam paused. "We went out into a house. I was scared...terrified." She half-shrugged, her hands clasped tightly in her lap. "And that's it. That's what I remember."

"When you think about it, what do you think was happening?"

"Maybe it was just a bad dream or something." Sam didn't sound like she believed that herself.

"Or maybe it really happened."

"Maybe. I don't know."

"When you were in the hospital with doctors, did you talk about this?"

"No. I didn't talk, and I didn't play their drawing games or anything else. They thought I didn't understand much. After a while they mostly parked me in the library and left me alone. I read a lot. I've never talked about this."

"There's a reason you want to now."

Sam's gaze focused intently out the window. "I don't know where to start. I have, I don't know…they're like random little slices of time."

"That makes sense. You don't have to put them in order. Is it okay if I keep asking questions?"

Sam's shoulder twitched. Vicky took it as assent. "Earlier you said something interesting, about being inside, but it wasn't a barn or garage. What was that like?"

"I was scared. I don't remember."

"What'd it smell like?"

"Cold. Old. Like dirt."

"Have you smelled it since? Something that reminds you of it?"

"Yeah. On a cave tour."

"You've thought about it, then. Do you think you were in a cave?"

"Maybe. Yeah. Dammit. Sorry. That's all I remember."

"There's nothing to be sorry about, Sam. Is it too upsetting to talk about this? I don't want to push you."

"No, it's good. Keep asking questions."

"Okay. You said you went out into a house. Out into. Were they connected? The cave and the house?"

Pause. "I don't know."

"Was there anything the same about them?"

"I'm not sure."

"That's fine." Vicky exuded reassurance. "Do you remember your parents?"

"Not really. Just my mom, a little."

"What was she like?"

"She made me feel good. We made each other laugh." Sam's voice was softer for a moment, then full-out tension returned. "We were going somewhere."

When the next pause had gone on long enough, Vicky asked, "Do you know where you were going?"

"No."

"Were you in a car?"

"I don't think so. I was sleeping. I've tried to remember, but that's it."

"Do you remember talking?"

Eventually, when Sam spoke again, she sounded surprised. "Oh! We were together in one seat. I think we were on a bus."

While Sam paused, Vicky started building a fairly elaborate mental image of a woman and child riding a bus at night, cuddled under their coats, surrounded by strangers, talking quietly in the dark as the bus rumbled past sleeping small towns.

"Mama was telling me about her sister. We were going to find her, I think." She shifted slightly. "You know how you don't know all that's going on when you're a kid."

A shudder traversed Sam's rigid body.

Time to move on, Vicky told herself. For now. "Okay, let me know when you want to stop. Take your time."

Vicky hoped it wouldn't damage Sam in any way, pressing her about obviously traumatic childhood events. But Sam had clearly survived a few battles in her life. She could take care of herself. Vicky carried on. "Tell me something else you remember."

Sam glanced toward Vicky, but her eyes didn't focus before her gaze returned to the window. "There was another time, I remember waking up right next to a woman. I couldn't move. I pretended I was still asleep, but I could see a little."

Sam had given up any pretense this was a dream.

"Was she the same woman from the house?"

"I'm not sure."

"Where were you?"

"We were moving. Driving."

"Was she driving?" Vicky made her questions sound gentle, merely interested, instead of voracious.

"No. A man was. She was moving things around, like she was trying to find something."

"Do you know what?"

"I didn't then, but I think it was a tape. She stuck it in the dash."

"Like a music tape? A cassette?"

"The bigger ones they used before."

"Eight-track. You were a kid in the '90s, right? Eight-tracks were big in the '70s. So it must have been an old car even then."

Vicky had always liked the name of that audio

technology. It said what it was. Sometimes she pictured people's lives as eight-track tapes. Physical changes, personalities, actions, histories, thoughts, secrets—all that and more on parallel tracks for some length of time. Some lives were always out front, like lead guitar or vocals, sometimes stronger, louder, sometimes less so, but always present. Other tracks were fainter, in the background, maybe setting a subtle part of the tempo or mood, but mostly not. Lives whose absence went almost entirely unnoticed, or at least uncommented-on.

That was how Vicky's mind worked, too, and right now the drums and bass guitar were leading, beating this is it, now. Something always changed when tracks diverged or intersected. Or someone's mind jumped to something forgotten. Or hidden.

Sam stared straight ahead. "It was bigger. A van, maybe. That's all I remember. I've tried." She fell silent.

If Vicky still had her phone, she would have put it where she could see the time, to keep a mental countdown to the fundraiser's eleven a.m. start. Other people were handling that now, so her attention was all on Sam. Almost all. It had to be close to ten, now.

Vicky twisted slightly and tugged at the yoga pants near her injury. Without a word, Sam turned, and with both hands gently tugged at the hem.

"Thanks, that feels much better." Vicky settled back and gazed at Sam. "It's good you've thought about this."

"Maybe. I usually try not to."

"That's understandable. Even so, you've thought about all this before, right? It must be so hard to have to relive it."

Sam ran both hands through her hair, from her forehead back to the nape of her neck. It was the first time Vicky had seen her make any self-grooming movement. She never seemed to need to.

Vicky softened her voice. "Can you tell me about another time with your mama?"

Chapter Thirty-Two

Sam Dumain

Sam turned back to the window. Vicky's questions were like probes tapping, touching, stimulating the pain and images and feelings she'd always managed to block. She considered this last question before nodding once. "We were on the ground, on cardboard. Mama was sleeping. It was dark except for one lantern."

"Was anyone else there?" Vicky's voice was gentle.

"Just Mama."

"Were you tied up?"

"No. Well, yes, at first, but not later."

"What was it like in there?"

Sam fortified herself against the wave of remembered pain. "Cold. Dark, except for the lantern."

Sam hated that her voice cracked. She needed to get through this. Waves of sensation crashed back—the fears of a child, her heart being eaten alive from the inside out, thousands of sharp teeth gnawing at her insides.

"I didn't want to leave Mama. But I had to get help. I crawled under a ledge where I could feel air coming in. There was kind of a tunnel. I could hear water running. I could barely fit at first, but it got bigger. I crawled out. It was horrible. I got out and found a knife. Then I went back to Mama in the cave. It was a cave."

Sam pushed away the memory of returning to

Mama. "There's more but I can't remember anything else."

"That's a hell of a lot already. Where'd you get the knife?"

"There was a house. No one was there. I took a knife. I was so scared."

She shook Mama, begged her to please wake up. But Mama's hands were so, so cold. She scolded herself for not getting a blanket. Her world shattered when she realized a blanket wouldn't help Mama now.

"What a brave girl, especially to go back. Try to picture it. It smelled like a cave, right?"

"Yes." Pause. "Then the woman was there."

"The woman from the van?"

"Yeah. By the door."

"Did she open the door?"

"I don't know. It was giant, thick. Metal."

"It was made of metal? How do you know?"

"I must have touched it. It was cold. It made a lot of noise."

"Like squeaky hinges?"

Sam was thrumming with tense energy. "Bigger than that—"

Chapter Thirty-Three

The Library

Wanting to remember every word Sam said, Vicky leaned forward.

Without warning, Sam lunged, knocking Vicky and her chair to the floor.

"What? What?" Vicky gasped under Sam's weight. God, what now? Her leg screamed. Her heart banged, rallying the rest of her body to prepare for action. "What happened?"

Sam rolled off her. "Stay down."

Vicky tried to sit up. "Shit! What happened?" She hated being confused about her circumstances.

Designated Deputy Merrill, who'd been stationed outside the office, rushed in, holding his gun in both hands. "What happened?" His eyes darted around the room.

"Get down," Sam hissed as she motioned him down.

Merrill crouched low.

"What?" Vicky and Merrill whispered in unison.

Sam pointed at the window. "I saw something."

"What?" Vicky grabbed a leg of her fallen chair and pulled herself up to sit, head bent low. "What? What was it?"

Sam was on her feet, squatting. Vicky fumbled for her crutches. Merrill and Sam each grabbed an arm. They dragged her away from the window and helped her stand next to the wall.

"Gun. I saw an arm with a gun." Sam's stunned expression was morphing into something fierce. "Back there, by the woods. It was aiming right at us. Goddammit, Vicky. Shit. Who's after you?"

"Back up." The deputy motioned for Sam to move away from the window before he spoke briskly into his radio. Report of man pointing gun behind the library, possible attempted shooting. No shots fired. No injuries.

"I saw an arm come up, holding a gun." Sam peered out the window and pointed. "Aiming right at us. Look, where those guys are."

Merrill took her place. Several men stood where the garden met the woods.

"We're fine. We're okay." Vicky tried to sound reassuring, mostly for her own benefit. "Nothing happened." She took deep breaths as pain and fear boomeranged throughout her body. Jesus! What the hell.

Merrill's radio crackled with Sheriff Linden's voice. *"Stand down. No shots fired. No shooter. Repeat. No active shooter."*

The deputy visibly relaxed. "Ten-four. No shots fired. Confirming, no injuries here."

Well, that was good news. Vicky was done with excitement for a while.

The deputy looked at Sam. "You saw a gun?" He sounded a little skeptical, which clearly offended Sam.

She stepped around him and pointed. "An arm with a handgun came up out of those bushes, aiming right at us."

He glanced at Vicky, who said, "I wasn't looking out. Sam reacted fast."

Vicky peered around the deputy. Mike, Pete, and the sheriff stood with several other people near the edge of the woods. Pete waved. She waved back. He broke away from the group and jogged toward the library.

Merrill pulled the curtain back farther. "Is that your phone?" He gestured at the sill, where sat a cell phone, the cheap prepaid kind. The small screen was lit up. The phone was on. Someone was listening.

The screen went dark as they watched. Vicky and Sam eyed each other before saying, "No."

The deputy spoke into his radio. "Sir, there's a cell phone here on the windowsill...yessir...I'll secure everything."

He asked Sam and Vicky. "Did you touch it?"

"No. Didn't know it was there." Vicky pivoted toward the door. "I'm going to see what happened." Sam was already moving. Vicky hobbled after her.

Outside, a good-sized crowd milled around in the street-turned-concert-venue. It seemed surreal that everything was so normal. The band was warming up. They sounded great.

Vicky took deep breaths to calm herself. Rick and Kerry stood on the low stage with several people. It looked like she was giving instructions.

Vicky's adrenaline rush receded. No flight or fight necessary, thank God. The booths weren't open yet, but people were lined up to buy cinnamon rolls. Beth and Tom from the RV campground were busy at the beverage booth—no alcohol, naturally, it being Sunday morning in Missouri and all.

A crowd formed at the donation and volunteer sign-up station where tickets for refreshments were for sale. It was good to see that arrangement working so beautifully. At the end of the block stood six portable outhouses and handwashing stations. Vicky had only arranged for two. Another instance of good thinking on someone's part.

Pete bounded up the low steps. Vicky put her arms out, elbows pinned in to hold her crutches. "We're fine."

He wrapped her in a hug. She melted into the comfort of his strong arms.

He kissed her twice. "Are you sure you're okay?"

"Who was it?" Sam was livid.

Keeping one arm around Vicky's waist, Pete shook his head. "Don. He claims he was just walking, holding his gun, and tripped."

Vicky had already cycled through panic, terror, and relief, and was now trying to channel her emotions into something more useful, like figuring out what was going on. "Don had a gun?"

"Yes. He had a pistol. Mike and I noticed him going off behind the library. He was acting squirrelly, so Mike followed him. I went around to come up on the other side." He gave Vicky another nice squeeze. "Are you sure you're okay?"

"We're fine. Badass Sam here saved me. It was over before I knew anything was happening."

"I was looking right there," said Sam. "I saw bushes move and an arm come up. I thought 'gun' and just reacted."

"Did I say thank you? Thank you, thank you." Vicky gave Sam a one-armed hug.

Sam seemed a bit standoffish. Or stunned. Definitely furious.

"Pete, do you believe him? That he wasn't going to shoot us?" Vicky wasn't one to always think the best of people but didn't want to believe Don would try to hurt her.

"It could have been an accident." There was a thin streak of skepticism in Pete's voice. "He was flat on the ground, had trouble getting up even with two of us helping him."

Good enough for now. "So everything's still a go?"

Pete motioned past the stage, outside the street barrier, toward Mike, Don, and Sheriff Linden who were walking toward the front of the library.

The deputy's radio squawked behind them. Vicky had forgotten about her Designated Deputy. He said Sheriff Linden would be right up to talk to them, then left.

No problem. Vicky's heart and breathing slowed to a brisk pace. "Pete, tell me more about Don when you got there."

"He was face down in the dirt. He needed help getting up. He kept saying he was fine, but he was crying and pale as can be. I was worried he might have a heart attack or stroke or something."

Skipping past a minor flash of guilt over Don's possible health scare, Vicky asked, "What'd he say about the gun?"

"He acted surprised to see it and said yeah, it was his, he must have dropped it when he fell."

Sam crossed her arms. "I guess if Don wanted to shoot us, he could have. He's a good shot. Or so I hear. Mostly from him."

Pete nodded. "Mike said the same thing. And that he wouldn't have used a puny old .22 pistol if he wanted to shoot someone, that he has other guns."

Vicky briefly wondered how much Pete knew about

guns. Did he have one? It had never come up.

Just then, Sheriff Linden arrived at the library steps. "Everyone okay?"

"We're fine," Vicky said.

"We need to talk." Linden sounded stern again.

Pete jumped in. "I was just telling them what happened, Sheriff." He motioned toward Linden. "The sheriff got there while we were helping Don up. The gun was still on the ground."

Sam glanced at her watch. "We need to get to work. Let's get this done."

Vicky turned to Linden. "Sheriff, can we talk later? Everything's fine." She sure as hell hoped that was true. "Look at all these people. You're needed out here to keep things secure."

Linden frowned. She leaned on her crutches to free both arms. She talked better when she could move her hands. "Pete and Sam need to make sure everything goes off okay. We're doing this for Rose. And the volunteers."

"Are you sure you'll be okay?" asked Pete.

"Yes, I'm fine." She loved the concern in his voice. "Sheriff, I'll wait right where you suggested earlier."

Linden glanced around before he gave one sharp nod.

"Great. Pete, before you go—" Vicky whispered urgently.

Pete leaned in and kissed her. "You got it. See you soon." He and Sam left, stepping around people who were using the steps as bleachers.

Linden surveyed the growing crowd with his steely lawman look. "Who knew where you were?"

"Anyone who was out here could've seen us go inside. But I don't know how they'd know to put that phone there."

"Any reason the old man would want to hurt you?"

"Not that I know of. You'll have to ask him."

Vicky paused to listen to Rick Carr on stage. He was doing a little pre-show tease, reminding folks that we're all here to help find little Rose Willwood, missing two weeks now, and to support the good people working so hard to bring her home. The coffee and cinnamon roll booths were now open. "Make sure you buy your tickets there at the volunteer signup booth before you get in line. Extra donations welcome."

Vicky and Linden stepped aside when George came out of the library. "Everyone's out." He locked the door. "Mike has a key if you need in, and I'll be around. Sheriff, Liz Ann said it's not her phone."

Linden talked into his radio and told Merrill to get forensics out to process the cell phone scene.

Good. Find out who was responsible for the mystery mobile. *Oh shit—did whoever was on the other end of the phone hear everything Sam told Vicky?*

"Sheriff, I do want to talk with you, but can we wait 'til after fundraiser is over? Nothing really happened. C'mon. We can sit together. Don can sit with us if you want. Was he listening in on that phone?"

"What are you up to?" Linden's question exuded the authority of his badge, title, and weapon, but also included curiosity and what Vicky chose to interpret as real interest.

"Can we first get through the fundraiser? Then I'll talk all you want. And then some, probably. All these people are here to help. The show's going to be on TV and everything. It's for Rose."

Linden tilted his head to talk into his radio. "Merrill.

Bring Don on up here." He gestured in Don's direction. "All right. Merrill will sit with the two of you."

****

Within minutes, Don settled in and started talking. His face was sweaty and flushed where it wasn't fish-belly pale. "I'm sorry to scare you, ma'am." He proceeded to describe in animated detail how he'd tripped, and his arm must've kinda flew up when he was trying to keep from falling. Purely accidental. "And then I fell anyway. Thank the Good Lord no one was hurt."

Vicky made a point of looking away. "Yes. Good thing."

Don failed to take the hint. He pointed to one end of the street and started telling her about each building and its history, going back to when somebody's grandfather had a store, where when Don was a kid he used to get licorice and Black Jack gum.

The man was seriously "working her last nerve," as they say in Texas. She finally had to ask him to tell her the rest later, that the fundraiser show was about to start. She did make a mental note to check whether Pixy Stix really were invented in St. Louis.

Chapter Thirty-Four

Joan Beck

Joan had to strain to hear over the noise of all these damn people. She stood in the scrub trees behind the library where she had a filtered view of the office window. She'd wandered around, acting like a fundraiser early bird to keep an eye on Vicky. Nosy scumbag. She never should have talked to that prying little snoop. Even showed her the bag. Damn. And she never did find out what all Vicky knew about her and Rick.

Joan could barely understand what was said on the damn burner phone. Damn Sara. At least the idiot had enough sense to tell her that nosy bitch Vicky was asking about her dear brother Bill. But Sara's brain was so meth-scrambled, she couldn't even put the phone somewhere good enough to hear clearly. Still, she was able to hear when one of those bitches said "cave." She heard that plain as day.

Time to put an end to this. She had just opened her bag, her winter gloved-hand fumbling with the flap, when something rustled behind her. Don ran—shuffled speedily, actually—toward her.

"Don, you idiot." Joan had pivoted to one side, stuck her foot out, then caught him by his jacket when he tripped. She was strong, but he was heavy. Best to keep him off-balance.

This could be good luck. She glanced around. They were several feet into the woods behind the library's back garden. No one was nearby.

"What're you doing, Joan?" His voice rasped. "I seen you lurking around. What the hell are you doing?"

"Oh, this about what you're doing." Joan chuckled a venomous chuckle.

"What? I'm not doing anything." Don inhaled wheezily as he bent and rubbed his knees.

"This is what you're gonna do. Now." Joan held up the handgun.

Don stepped back. "What the hell? Where'd you get that? Is that my—"

"Yeah, it's yours. You remember the last time you saw it. And who used it." Joan's voice was cutting and cruel. Don used to be part of that dirty bunch with the old sheriff and The Fucking Bastard Bill. This was perfect. He deserved it. Two birds, one stone.

The flush of exertion drained from Don's face, leaving behind pale gray skin. Fear widened his eyes and his mouth hung open in an almost cartoonish expression of shock.

"Yeah, you better be scared." Joan enjoyed it when her little collection of other people's secrets proved useful. She held decades of buried dirt. "The gun's not all I kept. You shoot that damn busybody. That's her on the right. Dead. I want her dead."

She thrust the pistol at him. He took it, stunned. Joan's voice was low and threatening. "Got that? You miss, and your dear wife spends the rest of her life in prison. Do it."

Someone was coming. Joan tugged her cap firmly over her bright white hair and hissed, "Now," as she melted into the trees.

She sidled around to the front of the library. There had to be several hundred people on the street, the most she'd ever seen in this little town. No one spoke or waved to her. She was good at avoiding people, not that many ever noticed her, anyway.

She stood near the back of the crowd and waited to hear a gunshot.

Joan almost gasped out loud when that bitch Vicky came out the library door with Sam, followed by a deputy. Goddammit. Don didn't do it. Well, he was going to pay, big time. If he thought his fake-sweet little wife was going to get away with killing her ex all those years ago— Huh. But what if he actually wanted her sent off to prison?

Joan scoffed silently when Rick took to the stage and started talking about the poor little missing girl. What a fake. Up there acting like a big shot, pretending he cares, when everyone knows he only thinks about himself. Always acting all innocent when he knew damn well what his sheriff daddy was up to. But he'd been paying for his daddy's deeds for quite a while now. She made sure of that. His payments added up nicely.

Dammit, Don. She should have taken care of things herself. And damn that goddam nosy little snake. She's gonna screw everything up. Everything. Goddammit. She should've taken out that prying little bitch on the highway, but she was quicker than she looked. Dammit. And it was pure bad luck that Mike showed up before she could rig the pipe bomb. She'd barely had time to leave it under the RV before she had to slip away.

Shit, now Vicky was looking Joan's way. Joan stepped behind two women who were talking about how hot Rick was. Hot little weasel, more like.

Goddamn Rick. If it weren't for him and his goddamn fancy bag, that bitch Vicky would never have even heard of Joan. She should've dropped that Alisa woman off at Rick's all those years ago. She must have escaped from his sheriff daddy's bunch. Rick should've had to clean up that mess.

But that damn reporter had been right there on his porch, sitting like she was just waiting for Joan to drive by and drop off a beat-up woman. Like she knew she was coming. And back now all this time later? Of all times. There must be more to her being here.

The sheriff arrived and talked with Vicky. Where the hell was Don? It was awful being around all these people. All this for one kid. Nobody had ever cared about her anywhere near that much, 'cept for Mama. She still missed Mama, the only person in her whole life who made her feel wanted. She was lonely without Mama.

"What are you up to?"

Joan glanced sideways. Mike. She didn't answer or pretend to be friendly. When they were young, Joan often felt a little fluttery around him. Not now. Life was simpler not liking anyone.

Mike spoke in a low, forceful growl. "Why are you here?"

"I'm here to support the community."

"Since when?" Mike's sarcasm was as clear as hers. "What'd you do? Did you put Don up to something?"

Joan didn't bother to answer. Mike continued, "And why were you at my place a few weeks ago? George saw you sneaking around when he returned some tools. What were you doing there?"

"Guess you should ask George."

"What're you gonna do tomorrow?"

"I'm going to a meeting, same as you."

Mike leaned in close and whispered, "We have a deal. You better not screw it up."

When his breath touched her, an unwelcome rush of heat swept through her body. Christ. Even now. "Leave me alone."

When she was in high school, half the girls were forever chasing after him, the sexy, smoldering loner. He'd been more man than boy, well-built, with whiskers and a distinctive widow's peak above his clear green eyes. He moved like a panther, sleek muscles rippling. Sure of himself, though a little rough around the edges. When her classmates talked about what they'd done or wanted to do with him, she couldn't help but imagine doing those things with him, and to him.

Not that she'd ever had the opportunity. She'd only touched him once. She would never forget it. She was sixteen and rushing to chemistry class when she tripped and fell down the last three steps. Classmates snickered. God, she despised them. Then Mike's hands were on her waist and elbow as he helped her to her feet. Off-balance, she tipped back against him, then jerked away when she realized who had helped her.

He asked if she was okay, and she muttered, "thanks" and rushed away, face burning. For years she'd relived the feeling of his body against hers.

"See you tomorrow." His low rumbling voice still stirred something deep in her.

She jerked her head in a nod. Now idiot Don was there with the troublemaking snoop and sheriff. That can't be good. Dammit. Dammit.

She eased away from the crowd. One more day, less

than twenty-four hours to go. She'd been counting down to tomorrow ever since she read Old Man Miller's will while doing mindless paperwork for the town law firm. The estate would be split equally among all descendants of Beck and Miller, the original owners. Her grandpa and Mike's. To collect, they were required to attend a meeting exactly one year after the last partner died. And they had to be present in order to collect.

She just had to show up for Monday's meeting, vote to sell the damn place, then close the deal with the frack sand company. Then she'd be rich and could finally get away from this hellhole.

Chapter Thirty-Five

The Fundraiser

Rick Carr opened the fundraiser with a touching video montage about the community joining together to find Little Rose Willwood. On stage, her mother trembled as she made a heartbreaking plea for help finding her daughter. The junior FBI agent followed and gave an update with no real new information. Sheriff Linden got up to thank the volunteers and ask anyone with information that might help find Rose to please speak up.

Rick was a talented emcee. The crowd absolutely loved it when he announced they were going to be broadcasting live in thirty seconds. He held up his hand and announced, "Standby" in a loud and authoritative voice, before switching to his ever-so-slightly over-the-top TV anchor/reporter persona.

People whispered about him growing up here. "Yes, right here in Walkers Corner," one said. "He used to be a cop. And now he's on TV news in St. Louis."

The band was a big hit with their lively blend of blues and almost poetic country rock. Copies of their new album were up for sale next to the donation booth with all proceeds going to the Rolls for Rose fund. They sold out long before the end of the show.

An hour later, Rick signed off. The show was over.

Don and Deputy Merrill both rose to help Vicky up from her seat next to the library wall.

Sheriff Linden appeared at Vicky's side and gave her elbow a light touch. "All right now, it's time we talk."

"Yes, thanks, I'll be back in a sec, okay? Really, just a minute. I need to thank people." And give Pete enough time to get the group together.

Sheriff Linden drew a deep breath, the very soul of patience. Vicky started unsteadily toward the stage. Kerry met her halfway.

"Omigod, Kerry. Thank you, thank you, thank you for all you've done."

Kerry returned Vicky's modified high-five. "It was good, wasn't it?"

"It was amazing. You're amazing." Vicky gestured, encompassing the lively groups of people milling around, neighbors and once-strangers mingling with the bakers, the band, TV people, cops, and politicians. "Look at all this."

"Crazy, huh? Did you love Rick's intro?" Kerry did an imitation of his adlib about the band, rock 'n roll, and the smell of cinnamon rolls in the morning.

"And check this out." Kerry held out her phone. "The response is fantastic. Donations are coming in faster and bigger than anyone hoped."

Rick broke away from his fans to join Kerry and Vicky. "Hi, Vick. Are you okay? How's the leg?"

"Not too bad. I got lucky."

She summarized the event casually, like it was no big deal that someone wanted her dead. The three of them—being news people—spent several minutes analyzing the RV explosion and possible scenarios before switching to fundraiser highlights. The benefit was, by any measure, a success. For now, anyway. In Vicky's unvoiced opinion it would succeed only when Rose was found safe and healthy, undamaged, or at least able to recover.

That was the only metric that mattered. Though it'd be good to find out about a few other things, too.

"I better get going. The sheriff wants to talk with me." Vicky gestured toward Linden, who watched her while talking on his phone. She half-turned to Rick. "Oh. Rick?" For a moment she channeled Columbo, the rumbled TV detective who always happened to remember he had just one last question before he left. "I wanted to ask you something. I meant to when we had coffee, but you had to leave."

Rick froze, probably bracing himself for whatever she was about to say in front of his boss.

"The other day, we were talking about Lisa on the Levee, when you were a deputy—you were at Joan Beck's that day, right?"

"What?" he acted perplexed. "The kid on the levee? What about her?"

"Joan mentioned you were at her house that day."

"Maybe. Long time ago." Rick did his charmingly sheepish grin thing. "How 'bout we get you on camera for a quick interview about the explosion? Won't take a minute."

"Not now. Just use the statement, okay?"

Pete had sent it out to the news media on her behalf before they left the hospital. It said she was shocked but fine, had confidence in the investigation, was grateful for all the help and good wishes, and that she looked forward to seeing everyone at the Rolls for Rose fundraiser today.

"All right, I guess. I gotta run." Rick shook her hand. "Glad you're okay."

"Thanks. Good to see you." For the last time, probably. Just as well. Some things were better called done and gone.

As Rick strode away, Kerry called after him, "You still need to turn a fresh story for the Ten." She put a hand on Vicky's shoulder. "I'll ask one more time, then I'll leave you alone. Let's get you to tell us what happened. You can also talk about the fundraiser."

Vicky had interviewed plenty of people who spoke too soon. She wasn't going to say anything on the record until she was ready. "You know I want to, but not yet. I will, but later. Not today." Vicky crossed her fingers for good luck and used them to blow Kerry a kiss. "I'll keep you posted."

"You better." Kerry pointed a finger in mock-warning, then left without another word.

Vicky watched Linden walk toward her. She didn't see Don and hoped he was with Pete. "Okay, Sheriff, I'm ready. Thanks for being so patient."

So far, she'd managed to avoid saying much of any substance to him. And despite her actions to the contrary, the gun scare had unnerved her, especially when it followed so soon after the RV explosion. She followed him to the library door, pausing along the way to thank the volunteers breaking down the booths, or loading furniture onto trucks, or doing general cleanup. It was early afternoon but had already been a long day after a very long night. People were ready to go home.

Linden held the door open for Vicky, then followed her inside where Don sat with Pete, Sam, and Mike at the table closest to the check-out desk. Perfect.

"Sheriff, do you mind if we just catch up on a few things first?" Vicky sounded nice as pie. "Y'all did such a great job with everything," she said to the group.

Linden's expression fell somewhere near the intersection of irritated, interested, and entertained. After a long, questioning look at Don, he sat. "Make it quick."

Mike locked the front door. Vicky settled into the seat Pete indicated. He helped her lift her injured leg onto another chair.

Don immediately began embellishing the story of how he'd tripped and how bad he felt if he'd scared anyone with his old pistol. "Thank the Good Lord no one was hurt. Shouldn't have brought it along, shouldn't have had it out, but things've been a little odd around here lately. I just wanted to be ready to help." He wiped his forehead with a blue bandana handkerchief. Vicky briefly recalled reading that the classic bandana's paisley design originated in India. Or was it Persia?

Don appeared jumpy and close to crying, but Vicky admired his talent for framing a story with his version of events, getting it out there first so it could hardly be repeated without his side in it.

Don finally caved to the sheriff's glare and unspoken order to be quiet. In the silence that followed, Vicky renewed her vow—made only to herself, fortunately—to mostly listen. She had asked Pete to feel free to speak up about anything, whatever seemed right, depending on the mood of the table, whatever it took to help get people talking.

That proved unnecessary.

Sam put both hands on the table. "I've been remembering things." She paused and took a breath as if to compose herself. She'd taken off her apron but still wore the clothes she'd worn while baking and selling cinnamon rolls. "Things I've tried not to think about since I was a kid. Vicky's been helping me remember."

She spoke softly. "I am, or I was, the girl they called Lisa. But Samantha is my real name."

Sheriff Linden opened his mouth, then clamped it shut just as fast. Don over-acted surprise with raised eyebrows and an open mouth. Pete and Mike just waited.

"Lisa on the Levee," Vicky confirmed.

"You knew." Sam pressed her lips into a tight semi-smile. "I wondered, with the questions you kept asking."

"You're the right age. You said you'd been in institutions. And you moved here." Vicky looked around the table. "Earlier, when we were in Liz Ann's office, Sam started to talk about what happened before she was found on the levee." She motioned to Sam to go on.

"When it happened, when the farmer found me," Sam said, "people kept asking who I was, how I got there. I couldn't answer 'cause I didn't know. Everything was blank. But now things are coming back; things that I've always tried to keep out of my mind."

Her voice grew stronger as she talked, succinctly summing up some of what she'd told Vicky: being with her mama on the bus, then in a cave, a tunnel, a strange house, the woman, escaping.

She sounded almost matter of fact, but it didn't take any imagination to know she'd been through something hellish. "I was put in a psych hospital for kids, then foster homes 'til I was eighteen. Then I was on my own."

Vicky was impressed by how effectively Sam communicated, especially for someone who'd spent eight years not saying a word. "Is that when you started talking again?"

"Yeah." Sam half-grinned. "Sometimes I miss not talking."

Vicky smiled. "You came back to Walkers Corner."

Sam and the sheriff exchanged a serious look. "I thought if anyone ever wanted to find me, I'd be here. I've never told anyone about this."

After a pause, Vicky said, "I need to say something."

Sheriff Linden made a go-ahead gesture that transitioned to a hold-on-now motion to Don. Don closed his mouth and scowled.

"I feel responsible, since I invited everyone here." Vicky aimed a shrug at the sheriff. "Thanks for coming. We're just talking, but everyone should remember Linden is a cop, and I'm planning to write a story." She grinned at Don. "And it's even possible Don might mention something about whatever he hears."

Don didn't seem amused. "I knew you weren't writing a travel article."

"Everyone knew that," Mike added.

"I *am* writing a travel article, about a place where a crime happened. Or crimes." It was true, though only part of Vicky's motivation. "I'm just saying, no one's obligated to say or answer anything."

Sheriff Linden frowned. Mike glanced around the table. "We're all grownups here."

"I want to keep going," said Sam. "Ask away."

"All right. So you pretended you couldn't talk?"

"I didn't want to talk about anything."

"Sounds like you had good reason."

Don jumped in. "I remember that, that little girl who showed up out of the blue. That was you? We searched everywhere, couldn't find any sign of where—"

Sheriff Linden didn't let him get going full speed. "Let her talk. What else?"

Sam shrugged. "That's it."

"Where'd all this happen?" Linden sounded impatient.

"I don't know."

The honed edge in the looks Sam and Linden exchanged suggested some history between the two. A pre-existing adversarial condition. And yet they had a diner backdoor knock.

Interesting. What was that all about. Maybe later.

"Does anyone know—was anything else going on around the same time? Anything unusual?" Vicky asked. "Sheriff, you were with the department back then, weren't you?"

Linden's face remained expressionless.

"Do you remember something else going on, about the time Lisa—I mean, Sam—was found?" she asked.

Linden shook his head. "I'm not here to answer questions."

"We're all just talking," said Pete.

"Look, we're all trying to help find Rose." Vicky spoke in a conciliatory voice. "Maybe there's a connection between Rose and Lisa. I mean Sam. Maybe if we all share information, we can find her."

The sheriff did not appear to be in a sharing mood. After a few moments of silent challenges crisscrossing the table, Mike spoke. "Okay, I'll tell you something unusual that happened the day Sam was found."

Finally. Vicky worried Mike wasn't going to tell his story.

"I found a woman out near the edge of the swamp. She was unconscious, been beat up bad. I took care of her some, but she ran off. Never saw her again."

Sheriff Linden leaned forward. "Who was she?"

"She never told me."

"And you didn't think to report that?"

"I thought about it and decided not to."

"Why?"

"Why? Because she didn't want to be found. She was real skittish. Scared. And it looked like she had good reason to be, like Sam." Mike's growly voice was now more downtown Chicago than rural Missouri. "That's the night it rained so hard, remember, Linden? And I got sent to search halfway across the county." He sounded like he was still sore about something.

"Now you just hold on," Don snapped, the befuddled old man persona on pause. "We was searching for her family for hours before you finally showed up, Mike. We was organized. We had them close-in grids covered already. Where was you that whole time, anyway?"

"I just told you. I got nothing to hide."

The sheriff was about to jump in, so Vicky spoke up. "Sheriff, you were a deputy back then. You and Rick Carr, when his father was sheriff. We talked once, out on the levee, right?"

Linden acted as though he had no idea what she was talking about. Vicky knew that act. "What'd you think of him?"

"Who?"

"The sheriff. I knew Rick from my time covering news stories, but his father wouldn't talk to reporters, other than canned comments at news conferences." Vicky was now certain the old sheriff had been a crook— or worse—but had no way of proving it.

257

Linden was good at waiting silently.

Don launched into a spirited defense of former Sheriff Carr. "He was a fine sheriff, a good man. He kept things under control. Place was thriving. Business was good."

He wiped his forehead again. He choked up a little as he described how Carr kept working even after he got lung cancer. "He took care of things right up 'til he died, must have been 'bout a year or so after that little girl was found, guess she's here all grown up now." Don took a long look at Sam. "Things were never the same after he died." He glanced at Sheriff Linden. "No offense."

Vicky kept her smile encouraging. "The other day, you mentioned you sometimes worked with the old sheriff, right, Don? He did other work, too, back then, didn't he?"

Don froze, no doubt scrambling to remember what-all he'd told her while they sat across from the sassafras tree. Vicky figured it must be difficult for a person to remember everything they said when they talked as much as Don Winters.

He mumbled, "Well, every now and then, I suppose. Don't remember what. Small stuff."

She spoke to Linden. "The state had an investigation going on here in the county, remember? That was right about the same time."

Linden frowned. "Don't know what you're talking about."

Vicky raised both eyebrows. "Hmm."

Sheriff Linden was in full intel-gathering mode. "What *are* you talking about?"

So was Vicky. Give a little, get a little. "Back in '99, when I worked TV news in St. Louis, a state grand jury was empaneled to investigate illegal distribution here in the county." Vicky gave Linden a challenging stare, as though she knew much more than a long-ago glimpse of a secret subpoena. "It involved the old sheriff."

Linden barely shook his head, no. Don stared at the table.

The silence stretched on so long Vicky almost jumped when Sam started talking again. "I was so scared. She made me promise never to talk about what happened."

"It's been almost ten years," said Vicky. "You can tell us."

After another long pause Sam spoke. "Alisa. Her name was Alisa. I promised I would never tell anyone."

Sam looked at everyone, one by one, ending with the sheriff. She seemed calm and sure. "Alisa said if I told anyone we would both go to jail for the rest of our lives. I hope that doesn't happen, but I need to get this out."

Sam glanced at Vicky, who said, "Take your time. Think about what you say."

Sheriff Linden made a go-ahead motion with his chin.

Sam seemed focused far beyond the library table. "There was a fight in the cave. Right by the door...a man was sitting on Alisa, hitting her. She was screaming for help...I had the knife. I jabbed it in his back as hard as I could. I felt it go in."

Her entire body was taut, even her spiked blonde tips seemed to stand taller. "His blood got all over me." A shadow crossed her face.

After a while, Vicky added, "And you were just a kid..."

"Alisa took me through the metal door into the house. The TV was on…" Sam's voice trailed off again.

"Later she took us back to the cave. I wouldn't go in, but she did. I was watching. The man attacked her again." Sam scoffed wryly. "Apparently he wasn't all the way dead. I ran away. I left my mama and ran away."

There was a quiver in Sam's voice, but it was more like the movement of a flexible metal rod than something that might break. "I think Alisa was searching my mother when the man attacked her again. She took something from Mama and put it in her pocket."

Vicky wanted to touch Sam's arm, but the chair she had her leg on was in the way. She murmured something encouraging instead. Sam stared ahead.

After a long silence, Pete said, "Can I show you something?" He'd been discreetly tapping on his laptop. Now he spun the screen to show the others a map. Pete spent a lot of time bouncing around Google Maps, searching for ponds and lakes that might be home to nice healthy bass. "I couldn't find anything on the Missouri cave websites. Probably too small."

He used his cursor to highlight locations. "Here's Walkers Corner. . . this is the highway to St. Louis. . . here's the river levee." He traversed the countryside, pointing virtually, then paused. "I'm not sure where Sam was found…?"

Sheriff Linden got up and moved closer to the screen, pointing at it with the tip of his pen. "The little girl was right about here, south of the farm-to-market road."

Pete marked the spot, then switched to satellite view. "Okay, you can see the area's still mostly fields and woods. It must have been wilder back then."

"Sam was found the same day Mike found Alisa," Vicky said. "I doubt a kid could've walked very far."

"Mike, where'd you find Alisa?" Pete asked.

Mike pointed at the screen. "Somewhere over here. See where this road splits? You can't see much through the trees." Using the tip of his pinkie finger, he traced a path along the wooded area. "My place is about where this ends."

Pete followed with his cursor, then zoomed out and pointed. "This line of trees must be the creek. Somewhere along here is probably where Sam crawled out of the cave."

As everyone contemplated the screen. Pete asked, "What's this at the other end of the split?"

"That's the old lodge," Mike said. "Near the bluff."

Pete traced the distance with his cursor. "About how far is it from your place?"

"It's almost two miles driving, less than half that if you cut through the woods. It's all part of the same big property."

Pete drew a line from the lodge to the spot the sheriff had previously indicated. "It looks like a couple of miles or so from the levee."

"Mike, do you take care of the lodge?" Vicky asked, as though she didn't know.

"The bank pays me a few bucks a month to keep an eye on things. I just watch it rot away. Can't stand the place. And before you ask, Sheriff, yes, I checked it when I heard about Rose. With one of your search teams."

Mike lifted his chin. "That reminds me of another odd thing. The same day the little girl—the same day Sam was found, Rick Carr came by my place to ask if I knew anything about her, which I didn't. Then we drove over to check the lodge."

Mike paused. "Rick's pa—old Sheriff Carr—was already there. He'd been inside, turned out he had a key. Claimed everything looked normal, which it did when I checked real quick, 'cept his footprints were all over the place, coming and going. They would've covered up tracks of anybody else who'd been there. Him being there felt real fishy."

Vicky glanced at Mike. "Is there a cave near the lodge?"

"Nothing big enough to be what Sam described." Mike frowned. "But in his last days, my grandpa started talking about a cave. I didn't think there was anything left that old man hadn't talked about, but he held onto that one thing until just before he died."

"What'd he say about it?" Vicky tried not to sound like she was accusing anybody of anything, but why was this just now coming up?

Mike's eyes locked Vicky's with a clear back-off warning. "Grandpa liked to talk. Even more than Don. Toward the end, Grandpa was rambling on. He wasn't making much sense."

Don scoffed. "You wouldn't've never found it anyways."

Attention swiveled to Don, who appeared almost anguished, but at the same time, somehow satisfied. His voice was shaky. He squeezed and twisted his bandana. "That ol' cave hain't been used in years. Mike's granddaddy wouldn't've told him nothin' about it." He paused. Don had a firm grasp of the dramatic. "That was the deal. We all agreed."

Vicky wanted to thrust a fist down Don's throat and

rip out the truth. If her theory was right, a human trafficking ring had been operating this whole time. "Rose could be in there!"

"Nah. Old man Miller, Beck, and Sheriff Carr was 'bout the only ones knew about it. And me." He appeared to enjoy knowing something they didn't, having something they wanted.

"We agreed to never talk about it." Don leaned back, showing all the signs of settling into a long and convoluted story now that he had everyone's attention. "Sheriff shut it all down 'fore he passed. With him gone, we was done with that business."

"What business?" Vicky asked.

Sheriff Linden stepped next to Don. "Where is it? The cave."

Looking irritated, Don shook his head. "It's hidden. I'd have to show you."

Linden put a hand on his shoulder. "Don. Tell me."

"It's all ancient history." Don winced as the sheriff's hand tightened. "Hey. I don't have to tell you anything."

Vicky piped up. "It'd be good to just tell us. What business? You told me before about bootlegging—"

"Oh, that was long ago." Don pulled away from Linden. "Old-timey days. We used it to store what-not 'fore we took it places." He glared defiantly at the sheriff. "Nuthin' you can do anything about now."

The sheriff replaced his hand on Don's shoulder. He towered over the old man. "Where's the cave, Don?"

Vicky could barely contain her impatience. Rose might be in there. Plus, she was hungry to know about the 'what-not' Don was hanging on to. Given enough time and Don's sheer love of gab, she could surely get him to reveal plenty about what—or who—he and his cohorts used to store, then move.

But she had no authority, bargaining chips, or time, so she settled for, "Come on, Don. Just tell us. Please. Where is it?"

Don stared at her for several seconds, then shrugged. "Oh, all right. It's at the lodge, but you'll never get in. It hain't been used for years. Like I told y'all, Sheriff Carr shut it all down 'fore he died."

"Where at the lodge?" Mike scowled. "There's no cave there."

Don seemed pleased with himself. "You'd have to know about it."

Sam leaned forward, both hands on the library table. "My mother's body is in there." She stood up.

Vicky lifted her injured leg off the chair. "And Rose might be, too."

Don frowned. "Nah. The entrance is hidden and locked up tight. No one's left knows how to open it. I don't."

The sheriff spoke into his radio. "Bet Merrill can."

Vicky pictured the wide-eyed young lawman. "Merrill? The deputy?"

"There wasn't no kind of lock his daddy couldn't break." Don sounded proud. "He was good at it. And he taught Merrill everything he knew."

"Good at it, right up 'til it got him killed." The sheriff's eyes said something to Don that interested Vicky. Maybe later.

She got to her feet. "Let's go."

Linden made a hold-on gesture. "Whoa, you're not coming. Just Mike."

Sam strode toward the door. "I'm coming with you."

"No." The sheriff pointed at Mike. "Just you, to let

us in." He pulled Don to his feet. "You. Let's go. You're going to tell me everything about the cave, then I'm taking you home. We'll have plenty to talk about later." The sheriff rushed him out.

Sam caught Mike's arm. "Hang on, Mike. What's the lodge address?" She and Pete had their thumbs poised over their phones. Vicky wished she still had hers.

"There's no mail address. I have a PO Box. I'll give you directions." Pete followed along on his phone's map as Mike told them how to get there.

"Mike. Hang on a sec." Vicky whispered fiercely. "You're in charge of the property. You can give us permission to be there. It's okay if we're on it, right?"

"Makes no difference to me," said Mike.

Vicky caught his arm. "And if Linden won't tell us what's in the cave, you can. You need to. Please. You have to."

Mike followed the sheriff. "I'll think about it."

Chapter Thirty-Six

Sunday Afternoon

Mike listened as the sheriff drove and questioned Don, who'd been sulking because they'd made him sit in back. He answered tersely, with none of his usual gabbing.

After they pulled into Don's driveway, Linden said, "Back wall, mudroom closet. Anything to add?"

Don's face gleamed damply in the dark back seat. "This ain't fair. I oughta be going with you, to show you." He sounded bitter.

Mike got out to open the rear door. "It's all right, man. We'll find it."

Grumbling, Don climbed out of the SUV. "You better not forget I told you all this, Hal. I didn't have to say a damn thing. You'd a' never found it without me."

"You should have told me a long time ago, Don," Sheriff Linden said. "Now you stay home 'til I get in touch."

It took a half hour to get to the lodge property road. Several bumpy minutes later, Mike pointed. "Best pull over before the split so we can check for tracks."

The sheriff parked. They got out and studied the ground. Mike pointed at tire tracks in the dirt and gravel drive. "Those are mine, those are your deputy's. Doesn't look like anyone's been here since, but it'd be quieter to go on foot, just in case."

****

After Mike, Don, and the sheriff left the library, Sam picked up her coat. "We better take your car. My truck doesn't have a back seat."

"Shit, it's by the diner," Pete said, "I'll go get it."

When he returned, Sam opened the back door for Vicky. Vicky wanted to ride shotgun, but her leg was killing her, and she needed to stretch out. She was slowing them down. Sam was familiar with these roads and her truck was better suited to them. But here they were, a half hour behind the sheriff and in a hybrid sedan, all because of Vicky.

No, she told herself, because of whoever the hell blew up the RV.

Other than Sam and Pete occasionally consulting on the route, no one spoke. Vicky welcomed the quiet. She was practically vibrating with excitement. Rose. God, Rose had to be there. She had to be okay.

Her mind raced, but Vicky's body wanted nothing but rest. She leaned back against the seat.

"Dammit! Those bastards!" Vicky jolted awake when Sam yelled. Christ, had she fallen asleep? Two patrol cars were parked at a V in the road, blocking any way forward. A deputy walked toward them. Pete rolled down his window.

The deputy leaned down and looked past Pete at Sam, then Vicky. "You Pete?" He didn't wait for an answer. "Sheriff said y'all'd be coming. Said to wait here. He'll tell you what's going on when he knows something."

Everyone objected. The deputy shrugged. "Possible crime scene."

"Can they do that?" Sam sounded agitated.

"Yes, they can." Vicky leaned closer to Pete's open window and used her professionally friendly voice. "Hi, just a sec, Deputy…? What's your name?" She hated that she couldn't see his badge. His ranger-style hat hid his eyes. What showed of his mouth wasn't smiling.

"Briggs." His manner wasn't hostile, but he was certainly humorless and unresponsive to sociable overtures. "I need you to wait in the car."

"Deputy Briggs. Hi. This is Sam and I'm Vicky. We were just in a meeting with Sheriff Linden and Mike Miller."

Briggs didn't seem impressed. "The sheriff's the one to talk to."

"When did you say he's coming to talk with us?"

"I didn't." The deputy gestured dismissively and walked back to his car.

Vicky tapped Pete's shoulder. "What time is it?"

"Ten 'til four."

"Hmm. It's already getting dark. Do you have a signal?"

Pete looked at his phone. "No bars." He started tapping on it anyway.

"There's no service out here," said Sam. "We can walk in, can't we?"

"Cops can legally keep us away from a crime scene," Vicky said. "But this isn't taped off. And Mike gave us permission to be on the property. But maybe we should give it a little while."

Vicky sincerely hoped her willingness to wait had nothing to do with her damn leg, which was now pulsing sharp bursts of heat. She wasn't doing very well with keeping it straight and slightly elevated. "I think

Linden's going to be fair with us."

"Why would you think that?" Sam half-turned in her seat. "You're the one who doesn't trust anyone."

"That's not really how it is with me. Anyway, Linden knows he wouldn't be here now if we hadn't all talked. I think he's a fair guy. And Mike's with him."

Sam made a noise something like a scoff, something like an ugh of disgust, then said, "Who's this now?"

A van parked behind them. Briggs came up to Pete's window.

The deputy took another good look around the car. "Sheriff said to tell you there's no sign anybody's been up there. Mike's on his way here to take the state lab boys in, that's them here now. And no, you can't go with them." He didn't wait for a response, just slapped the car roof as he left.

"Such a sweet guy." Vicky chuckled. "I'm going to see what's going on." She opened the door behind her and scooted backward until she could swing her good foot onto the ground. She held onto the open door and gently, carefully, pulled her injured leg out. It wasn't graceful but she was standing.

Sam handed Vicky's crutches across the roof to Pete, who stood next to Vicky, clearly ready to intervene if she got into trouble. She was glad she didn't need the help.

Deputy Briggs stood with two men in coveralls. He glared at Vicky as she approached the trio.

"Hi, I'm Vicky Robeson." She extended a hand to the older of the two new arrivals, who shook it. "This is Pete, and Sam."

The newcomers—one in his grizzled fifties, the other a decade younger—nodded.

Vicky focused on the senior of the two. "We've been talking with the sheriff—"

"Who said to wait here," Briggs barked.

"My leg was killing me. I had to get up and move around." Vicky returned his glare with a smile. "We're not going to hurt anything." She addressed the investigators. "Sam here's the one who told him about the cave."

The crime scene men turned to Briggs, who shook his head. Vicky tried a couple more fruitless approaches, then gave up. It used to be easier to get cops to at least banter when she could say she was with a TV station.

"Let's talk." Mike spoke from beside Vicky.

Vicky jumped. "Jeez, where'd you come from? You're like a ghost."

Pete and Sam looked as startled as she was. The late afternoon sun had faded, and deep shadows congealed with the thick woods. Still, there was enough light that she should have seen him coming. She gave herself a little mental kick. Apparently, her powers of observation were softening along with the rest of her.

Deputy Briggs ordered them to return to their car. Mike said, "They're okay." When everyone was circled around him, Mike continued. "All right. No one's been in the lodge but me and a deputy a few days ago. We found the cave entrance. It's covered with dust. Linden wants the state forensic boys here to take a look before we open it up. It's going to be a few hours. You might as well go get some rest. I'll let you know if anything changes."

At Sam's protest, Mike raised a hand. "We all get it. But there's no sign Rose or anyone else has been there, none at all. I would tell you. And if your mama's in there, we're way too late to help her. Linden said he's going to do things by the book."

Glancing at the forensics team, Mike tilted his head. "Ready? I'll ride with you."

Briggs moved his vehicle to clear the driveway. After the van disappeared around a bend, Vicky returned to her car and struggled into the backseat. The adrenaline that had fueled her for the last many hours seeped away, leaving her drained and dejected, allowing the physical shock and pain to finally have full say.

Pete and Sam got into the front seat. "Guess I got this wrong." Vicky's voice was low and controlled.

"We don't know that, Vick," Sam said. "And you helped me remember some hard things. Whatever's here, I know more now than I did."

"Vick, why don't you try to sleep?" Pete suggested. "We can wait here if you want. I'll wake you up if anything happens."

"Okay, thanks." She sank against the rear window. Outside was slate gray, dark, shadowy, as gloomy as her mood. She took a deep breath, trying to fill the chasm in her chest. She'd been so hopeful Rose was there, in the cave. Shit. She closed her eyes to think.

****

Vicky jerked awake. It took a moment to remember where she was. "Pete?" she whispered. "You awake?"

"Yeah." He angled the rearview mirror to look at her. She could see the pale gleam of his face, but not what was in his eyes.

"What time is it?" She spoke softly so she wouldn't wake Sam.

"Nine. We've been here almost five hours."

"I guess I fell asleep. I've been thinking about

something."

"I've been doing some thinking, too." There was an unfamiliar trace of harshness in Pete's tone. "I don't understand why you didn't tell me about your parents. We've been seeing each other for months. That's a pretty monumental event to not mention."

Ah hell. He'd been sitting here in the dark thinking about her. About them. Vicky sighed. "It's complicated."

"Try me. Bet I can handle it."

"I know. I'm not sure *I* can."

"Just say what it is."

"It's not like yes or no. Did you ever diagram sentences? A teacher made us do that to learn how to form sentences. You draw a line with places for the subject, verb, and object, then add lines under with info like adjectives and phrases. Every word in a sentence has a place it belongs."

"So we're going to talk about grammar instead of what's happening with us?"

"Sometimes I wish life were like that."

Silence.

"I would have told you, just later. I wasn't trying to hide anything. I just wasn't ready. Can we talk after all this is over?"

No answer. Damn. She'd hurt him. Well, that was about to get way worse. "About that, and something else that's come up. This is a terrible time to mention it, especially now, but a station in Dallas offered me their news director job. They want to know by Monday."

"Tomorrow." He wasn't asking. "This has been in the works for a while."

"Long before we went camping. I've been putting them off."

"And what'd you decide?"

"I haven't decided. But that's not what I meant—"

"You decided not to tell me. That says something."

"C'mon, Pete. We'll talk about everything after all this, I promise."

"Yeah."

Vicky leaned back against the seat. Man, she hadn't gotten much right lately. "Pete, I think I've been looking at things all wrong."

He turned to face her across the back of the seat. "Me, too."

"What?" Vicky reminded herself to whisper. "I think I decided something too soon."

"Me too, maybe."

Vicky asked again, with real curiosity. "What?"

"I thought we trusted each other."

"Ah, Pete. Can we talk about this when Sam's not listening?"

"I'm not trying to listen." Sam sat up straight in the front seat. "But I don't blame Pete for being pissed."

"I don't either." Vicky considered whether an apology was in order. Her life, her story, her choice. But still. "Sorry. I'm used to keeping things to myself. Pete, you know I want you in my life and I know you want me in yours."

She squeezed his shoulder. "But I remembered something. It might be urgent. I was convinced human traffickers had been operating here for years, that Sam and Alisa escaped from them, and now they took Rose. I locked in on that and missed something. Tell me what you think of this, okay?"

"I'm going to get some air," Pete said.

"Pete, wait. Flip the inside light off first, okay? So

Briggs doesn't see. I'm getting out too. I need to talk with Mike."

Pete sat back. "About what?"

"When he and I were making rolls, he mentioned his grandpa's will. But he didn't tell me who the beneficiaries are. I'm going to ask him."

"I'll go with you," said Sam.

"Me too," Pete replied. "The ground is pretty rough. Are you sure you're okay?"

"Yep. I'm fine," she fibbed. "Hardly hurts."

They quietly got out. No movement from Deputy Briggs's car. The night was full dark and absolutely silent, other than the soft thuds of three car doors quietly closed, and the faint sounds of their footsteps.

Sam took the lead as they walked, swinging their only flashlight at the ground in front of, then behind her for Vicky. Pete made do in the dark. No one spoke.

Vicky suppressed her gasps. Sam didn't seem to be cutting her any slack. Moving on crutches took upper body strength that she lacked at the moment. The stabbing pain in her leg didn't help.

Vicky was mid-swing when Sam stopped abruptly. She almost fell into her. Mike appeared in front of them.

Sam looked around. "Are we there already?"

Mike scoffed. "At the lodge? You're not even halfway. What are you doing here?"

Vicky said, "I need to ask you something—"

"Have they opened up the cave?" Sam vibrated impatience.

"I came to tell you. Don was right. They used an old safe to lock the cave."

Sam let out a deep breath. "So there really was a metal door."

Mike nodded. "Just like you said, right where Don said, hidden behind a closet wall. Behind a bunch of dusty boxes. No one's touched anything for years."

Vicky hesitated. "You never knew about it?"

"No. So what'd you want?"

"While we were making rolls—was that really just last night? —you mentioned your grandpa's will."

Mike regarded her silently.

"You said the property goes to a trust?" It was too dark to see his face clearly, not that she'd had much luck reading him even in sunlight. "When I researched property records near where Lisa was found, a big chunk was in the name of a trust. I couldn't find out who owns it."

Mike was silent.

"Mike. Come on. Is this a secret?" Vicky wanted to demand he explain, but managed to hold herself back, to speak in a friendly, encouraging way. "You almost told me when we were in the kitchen Saturday."

She could see Mike's eyes but still couldn't tell what he was thinking. "Mike. Please."

He shrugged. "You asked who the beneficiaries were." He paused. "This is absolutely none of your business, but I got nothing to hide. Basically, the trust was set up by the original business partners, Grandpa Miller and Bill Beck. On the anniversary of the last one's death, there'll be a meeting to divvy up the estate among all their blood descendants."

Vicky's mind revved. "Beck. Like Joan Beck?"

"Yep."

"Who all is there besides you two?"

"We're it. Our parents are all long gone. Her brother got killed driving drunk."

"What happens now? You split it?"

"There's a meeting with Grandpa's bank and lawyer. We have to be present to collect our shares. Then we can vote whether to sell or keep the property."

"When's the meeting? The vote?"

"Monday."

"This Monday? Tomorrow?"

"Yeah."

"What's going to happen?"

"We'll find out tomorrow."

"What do you want to happen?"

Sam said, "Come on, Vicky. He doesn't need to be interrogated."

"I'm just asking questions. He doesn't have to answer." Vicky looked at Mike. "I'm kinda surprised this didn't come up before."

Vicky paused to allow time for Mike to explain, which he did not do.

"I met her. Joan. Interesting lady. And her dog Ruby. We had coffee and cookies at her place. How well do you know her, Mike?"

Mike micro-lifted a shoulder. "We don't have cookies and coffee. There was bad blood between our families." He stepped back from the others. "Sounds like Linden's coming." It was several seconds before footsteps crunched in gravel. A flashlight beam approached their feet.

"Miller? Why'd you—" The sheriff ran his flashlight over Sam, Vicky, and Pete. "Look. You can't be here. I told you I would tell you when I know something. I was on my way now—"

Sam interrupted. "What'd you find?"

Sheriff Linden shook his head. "Y'all need to listen

for a change. I mean it. We can't have a bunch of civilians traipsing around a crime scene. I don't want to have to arrest you."

"We get it," Vicky said. "I needed to talk to Mike, and they came with me. What kind of crime are you looking at?"

"Don't know yet. But if anyone's arrested, I don't want some damn lawyer raising hell about you being here."

"We get it. Really. Why don't you tell us what you found?" Vicky raised her hand in a wait-a-sec motion when Linden shook his head. "C'mon. You wouldn't even be here if it weren't for us."

Linden shook his head again, but Vicky sensed some give in his demeanor. "Please. Just the gist."

"I can't have this getting out 'til I know what we're dealing with."

Sam leaned forward, her voice sharp. "C'mon, Hal. You're dealing with dead bodies in a cave. One of them is my mother. Right?"

Interesting that the two of them were on a first name basis. "Just tell her, Sheriff. She's waited nine years to know."

Linden had his hands on his hips, flashlight pointed down. He was stern and imposing. "You can't repeat any of this."

Vicky was too tired and ramped up to be impressed. "This is all going to come out anyway. Why not make sure it gets out right? Tell us, then hold a news conference about what you found."

"I'm not doing any news conference."

"Someone'll have to. At least put out a statement. But just tell Sam, Sheriff, whether what you found backed up what she remembered?"

Sheriff Linden looked at Sam. "All right. Yes, there's three bodies. Based what they're wearing, it appears to be a man and two women. One of the women was under a pile of rocks. That's all I'm going to tell you. Period."

Vicky was the first to speak. "Guess it's too soon to know who the other woman is. Was. Sheriff, people need to know about this. Your website's not set up for that, is it? Do you text? Or, you could call a reporter. Issue a press release. Three bodies, not recent. That's all you need to say. Or I could tell someone for you. Let me know."

Vicky nodded at the sheriff as if he had agreed to something. "By the way, just before you got here, Mike was telling us about his grandfather's will."

As soon as the words left Vicky's mouth, Linden and Sam pointed their flashlights toward Mike. He put up a hand to block the light. "Turn those off so we can see. The moon's out."

Vicky kept going, trying to sound friendly. "Did you and Joan talk at the fundraiser about the meeting of the beneficiaries?"

Vicky's eyes took a few seconds to readjust to the darkness, but she didn't need light to know Mike was radiating anger.

"It's none of your business who I talk to," he barked.

Interesting that the question bothered him. "I saw you with her in the crowd."

Linden's hands moved back onto his hips. "Joan? Joan who? Beck?"

Vicky looked at Mike. "Tell him about the meeting tomorrow. Come on. We're all sharing information."

Mike bristled. "What've you shared, really? Theories and speculation. So you worked on the levee girl story—who now says she's standing right here. That and your woe-is-little-me story."

Vicky's one syllable laugh punctured the silence that held his words. She couldn't help it. "Is that how I came across? Didn't mean to."

The sheriff turned back toward the lodge. "Y'all don't need to be here. Time to clear out."

No one said a word on the way to the car. Vicky was ready to collapse by the time they arrived.

"Okay. Stay or go?" Pete didn't seem angry anymore, just subdued. He opened the rear door and took the crutches she handed him.

"If we leave, we can't be sure we'll know what's going on. Plus, we'll never get a better parking spot." Vicky maneuvered into the back seat. "Kidding."

Chapter Thirty-Seven

Early Monday morning

The night softened and succumbed to first light. From the back seat, Vicky shook Pete's shoulder as Mike and Sheriff Linden strode near her car, still parked near the lodge.

"Pete, Sam, wake up. The sheriff's leaving."

Pete mumbled and sat up behind the wheel.

Sam jerked up straight in the passenger seat. "Oh, I'm going to catch a ride. I need to get to work."

"Just a sec." Vicky buzzed down the rear window. "Morning, Sheriff, did you find anything new?"

Mike kept moving. Sheriff Linden stopped. "No more bodies, if that's what you mean. Why are you still here?"

"Waiting for you."

"I'm taking Mike to his truck, then I'm going to get some sleep."

"We were about to do the same." She sounded casual. "We'll see you later."

The sheriff walked away without responding. Mike hadn't even paused. Vicky said, "Sam, we can drop you. Do you really need to go in today? You must be wiped out."

Sam gave Vicky a long look before turning back in her seat. No one spoke on the drive to the diner. When they arrived, it took a moment for Vicky to realize the RV was gone. All that was left of the explosion was a blackened portion of parking lot, still cordoned off, and the lingering oily stench of melted plastic and smoke. And the stitches in Vicky's leg.

Sam got out. "Thank God, or whoever cleaned that up. I'm ready for things to get back to normal. See you later." She marched to the back door of her cafe.

Vicky resisted saying things were nowhere near normal, and no telling when they would be. Finding the cave both answered questions and created more. It vented some pressure but, with Rose still missing, there was plenty more building.

And now, the presence of something new and unpleasant hunched between Vicky and Pete, waited to be unleashed. No telling what kind of damage this beast would inflict if it broke free.

Pete restarted the car. "Where to?" He sounded like his usual amiable self.

Thank God. Yes. Let's leave it alone.

"How about we go to Liz Ann's, get cleaned up, and nap for a couple hours? Then I'm going to find that meeting about the will Mike told us about."

"Sure."

Neither spoke on the way to the librarian's comfortable two-bedroom bungalow. Their host was already up and about, ready for the day. She greeted them at the door. "Where've you been all night? Poor things, you look exhausted. Come have pancakes. The griddle's warm."

She ignored their claims they weren't hungry, and in fact they each ate a short stack as they filled her in on a few of the night's developments. She said nothing about the fact that Vicky and Pete talked only to her, not each other, and assured them they were welcome to stay with her however long they liked.

"Thanks, Liz Ann," said Vicky. "I wonder…I'm trying to find a legal meeting that's scheduled for this morning. Do you know—"

"There's only one lawyer in town. He has a big conference room in back."

She said his office was in a brick building, conveniently located across the street from Sam's diner. She cheerfully mentioned an amorous after-hours "debriefing" she and the attorney had once enjoyed there. Vicky was too wiped out to think of any response.

After separate showers, a few hours of sleep. and even fewer words spoken, Pete drove Vicky to the diner. Along the way, she borrowed his phone to send a few texts.

The phone signaled an incoming message. "Go ahead," Pete said. "It's gotta be for you."

Vicky read the text. "Okay, good. Sam says Don's at the café." She deleted her messages and put the phone in the cupholder. "Thanks. I'll get a new phone later today or tomorrow."

At the diner, Pete pulled over to the curb but didn't park. "I'm going to check on the RV."

"Okay." Vicky squirmed her way out of the back seat behind him. She picked up a single crutch. "I think I can get by with just one of these now."

Pete lowered his window. "You seem to be getting around pretty well." He paused, then looked up at her. "If you're doing okay, I'll go ahead and take that trip south I talked about. I need some time to think. Mike said he'd take me to get a rental car before his meeting."

Ow, what a punch to the gut. "Sure, that's good. Or you can take my car if you want." She didn't trust herself to say any more.

"I'm not sure how long I'll be gone." His tone was gentle, and his eyes were warm and caring. "You sure you're okay? You're staying with Liz Ann, right?"

"Yes, I'm fine. Don't worry about me." Omigod. She wanted to fall into those gorgeous eyes and make everything better between them. Why hadn't she been open with him? Why was she like this?

"I'll leave your car at her house."

"Perfect. Sounds good." Inside, she was falling all right, falling and flailing, about to hit whatever rocky calamity lay below. Now? He was leaving *now?*

"I'll come back by after I get the rental." Pete's head was tilted slightly upward, in good position for Vicky to give him a kiss to remember. But before she could get that far, Pete gave her a slight grin and an air kiss. "I'm blocking traffic. See you soon." He drove away.

Well, that was a kick in the gut. She clearly had not been paying enough attention to what was going on with Pete. She didn't deserve him. She'd never felt like this about anyone before. He was not someone to be taken for granted. She would make up for it when he came back. She was already aching at his absence by the time he turned the corner.

The diner was half empty when Vicky entered.

"Hi, Vick." Sam pointed with her chin toward a back table. "Sara just got here. She's with Don."

"Perfect. Thanks." She could watch the lawyer's office, keep an eye on Don, and get that damn Sara to 'fess up about what-all she's hiding. "Have you talked with Rita?"

"Yes, she's back at work today. Said she can't stand sitting around."

"Good." Vicky asked for the bill at the same time she ordered.

She had a nervous second breakfast of coffee and a side of grits with milk, butter, and a little sugar. The first time Sam watched her do that, she joked that milk and sugar had no business on grits. Vicky didn't care. That's how she liked them.

Don and Sara were deep in discussion when Vicky gathered her crutch and limped toward their table. As she approached, Don said, "Joan's never gonna back—"

Vicky smiled. "Hi, good morning. How're y'all doing?" Silence carved their faces like stone. "Don, you okay after your fall yesterday?"

He shrugged. Sara's forehead creased as she looked at him, then back up at Vicky. Her eyes were red and watery. A rim of hazel surrounded hugely dilated, eerie black pupils.

"Hello, Sara. Good to see you again." Vicky wondered how stress and guilt interacted with whatever drug she was on. "Mind if I join you for a minute?"

Don started making getting-up motions. "I'm leaving."

"Hang on, Don, please. I'd like to talk with both of you."

"But we have to—" said Sara.

Vicky slid into the booth next to her. Good. She could still see the lawyer's building. "Let's talk about the burner phone you left in Liz Ann's office."

Sara froze with one arm already in her jacket. Good. Vicky's theory was right. Don stopped working his way to standing, clearly interested.

"Don, I'm going to take you at your word you weren't going to shoot me or anyone else. For now, anyway. But the two of you need to come clean."

Sara sat unmoving, jacket half-on. Don resembled a statue of an old man frozen in the middle of getting up, one arm braced on the table.

"Sara, you knew Sam and I were going to Liz Ann's office. You put the phone on the windowsill. You were rushing out when we got there. Why'd you do that?"

Sara stared with hollow, almost alien eyes. Impossible to read.

"It wasn't you listening in, though, right? Who was it?"

Sara blinked hard and tightened her lips before she looked at Don, then down at the table.

"Don. You must know more history of all this than anyone else around here. You act like a nice guy. But you knew all about the cave and smuggling, and kept quiet about it all these years, even with a little girl missing."

More silence. Okay. She could work with that. "And when Lisa turned up, you must have thought of the cave. It was still being used back then, wasn't it? You knew what was going on, but you didn't speak up? Then Rose goes missing and you still don't say a word about it. Why?"

She felt herself ramping up and paused to slow her momentum. "Yes, it turns out she wasn't there, but you should've made certain that someone checked the cave. Too many secrets can rot your soul, Don. At least around the edges."

Don stared at the table. The aw-shucks was all gone out of him.

"Who's pressuring you? The two of you?"

Don and Sara whipped looks at each other. Ah. A stab in the dark that nicked the target. "Someone has something on you two."

"How do—"

Don interrupted Sara before she could say any more. "Shut up. She's bluffing. She doesn't know a damn thing."

Vicky waited, ever more certain. After a moment, Don stood. "I'm leaving." He shuffled toward the door, looking older than he did the day before.

Good. Sara was more likely to talk now that they were alone.

When Vicky tapped a finger in Sara's direction, she jerked back like she'd been burned. "Sara. Who told you to put the phone there?"

"You don't know anything."

"But you do, and you need to talk about it. You know you do. You love Rose. Your own sister's kid."

Sara's shoulders shook.

Vicky shifted to face her. "I know you're super stressed. That's completely understandable. You've been through a lot. You and your sister." She patted Sara's arm once. "It must be so hard for you."

She spent a few more minutes being warm, understanding, and sympathetic. Sara gradually seemed slightly less tense but said almost nothing.

"What's with you and Don?" Vicky made the question sound casual. "You warned me off him when you came out to the RV that night. But, yet here you are together."

Sara scratched at her hand. "I'm not going to talk about any of this." She sounded more scared than stubborn. Skittish even.

"Sara, I can see something's eating at you. Just say what you know, whatever it is. You don't need to tell all of it. Just about the phone. You can tell me. But the sheriff needs to know who you planted it for."

Sara crossed her arms and hunched into herself. Her half-on leather jacket drooped from her shoulder. "I don't know what you're talking about."

"Sure you do. Just say who you did it for. You know it could have something to do with Rose."

Sara put her forearms on the table and hunched even deeper. She made sounds that might have been stifled sobs, might have been angry grunts, might have been a deeply muttered word or two.

Tough. Vicky didn't care which. She'd done enough persuading and prodding. "If you don't tell the sheriff then I will. The cops need to know you put the phone in the office to spy on Sam and me. You did it for someone else. You were just kinda like a messenger."

Sara sat up. Her eyes were still red and dilated, but less so than earlier. She appeared to be paying attention, poised for something to happen, survival instincts on alert.

"Sara, the sheriff's going to find out one way or another. It's better if you tell him."

"No."

"How about if I say you want to tell him something. I can sit with you while you talk to him."

After a long moment, Sara nodded slowly.

"Okay, so you're going to tell him?" Vicky put her hand out, palm up. "It'll be okay. Let me borrow your phone. Mine's melted."

Sara slowly handed it to her. Vicky tapped in a

number from memory. "Sheriff? Hi, it's Vicky Robeson. I need to talk with you about a couple things…in person's better…I'm at the diner, here with Sara. This is her phone. She has something to tell you. Uh-huh. No, she should tell you. Yes…Okay. See you then."

She glanced at Sara. "He'll be here in about a half hour." Vicky handed back the phone. "It'll be okay, Sara. Just tell him what happened. Even if it's only about planting the phone."

On the opposite side of the street, three men in suits approached the lawyer's building. The lawyers or bankers, no doubt, meeting in advance. Unlikely they'd let her even into the building, much less the meeting. She needed to catch Joan either on her way in or way out.

"Wait right here, okay, Sara? I need to go outside. Can I borrow your phone?"

Sara jerked a hand in a get-lost gesture. Okay then, no phone. Vicky prodded a promise out of Sara that she would stay right where she was. She grasped her crutch and made her way toward the door. She got stuck behind a group of two women, several kids, and an adorable toddler getting ready to leave. The diner door opened and, like everyone else in the room, Vicky looked to see who was coming in.

Joan Beck frowned and scanned the room.

From her spot at the register, Sam asked, "Can I help you?"

"You seen Don Winters?" Joan asked, then saw Vicky and took three sharp steps straight toward her.

Vicky put out her hand. "Hello, Joan. Good. You got my messages."

"Don't give me that friendly bullshit." Joan's voice was low and threatening, teeth clenched and eyes squinted in the manner of Clint Eastwood at his movie badass best. She loomed over Vicky, fists clenched. In some real-life tough situations Joan could likely handle herself as well as Clint, maybe better in some.

Vicky resisted the urge to step back. She dropped her hand. "Come on, Joan. I don't want this to sound like it's about to, but why don't we step outside?" She gestured toward the diners. "So we can talk without an audience?"

"Shut up. Your BS charm won't work twice."

Joan spread her fingers, then clenched them again. She looked angry, jumpy, nervous—like she was about to fall apart.

Vicky gestured at the small television behind the register. "Oh, wait." The morning news was on. "I want to hear what he's saying." She leaned across the counter. "Sam, can you turn that up?"

By the time Sam found the remote, the morning news anchor was assuring the audience that the news team had exclusive details, stay tuned right here or go to the station website for the latest, and, "Now, here's Monica, looks like we're in for a biiiigg change in the weather?"

Vicky wanted news. She missed her phone and laptop. She'd have to stop by the library later to get caught up.

"What'd he say?" Sam asked.

"I didn't hear. Their graphic said, 'Cave Discovery' with a map, just a dot in the middle of Missouri, no reference point, not a single road or city. It could have been anywhere in the state."

Sam looked amused. "Well, you already know where it is."

"It was still a terrible map. Sam, you know Joan, don't you?"

The women barely acknowledged each other. Vicky glanced past Joan. Sara was tucked deeper in the booth. She had her jacket on and head down. Laying low. Good. Those two together would be like gasoline and lit matches.

"Sam, Joan was saying today's meeting about the will is none of my business."

"Well, might be a little late for that." Sam played along beautifully. "You still going, Vick?"

"Absolutely."

"What?" The fury on Joan's face intensified but she seemed unsure where to direct it, her eyes darting between Sam and Vicky. "What? No way in hell you're coming."

"Yes, I am." Vicky gave it a split second before she bluffed. "And by the way, Joan, I now know the real reason you didn't tell anyone about your mystery visitor all those years ago."

"You don't know a goddam thing."

"I know what you did back then." As long as she was gambling, she might as well kick up the stakes. "And I know what you're up to now. You have more than a half hour before your meeting. Let's go out. I'll tell you what I know."

"This is none of your business."

"Yeah. I heard you. I'll be out front." Vicky jerked the door open. She was sick of this. Sick of hurting, sick of uncertainty, sick of being afraid. Sick of feeling guilty. She was done being diplomatic.

Outside the diner, she positioned herself so she could watch the door. Joan followed. They faced each other on the sidewalk near the free newspaper racks.

Vicky let her voice speak for the truly pissed-off part of her. "I've been lied to, had a gun pointed at me, almost got blown up. So this is all my business now. Anything you'd like to say?"

Joan let her eyes do the talking, with a churning mix of reassessment, anger, and something that might include fear. Wariness, at least. Certainly hatred.

"No?" There was no clock in view, but it was time to get some answers. This might be the only chance she'd get. "I'll tell you what I know." Or suspect, anyway.

Where to start, what to say? "That news story about the cave—they found three bodies there. The entrance is inside the lodge, on the property next to yours. The place was used for all kinds of shady doings. And you knew that."

Joan glanced away from Vicky to watch a sheriff department SUV and a large pickup parking in the next block.

Vicky kept her voice low. "Alisa escaped from there and you helped her. The levee girl was with her. Did you know it turns out the girl is Sam?"

Joan's stare jerked toward the café before returning to watch two groups of people—most in uniform—exit the vehicles and walk toward the diner.

"That's right. Sam. From the diner."

"There's too many people here." Joan strode away. "Leave me alone."

Chapter Thirty-Eight

Joan Beck
Monday Morning

Joan stalked away from Vicky. She hadn't felt such loathing since she'd killed The Fucking Bastard. No regrets there—he deserved it. But this goddam reporter was going to destroy her future, right when everything about her life was about to get better? No fucking way.

She was going to get away from this godforsaken place and live life large. She could live on an island. She could spend Christmas in New York City, take cooking lessons in Italy or dance classes in Spain, or whatever the hell else she wanted to do. She'd have plenty of money. She could do all the things she hadn't been able to do in her shitty life. She just needed to get to the meeting, collect her inheritance, and vote to sell the goddam property. Then she could sign the papers and start her new life with a nice, fat check from the frack sand people.

She'd been planning for months. Then a few weeks ago, on an errand in Jefferson City, everything had changed. She'd spotted a woman and child—surely mother and daughter—coming toward her. Something about the kid caught her eye. She was moving a frisbee hand to hand like she wanted to throw it, and frowning at the woman talking on her phone.

Joan had realized what it was when they drew near. The girl was the spitting image of her neighbor, Mike Miller—same long lean build, only small and female, with dark frowning eyebrows below a distinctive widow's peak made prominent by hair pulled back in a tight ponytail. She moved like him, too. Smooth, and fluid, like a cat.

What the hell. Joan had taken out her phone like she'd gotten a message. She took a couple of quick photos, then slowly followed them as they entered the state records building. Better see what this was all about.

Inside, she'd trailed them up the worn granite steps to the Department of Vital Records. She pretended to examine a display of pamphlets as the woman spoke with the elderly male clerk. He appeared to be hard of hearing, and twice asked the woman to speak up. She requested information about how to correct a birth certificate.

Joan had picked up some forms she had no use for, then left and crossed the street to wait. They came out— the woman carrying rolled-up paper—and went to a nearby drugstore. Joan waited several minutes, then entered the store, and prowled the aisles. They stood near a display in front of the pharmacist's counter, the woman looking intently at a box in her hand.

She had lingered a couple of aisles away, examining cold and allergy medications. After the pair proceeded toward the front of the store, Joan wandered by to see what they'd been looking at. A display of drug and DNA paternity test kits. Hm. She picked up some vitamins she didn't need before heading to checkout. When she approached the counter, the woman was talking to the clerk. The girl stared at Joan, unfriendly and suspicious. Her eyes were a vivid green.

Joan had forced herself to smile. She wasn't used to being around kids, much less smiling at them. The girl tugged at the woman's sleeve and said something. The woman glanced at Joan, said something to the girl, and pulled her closer.

Joan said, "Oh, hello, there. We've met, haven't we? You look so familiar."

"Oh, yes. Hello." The woman gave Joan a tentative smile, the kind people give when they think they should recognize someone but don't. "Walkers Corner, maybe? The diner? I work there."

"That's it. I thought so." Joan hadn't been to the diner in months. She placed her basket on the counter. "I'm Joan Beck. I live near there."

"Rita Willwood. So nice to meet you. See you again, I mean. This is Rose."

The girl scowled at Joan with icy green eyes.

"Well, see you at the diner." Joan turned toward the clerk.

A few miles into the nearly ninety-minute drive home—her pickup and mind both racing—Joan had to force herself to let up on the accelerator.

Was that girl Mike's kid? She looked just like him, with those eyes and widow's peak. That meant the girl would get a third of the inheritance. That must be why she and her mom were here. Damn Mike never mentioned a kid.

She wasn't about to give up one dime of her half. She just needed to make sure the girl missed the meeting. The girl was small, she could handle her. No one would ever suspect her, or even think of her. Why would they? She could keep her in the basement, in The Fucking Bastard's old hidey-hole, then drop her somewhere after she left town. Kids go missing all the time. The mom wasn't anyone important, wasn't even from around here.

But in the days after she took the girl, as she cared for her in the basement, Joan decided to keep her. She didn't like being around a lot of people, but just one kid might be okay. Then she'd have someone to travel with, to talk with, to care about. Someone who would care about her, too. Maybe not right away. She'd been so lonely since Mama died. She and the girl could be like a family. Mike's daughter would be her daughter.

****

Joan glanced back at the lawyer's office as she approached her truck. This was her chance to finally make her life what she wanted it to be. She deserved it. It was all within reach—money, a fresh start. Even a family. She could almost taste it, breathe it, feel it. It was her turn. She just had to get through this day.

But now, dammit, that nosy little bitch could ruin it all. What did she mean, she knew what Joan had done back then? How the hell could she possibly know Joan killed The Fucking Bastard? No matter. All she had to do was get to the meeting, do the deal, and get away from this hellish place. Everything was so close. She just had to get rid of that damn Vicky Robeson.

****

Vicky glanced around as she spun on her crutch to follow Joan. Sara came out of the diner and held the door open for the group from the SUV. Dammit, she better not leave.

Joan disappeared around a brick storefront. Vicky rushed to catch up. Taking the corner, she almost collided with Joan, who stood near the passenger door of a shiny new silver pickup backed up beside the building.

The engine was running. It was quite an upgrade from the old beater behind Joan's house.

"Is this your truck? Oh. I guess it is. There's Ruby." Clearly on duty, the rottweiler stood in the truck bed, her front paws up on something that put her head well above the level of Vicky's.

"Hello there, Ruby." Damn, what a big, scary dog. "Joan, I was about to say I know that was you in the truck years ago, when I was on Rick's porch, with Alisa in the back. Interesting you didn't mention that when we were talking in your kitchen.."

Joan had one hand in the bed of the truck. Vicky edged closer, though to see what Joan was doing she'd have to pass practically under Ruby's drooling jaw. It was bad enough to be terrified of the animal—she didn't want to get slimed, too.

"Why didn't you finish your story about helping Alisa? You left off the ending." She paused to calm her breath. "Because you didn't want me to connect you and her with Rick, right? Because your fathers were in the same dirty business. And maybe you, too. You only talked to me to find out what Rick told me. Do you have something on him, too?"

"You don't know what you're talking about."

Ruby dropped down from whatever she was standing on. Vicky stood on tiptoe. Two big suitcases lay next to a large metal toolbox built-in behind the cab window. There was a row of dime-sized holes near the lid overhang.

Uh oh.

296

Chapter Thirty-Nine

Monday Morning Showdown

Vicky looked from the truck toolbox back to Joan and Ruby. She debated a split-second before deciding to go all in. "The sheriff's on his way. I'm going to tell him you blew up the RV."

Rage snarled Joan's face. She whipped her arm up from the truck bed and pointed a handgun at Vicky. "Goddamn you."

Oh shit. Vicky automatically raised her hands in the classic surrender position, though with one arm at her side, holding onto the crutch, the effort was half-assed. At least they were out in public. Surely Joan wouldn't shoot. No way. Surely not. Not after they'd built up rapport over cookies and shared secrets.

Joan punched the handgun into Vicky's side. "Put your hands down."

"Come on, Joan. Please. What are you going to do? Put that away. You need to get to your meeting."

Perhaps she shouldn't have pushed Joan about Alisa and Rick. Or needled her about the meeting. Or bluffed about knowing what Joan was up to. That had clearly struck a nerve.

And now it was clear why.

Nine or ten minutes had passed since the suits entered the lawyer's office. Sheriff Linden was still a good twenty minutes out.

"Joan, come on. Think about it. What good would it do to shoot me? It'd make a big mess and you'd have to do something with my body." Vicky gave a nervous chuckle. "Then you'd never make it to your meeting on time. That's the important thing now. It's fine, I'll wait here for you."

Joan opened the passenger door. "Get in."

"I'm fine here."

Joan slapped her thigh. "Ruby." The dog immediately jumped to the sidewalk, her eyes on Joan. "Guard."

Ruby snapped to high alert, ears lifted, muscles taut, teeth bared. Saliva dripped from the right side of her gaping mouth. Vicky wasn't one to stereotype, but this kind of dog was fierce, bred to guard and protect. In this case, Joan.

"Get in, or I'll put her on you. Or shoot you. Or both."

Ruby growled on cue. Her drool formed a string halfway to the ground.

"You're driving." Joan prodded Vicky with the gun. "Get in."

"I can't go. But when you come back, I'll tell you the rest of what I know." Vicky gestured with her crutch. "Can you please not point that gun at me?"

"Don't be stupid. Get in. We're going somewhere to talk."

Sure, or somewhere less conspicuous to kill me. Vicky could barely breathe. She had always fervently believed in the rule about never getting into a vehicle with the bad guy, but that was before someone had a gun aimed at her gut. She edged around to stand inside the open door.

"Where're we going?"

"Shut up and get in."

"You don't have much time." Vicky glanced around the cab and located the handle above the door. No running board. A long step up to the seat. With her damnably short legs, one injured. Awkward.

Joan stood outside the open passenger door, gun in one hand, Ruby behind her. "Move it."

"Really, Joan, you don't want to risk being late. You have to be there to get your share." Vicky backed up against the passenger seat. "Ha, the seat's so high up, this'll take me a sec."

Gripping the overhead handle, Vicky clumsily pulled her crutch close, put one foot on the floorboard, and prepared to haul herself up. Joan backed up one step to make room.

With a kick and a shove, Vicky threw herself onto the bench seat as she whipped her crutch up to smash Joan's hand. Years of yoga tree poses and planks paid off—the handgun and crutch went flying. She dragged herself up behind the wheel and jerked the gear shift into drive—thank God the truck was running.

She jammed on the gas. Crouched, head low, she tore out of the alley, turning into the street as the open door slammed shut and tires screeched. Or was that Joan yelling? Shit, should have gone toward the diner. Breathing hard, Vicky cautiously raised her head, then jerked back down at the harsh bang of a gunshot from behind. A hole appeared in the windshield.

She stole a glimpse out the back. The rear window had a similar hole, surrounded by a spiderweb of cracks. Joan had one leg over the tailgate, holding on with one hand while the other held the gun.

Vicky slammed on the brakes, then the gas, swerving, trying to topple Joan. A glance in the rearview mirror showed Joan hanging on, still coming, her face contorted with rage and hate. A car in the other lane left little room to maneuver. Vicky was quickly running out of town. Main Street was about to turn into a country road. She needed to be around people. Someone must have heard the gunshot.

Vicky glanced in the side mirror. Oh great. Ruby was chasing them. That would make it tough to stop and jump out, even if she managed to dislodge Joan, who now had both feet inside the truck bed, holding on with her left hand, pointing the gun with her right.

Coming up to the road that went to the campground, Vicky hit the brakes, spun the wheel, and cut a sharp U-turn to the right. Somehow Joan managed to drop to her knees and hold on. Dammit. She was like the melting metal robot in that cyborg movie.

As she sped back toward town, Ruby was running full tilt toward the truck. The dog had a bad hip or leg. An odd gait, anyway. Vicky had an instant debate with herself about whether to mow down that part of her problem, but instead swerved to miss the dog. She bumped up onto the sidewalk and back down to the street. It wasn't Ruby's fault her owner was a kidnapper and maniacal would-be killer.

Now blocks from the diner, she laid on the horn, blasting at people about to cross the street. They scattered. Vicky wondered if Sheriff Linden had arrived yet. At least now for sure someone would report a pickup barreling through town with a crazy driver and a madwoman waving a gun in back.

Just past the diner, Vicky slammed on the brakes and jerked the wheel to miss a car backing out of a parking space. But she didn't quite miss. The vehicles collided in a cacophony of crunching steel and blasting horns.

Her scream echoed, the entire front of her body in agony. Eyes burning, she shoved the deflating airbag aside and yanked the door handle, searching for Joan, her mind racing, her ears ringing. The door was jammed by the rear end of the car she'd hit. Trapped.

A man opened the passenger door. "Are you hurt? Are you okay?"

"Whoa. Yeah. God." She turned to look for Joan, but her body shrieked at her to stop. "Help me get out, okay? Is there someone in back?"

The man glanced at the truck bed. "No. Are you sure you're okay to move?" Several people crowded behind him.

"Yes! Get me out. Quick. Please."

"All right, all right." He slid his arms under her and gently pulled her to the passenger door. "Can you stand?"

"Yes, yes. Help me out." He helped her to her feet.

"Thanks." She leaned against the truck. Damn she was dizzy. She scanned the people gathered around the two vehicles. Sam was there, and Rita stood next to Sara.

Shit. Where was Joan? "Is anyone hurt?"

A woman's voice came from the other side of Joan's pickup. "I'm fine. But it looks like you totaled my car."

"I'm sorry." Vicky looked toward the other driver. "Glad you—"

Her rescuer jerked away, saying "Okay, okay."

Vicky spun back to see him lifting his hands,

backing away from Joan and her gun. Dammit. Joan grabbed Vicky's arm and pressed the gun into her face. How the hell had she held on to it through all of that?

"Damn you. Damn you." Blood covered Joan's face. Good. At least she was hurt, too.

Tears filled Joan's ice-blue eyes. "All of you back there, move around where I can see you." The dozen or so bystanders shuffled toward the diner.

"Come on, Joan. Don't," Vicky gasped. "It's over. And now there're all these witnesses."

Three or four people put their hands in their jackets or bags as they backed away. Vicky raised her hand. "Everybody, calm down. It's okay! Nobody shoot or anything. Do what she says, okay? Please." Her heart hammered. "Joan, come on. Let's not make things any worse."

Joan responded by jamming the gun deeper into Vicky's jaw. In the silence that followed, Vicky assessed her situation. Clearly not great. Where was the sheriff? She wanted a SWAT team stealthily moving into position in front, back, and overhead, in a classic police standoff scenario.

But that wasn't going to happen. There would be no military-grade command post vehicle, no cameras or listening devices, no helicopter hovering overhead, no trained negotiator building a bond with Joan.

Vicky spoke in a low, soft voice, which was all she was capable of anyway. "Joan, listen." It sounded more like "oan ith-n," but Joan eased up with the gun enough for Vicky to say, "Joan, you need to go to your meeting. There's still time. Then at least you'll get your inheritance and still have a chance to enjoy it."

Joan growled, "Why couldn't you leave me the hell

alone?"

"You need to be there, or you won't get your share. It's yours."

"How do you know about that?"

"What's the difference? No matter what, you need to be there at ten. Then you can deal with anything else, including the cops. Getting your share is what's important right now." That, and getting Joan away from the truck. And the gun away from Vicky's head.

The pressure of the gun lessened slightly, which made it easier to talk. Vicky continued in her low, encouraging tone. "It's okay, Joan. You just panicked. But you need to be there to get your share. You'll lose that chance if you're not there. You only have a few minutes."

Vicky willed Joan to concentrate on the future instead of the immediate situation, which was looking increasingly unfavorable for all involved. "You have to be there to get your share."

A thin, sharp voice interrupted Vicky's mantra. "Joan, what're you gonna do here?"

Oh hell. Sara. She stood between Joan and the diner. Wild eyes, messed up hair, hand inside her leather bag. Vicky thought—hoped, to be honest—that Joan would point the gun at Sara instead of her.

Sara cried, "I'm not going to take the blame for this."

"Shut up, Sara. Just shut up." Joan's grip tightened and the gun poked deeper into Vicky's face. The steel was hot. She'd been this terrified only once before, when she was a child, and back then she didn't fully comprehend the possibility of actually dying.

Sara kept spewing, disgorging a fast, choppy stream

of words. "She said she just wanted to give Rose a present, that she's like her aunt, too"—she glanced at her sister— "since her brother was married to Rita."

"Shut the hell up, Sara." Joan's low voice vibrated through the gun pressed against Vicky's face.

"She told me to call her whenever she could see Rose alone."

"Shut up, you goddam tweaker." Joan's growl sounded deadly.

"I never thought she'd take her! Honest, I didn't!" Sara looked at Rita and shrieked, words rushing to escape. "I'm sorry! I freaked out. What was I supposed to do? Tell you I helped someone kidnap your kid?"

Sara pulled out a handgun. "You're a blackmailing bitch!"

The instant Joan lifted her gun from Vicky's face to aim at Sara, Vicky launched. She didn't think but might have prayed. She heaved against Joan, ramming her with all her might. She grabbed the weapon and shoved it toward the sky.

Crack! Sara and half the crowd dropped to the ground screaming, "Shit!"

The blast of gunshot drove all thought from Vicky's mind as she tangled in a twisting jumble of struggling arms and hands and bodies. Her injured leg screamed. She fought through deadened waves of throbbing sound and sensation.

"Her gun's there, Sheriff," said Sam. "You can let go, Vick. We've got her."

Sheriff Linden, gun drawn, pushed Joan's weapon away with his foot. Deputy Merrill handcuffed her, face down on the pavement. She screeched an ungodly noise, a fierce guttural sound.

"You okay?" Sam helped Vicky to her feet. "You okay, Vick?"

"I can barely hear you." Vicky took a deep breath as she scanned her body. Everything hurt but no major new injuries. "Yay. I'm not dead. Is everyone okay? Did anyone get hit?"

"Looks like everyone's all right." Sam looked as though she couldn't believe what just happened. Vicky suspected she had the same expression on her face.

Joan's howls quieted to an eerily liquid, visceral moan. Vicky was reminded of a nature show that caught the sound of a zebra taken down by hyenas, its hindquarters being eaten while it kept trying to run.

Vicky took deep, calming yoga breaths. Breathing had never before been so wonderful. One more deep exhale, then she pointed to the back of the truck. "Sheriff, the toolbox. Check the toolbox. I think Rose is inside."

Please, please let her be okay. Please God.

A rush of excited comments flowed through the crowd.

"She's in there?" Sam squeezed Vicky's shoulders. "Rose is in there?"

Rita rushed to the truck. "Rose? Rose?" Vicky and Sam put their arms around her and held her tight.

"Please, God, I think so, I hope so," Vicky whispered. "Looked like Joan was leaving town. And it's weird there'd be holes drilled in a toolbox like that."

Without a word, Sheriff Linden reached in to lift the lid. It didn't budge. He told Deputy Merrill, "Put Joan in my truck and get the bolt cutters. All you people, back up now."

Another deputy pulled Sara toward the sheriff.

Linden shackled her hands behind her as she twitched and jerked, futilely trying to yank away. Then the fight seeped out of her, her shoulders slumped, and she sobbed.

"What the hell, Sara?" Sam punched Sara's shoulder. "How could you?"

Vicky leaned around Sam. "Sara. I'm glad you're okay." Vicky didn't like asking in front of everyone, but who knows when she'd have another chance. "Why'd you help her?"

She didn't really expect an answer, but words tumbled out of Sara's mouth between fast, shallow breaths. "I'm not going to take the hit for this. She's crazy. I'll tell you and everyone else what happened."

"Good. But Sara, you're gonna need a lawyer."

"After what I put my own sister through? And that poor kid? God, I hope she's okay. I don't care. I'll tell everything." Tears streamed down Sara's face, mingling with the sweat from her forehead and the snot from her nose. "She said she had to make sure Rose wasn't at some meeting, or she'd lose out on a lot of money."

"Today's meeting?"

"I don't know! Shit. All this for a few bucks."

"Well, this part's over now." Vicky reassured herself right along with Sara. "Things can still work out okay. Was Don helping Joan, too?"

Sam took a napkin from her apron and wiped Sara's face. Sara didn't seem to notice. "Don, that asshole. You can't trust anything he says. He tells Joan stuff. She's a blackmailer. She has shit on lots of people."

Linden ordered the deputy holding Sara to put her in his unit. As he led her away, she cried, "I'm sorry, Rita! I didn't know anything like this would happen."

Rita turned away.

Merrill returned with a long metal tool and handed it to Linden, who ordered "Everybody back up." Rita, Vicky, and Sam ignored him.

The sheriff hoisted himself onto the truck bed. Rita tried to climb up behind him. Linden said, "Please, Rita, wait."

She sagged between Vicky and Sam. She cried softly. "Rose, my baby, please God."

There were two large padlocks on the toolbox, which stretched the width of the pickup. Linden snapped the lock farthest from Vicky. Someone murmured, "Please, please, God please, let her be okay." It took a moment to realize it was her own voice.

Several people screamed and the watching crowd jumped apart. Ruby rushed limping to the truck, snarling and barking, teeth snapping, sides heaving. Merrill and the other deputy pulled their guns. Sheriff Linden raised the bolt cutter like an axe.

"No! Don't hurt her!" Several people—including Vicky—yelled at the officers. Ruby jumped, trying to get into the pickup bed, but fell back, growling, then barking furiously as she tried again. She was having trouble with her hind legs.

Poor Ruby looked fierce but confused, her owner nowhere in sight. Merrill talked quietly to the dog while the other deputy got a snare pole. Ruby calmed down until the noose was around her neck, then resumed barking and snarling while twisting frantically, trying to escape. The deputy walked her away from the truck.

There was an audible snap as Sheriff Linden cut the second lock. He glanced at Rita once before he slowly lifted the lid. His face hardened. He took a visibly deep breath, then reached in with both hands. A moment later, he looked up with a huge grin. "She's here! She's alive. Merrill, get an ambulance."

His eyes reddened as he glanced at Rita. She shoved Vicky and Sam aside and climbed up onto the bed of the pickup, screaming, "Rose, thank God, Rose!"

Vicky didn't even try to stop weeping. Linden lifted out a small child. Her head lolled back. She was unconscious, hands and feet duct-taped together.

The sheriff said again, "She's alive," as Rita sobbed and clutched her daughter.

Chapter Forty

Midday Monday

Rita refused to let go of Rose when the emergency team tried to put her on the gurney. She carried her to the ambulance and got in with her, crying, laughing, calling her name, stroking her tangled dark hair.

The sheriff and second deputy left with Joan, still moaning, and Sara, still cussing. Deputy Merrill began taking names of witnesses, many of whom had tears in their eyes. Vicky exchanged insurance information with the driver of the car she hit.

Sam smoothed her apron and shouted over the hubbub. "Sorry, I need everyone to get your stuff and clear out. The diner's closing. Don't worry about your checks."

She put her arm around Vicky and helped her limp toward the diner. Vicky scanned the crowd. No sign of Pete, or Mike, or Don. Man, Don was going to be mad he missed all this. Be hard to put himself in the middle of this part of the story.

"What about my breakfast?" An old man in the crowd called out. "I want my eggs and sausage."

Sam waved at him, smiling. "We'll open as usual in the morning. Thanks for coming."

"Dammit. Things were just getting interesting around here." There was more good-natured grumbling from people in the crowd, who took their time leaving. The adrenaline rush had created energy some apparently didn't want to end. Vicky suspected a couple might even feel a little regretful that there had been no major bloodshed after all the high drama and danger.

****

The diner was empty except for Sam, Vicky, and Deputy Merrill, who'd taken Vicky's preliminary statement. Vicky wondered what happened at the meeting that Joan had obviously missed. When he opened the door to leave, the deputy leaned back in to say, "There's people here say they need to see Miz Robeson."

Pete, Mike, and Liz Ann crowded through the door. After minutes of hugs and excited comments, they all settled into the corner table that gave the cafe its name. Pete and Mike were both deeply disappointed they'd missed the entire event. Mike had dropped Pete to pick up a rental car, then gone on to the beneficiary meeting. In the lawyer's back office he hadn't heard the gunshots or the sounds of the crash.

Pete said something uncharacteristically vague about the slow rental car clerk and having to see about the RV before he hit the road.

Surely he hadn't come back just to say goodbye?

"Then Vicky shoved her, hard." Sam demonstrated as she recounted what Vicky had mentally labeled Showdown at the Corner Café, even though it'd happened a half block away. "I was hoping she would do something like that, but afraid she would, too."

Liz Ann squeezed Vicky's arm. "That took some guts."

Vicky shook her head. "Actually, I just didn't want

to die."

"I'd have peed my pants." Liz Ann gave an exaggerated shudder.

Vicky's grin was slightly loopy. "Good thing I'm wearing dark jeans." She'd finally caught up on her pain meds and was now thoroughly relaxed.

"I had no idea Joan would pull something like that," Mike said. "I figured we'd have our vote, do the deal, and be done with it."

"I guess I goaded her a bit." Vicky hadn't entirely decided whether that had been a mistake. "Was it just you at the meeting, then?"

Mike shrugged slightly.

"So you got it all? All the property, even Joan's place?" Sam sounded thoughtful. "And all the frack sand money too?"

Mike frowned. "That's nobody's business—"

There was a familiar, rhythmic knock at the door. "Sam? It's Hal Linden."

Sam slid out of the booth to open the door for the sheriff. They spoke briefly, heads close. He took off his hat and walked to the corner booth. "I just came from the hospital. It looks like Rose is going to be fine. She'd been drugged and tied up—could have been for the whole two weeks—but doctors say otherwise she appears physically unhurt. Her mama said to say thank you to Miz Robeson." He tipped his head at Vicky. "Thank you."

She sagged with relief. "Call me Vicky."

Liz Ann hugged her, laughing. "Thank you, Miz Robeson."

"Have a seat." Sam got the coffeepot and a mug before returning to the booth.

"Is Rose awake?" Vicky asked.

"She's awake and talking. She's mad. Girl's a little spitfire." He sat down as Sam poured coffee. "She's safe, thanks to y'all, especially you, Miz Robeson."

"Vicky."

"Vicky. Though things could have gone wrong, real wrong. You should've come to us instead of confronting her."

"I know you have to say that, but it wasn't exactly planned."

"We'll need to get a formal statement from you tomorrow. In the meantime, I wanted to follow up on a few things."

"Sure. Was Rose in the toolbox the whole time?"

"It looks like she kept her in a hidey-hole under her root cellar floor."

"Omigod, was that poor girl there when I was at Joan's?" Vicky immediately did her usual instant self-appraisal, a reaction she attributed to decades working in live television news. She might have sounded a bit self-centered.

"That seems likely," Linden said.

Mike frowned. "She's a hard case, but I never expected her to do anything like this."

"Hal, has she said why she did it?" Sam asked.

"She still hasn't said a word, just moans. Sara's talking. She claims Joan tricked her."

Vicky felt sorry for Sara, who seemed like someone who started off okay, then took a wrong turn or two and ended up in dangerous waters way over her head. "She needs a lawyer."

"We read her her rights." Sheriff Linden did not seem the least bit sympathetic.

"Still." Vicky shook her head. "Man, I've tried to remember everything we talked about when I was out at Joan's place. I thought she was just tired of holding things in. Now I wonder if she was playing some weird game, talking to me, all the time with Rose in her basement."

"Maybe." Linden shrugged. "Doubt you could have heard her, even if she'd been screaming her head off. Joan's daddy built that hole solid, to hide stuff."

"Even so, it was brazen of her to let you in her house while she had Rose," said Pete.

"She kept checking the time. I thought she just wanted to get rid of me, but she must have been keeping track of when Rose would wake up."

"Strange she talked to you at all," said Mike.

"I think Joan was trying to find out what I knew, what people had told me. It's a good thing she's one of the first people I talked to. About all I knew then was that Kerry saw a leather bag on her porch."

"Maybe she was trying to get close to you, so you wouldn't suspect her," said Liz Ann.

"Maybe." Vicky was disappointed she hadn't caught on to Joan when she first sat in her kitchen. "It kinda worked, for a while."

The sheriff said, "Mike, seems Joan might have the idea you're Rose's daddy."

"What? Me? No way." Mike frowned. "Why?"

Vicky asked, "Are you?"

"No chance." Mike shook his head.

"She had paperwork in her truck," Linden said. "A DNA report with your name on it."

"What? That's ridiculous. I don't have any kids." Mike was either sincerely perplexed, or a particularly good actor.

Vicky nodded an 'aha' kind of nod. "Oh, so it was Joan you and George were talking about in the diner. Who he'd seen sneaking around your place? She might have been getting something for a DNA sample."

Mike shook his head. "I had a feeling you were listening to us. Man, you *are* nosy."

"I couldn't help but hear. Hey, so Sara said Joan wanted to keep Rose away from some meeting, which must have been the beneficiary meeting. Why else would she do that, Mike?"

"Guess you'll need to ask her."

"Maybe Joan thought she'd have to give up a share of the estate to your daughter." Vicky tilted her head. That made sense.

"I don't have a daughter."

A few silent seconds ticked by before Vicky spoke. "You do know her Mom, though, right? Rita?"

Mike shook his head impatiently. "Dammit. This is nobody's damn business. I told you about the will. I'm not hiding anything. Grandpa was always after me, telling me to have a bunch of kids so we'd get a bigger share of the land after he was gone. I don't want kids. Never did. Got myself fixed in my twenties."

He looked around like he was daring someone to comment.

Sam spoke up. "Mike isn't Rose's father. Rita's ex who lives in Colorado is. The sheriff here questioned him when she went missing." She said to Linden, "Rita told me."

Linden was silent, didn't confirm or deny, though a ghost of a grin danced under his serious demeanor. Vicky was almost certain there was something going on between him and Sam. They'd make a nice couple.

"Not to gossip," said Sam, "but Rita's getting back together with the dad. He's paying back child support. She's getting him added to Rose's birth certificate. In fact, Rita was meeting with her lawyer about that when Rose was kidnapped."

"So." Vicky lifted both hands. "Maybe Joan just wanted to know for sure whether Mike was dad. Guess that'll all come out later."

Pete asked, "Sheriff, was it Joan who blew up my RV?"

"We're still investigating."

"She didn't deny it," said Vicky. "She must have been trying to scare us off, afraid we'd mess up the frack deal."

Liz Ann piped up, "Who else would've done it?"

"Don maybe?" Pete turned to Sam. "He got here awful fast when you called 9-1-1."

"Don swears he had nothing to do with that, and he's sticking to his story about his gun." Linden sipped his coffee. "We'll be digging into his older stuff, especially the cave."

"He's a nosy old fart who talks too much," said Sam, "but I don't see him trying to blow someone up."

"He did say he called Rick Carr to tell him Miz Robeson was in town, but he always told Rick whenever something was going on." Linden was downright chatty, possibly due to a combination of stress, exhaustion, and exhilaration.

"Huh. Rick didn't mention that." Vicky was sick of thinking about him. It was up to Kerry and the sheriff to look into Rick, his father, and any misdeeds. "Bet Don's got plenty more to say about what's gone on around here.

And it's interesting Sara called Joan a blackmailer."

"Did Joan have anything to do with the cave?" asked Sam.

"Don't know yet," Linden replied. "Don says her daddy did, so could be."

"Have you been able to find out anything about the people in the cave?" Normally Vicky would have said bodies, but she was trying to be sensitive to Sam's feelings.

That proved unnecessary. Sam asked, "Yeah, did you ID the bodies?"

"We're not ready to release names yet." Sheriff Linden sat back. "So don't repeat this."

Vicky didn't hesitate. She agreed along with everyone else.

"Sam, I wanted you to hear this from me." Linden put his hand near hers on the table. "One of the women's been there years longer than the others. We're working on a DNA match, but according to the driver's license on her, it looks to be Phil and Jennie Hanford's girl. I know you were close to them."

Linden glanced away from Sam to address the others. "They built this diner. Their daughter disappeared years ago."

Sam's face was impassive. "Phil and Jennie never believed she just up and left them. What about the others?"

Sheriff Linden shook his head. Vicky cajoled, "C'mon, Sheriff. You might as well tell us. It's all going to come out, anyway."

Linden looked around the table.

Sam added, "C'mon, Hal. Who were they?"

The sheriff frowned at Vicky. "This stays quiet for

now." She dipped her chin a fraction.

"The man's ID says he was Randolph Tripp. Don says a fella by that name used to come around, back when they used the cave to store booze and cigarettes."

"And kidnapped women," Vicky added. "So, the other woman is Sam's mom."

"Probably, but she had no ID, and she was too far gone for fingerprints."

"Marsha." Sam took a deep breath. "Marsha Sutton. My mama's name was Marsha Sutton."

Chapter Forty-One

Monday November 2008 - Los Angeles

The new Marsha Sutton drove expertly, as she did most things, though creeping along at twelve miles an hour didn't require much skill. She listened to the news while sitting in Monday midday traffic on L.A.'s 405 freeway. The radio newscaster ended with happy news about a ten-year-old Missouri girl found alive that morning after being missing for two weeks.

Marsha took off her vintage designer sunglasses to flip through radio stations. She always paid attention to Missouri news, especially about anything to do with girls. Another station reported the same thing, almost word for word. Missouri was half a country and most of a world away from where she sat now. L.A. radio news reflected that. It wasn't a big story here.

She broke her personal rule and the newly enacted California law to check the news feed on her phone. Not much more information there, other than it'd happened in Walkers Corner, Missouri.

Oh, no. Walkers Corner.

As she inched along the freeway in her near-vintage BMW, tailgating a silver Tesla, she scanned the St. Louis news websites, which rehashed how Rose Willwood disappeared from outside her home two weeks ago. She was rescued after some kind of chase. A woman suspect was in custody.

One TV station website claimed to have exclusive information—that their unidentified source close to the investigation said the girl's rescue might be connected to bodies found in a nearby cave.

Marsha drove forward a few feet, then briefly closed her eyes. A near-decade had done little to fade the horror of the cave. She had packed it all away: Tripp, the van, the girl, the cave—all locked up tight in the darkest corner of her mind's basement. Now the box was open. Memories rushed out and dragged her back to when she was nineteen and someone else. Back to when she was Alisa.

****

Alisa had watched Tripp in the van's side mirror while he pumped gas. He straightened up, alert. She followed his predatory stare. A woman and young girl had just stepped off the bus at the outdoor station—a single counter, a couple of benches, restrooms around back.

When he got back in, he told Alisa what she was gonna do if she didn't want to die. She got as far as, "Oh, no, I—"

He backhanded her with a closed fist. She could taste blood from her swelling lip. No point in fighting it. "Okay, I will, Tripp. I'll help." Maybe it was better that the girl and her mother stayed together, anyway.

Tripp drove behind the bus station. He parked next to the restrooms, ordered Alisa out, and opened the van's side door. They waited.

The girl and woman walked out of the restroom. Tripp sneaked up from behind and smashed his flashlight into that poor woman's head. Alisa grabbed the girl around her waist and covered her mouth. The girl was small but strong. She almost got away as Alisa dragged her to the van's open side door. Tripp was halfway in the van, one knee on the woman. He grabbed the girl, cursing at her frantic struggles to get away, her small limbs kicking and flailing as she screamed, "Mama! Mama!"

He punched her head until she lay flat, unconscious, as still as her mother beside her. He tied them both up, then drove at least an hour before he pulled into the parking lot of a lonely country store. He stopped near the payphone and said, "Don't move." Alisa didn't. There was nowhere to go.

Tripp was on the phone for several minutes before he hung up and entered the store. Alisa could see him eyeing her through the window.

He returned with a grocery sack and a six-pack. He popped a flip-top and gulped down a beer, then tossed the can at her before he started the van. She didn't flinch. He always did that. It was normal. Not like grabbing that poor woman and little girl.

"Tripp?"

"What?"

"Sorry, but the girl was moving around while you were in the store."

"Yeah?" Tripp poked the small form under an old blanket behind the front seats. She didn't move.

"If you want, I could hold her, in case she wakes up again. I can keep her quiet. She'll still be tied up."

Tripp looked at her suspiciously, then jerked his head to tell her to do it. He started driving while Alisa awkwardly pulled the limp child over the console onto her lap. She tugged the blanket over the motionless child and held her tight, trying to comfort the poor girl, and herself.

They drove past fields, with sporadic glimpses of the dim lights of houses. There were fewer and fewer cars, until they were the only ones on the dark road. Pockets of mist flowed together until the van was enveloped in fog and darkness.

Tripp emptied two more beers before Alisa worked up the courage to speak. "Where are we going?"

"Shut the fuck up."

She did. It was better to obey him. They hadn't passed another vehicle for at least a half hour. The woman whimpered in the back. Tripp didn't seem to notice. He slowed down, hunched over, peering into the foggy darkness, then jerked the wheel hard to turn onto a gravel road.

Alisa held tight onto the girl while grasping the door handle to stay on the seat. There was a thump that must have been the woman getting tossed around. She peered through the cracked windshield at what little the dim headlights revealed. Dark fingers of shadowy trees and bushes scratched at the van.

The van slowed until it was barely moving. The headlights swept past an SUV before Tripp stopped next to the open door of a building. Two men stood there. Tripp got out and the three men talked for a few minutes before the skinny one in a Smokey Bear hat got in the big SUV and drove off.

Alisa sat motionless as Tripp opened the sliding door behind her. He dragged the woman out and dropped her next to the van. She didn't move. He opened Alisa's door and picked up the girl by her waistband with one hand, like he would a bag. The girl whimpered and writhed to get away. The men chuckled. The other man picked up the unmoving woman.

Tripp jerked his head at Alisa. "Bring the bags."

She picked up his duffel and the grocery sack and followed him toward a long, low building. Inside, the men set their captives on the floor of a dingy, dimly lit mudroom. A rough bench sat against one wall, across from an uneven stack of old cardboard boxes next to what looked like a closet door.

The other man said, "I'll be back in a day or two."

Tripp handed him the van keys. "Fill it up before you bring it back."

After the stranger left, Tripp closed the outside door. He ordered Alisa to turn around and keep an eye on the girl and her mother. She did, but that didn't keep her from listening and trying to see what Tripp was doing. He did something in the closet that sounded like metal screaming. He came out and ordered her to make him something to eat. She made her way down a long hallway, found her way to the filthy kitchen, and did what she was told.

That was the last she'd seen of the girl and woman until hours later. Tripp finished off the cold pizza she'd found in the kitchen, along with sandwiches she made. Then he shoved her into a windowless room. He grabbed her breast and twisted hard. She didn't have to be told to take off her clothes. He'd rip them apart if she didn't.

She automatically separated her mind from her body. He yanked her hair and fell on her like an animal devouring prey. "One last time, baby," he snarled.

The next morning, she had cowered in bed. His eyes and grin were even nastier than usual. "All right. C'mon."

Alisa hated Tripp with every cell in her body. She'd braced herself for this ever since he'd spotted the girl at the bus station.

He grabbed her arm and dragged her down the hall, ignoring her cries and attempts to clutch the bed, the doorways, anything to save her from whatever evil he had in mind. She cried and begged, promised she'd be good and do everything, anything, he wanted.

He jerked her to the mudroom where she'd last seen the captives. She screamed and wrenched away. He kicked the breath out of her, then leaned over and punched her face. Blood oozed into her eyes. He dragged her into the closet, then heaved her through another door.

She fell onto hard dirt, scrabbling, trying to get to her feet. The space was low and dark except for a lantern hanging from the ceiling. Rough rock walls—she was in a cave. The woman and girl she'd helped kidnap lay on the ground.

Tripp kicked her again, then stood over her. He described how creatures would eat her ugly, rotting body. She was getting too old to be good for anything anyway.

****

A horn blared. Marsha jerked away from the tentacles of memory. Shit. Her rearview mirror was full of grill belonging to an obnoxiously ornate SUV. She needed to get off the road. She bullied and pleaded her way to the shoulder. She crept along to the first exit and parked on a side street.

Marsha started to run her fingers through her highlighted brown hair, then stopped before she messed up her carefully casual bun. Deep breaths. She had a lot going on today. She needed to be calm and look

323

professional. She rubbed her neck instead. Her skin was cold and sweaty. She fought to fend off the memories, but her mind would not allow that.

She stared sightlessly at the industrial neighborhood, breathing deeply, sinking into her body, letting herself remember, reliving the terror. She could feel again the dirt and grit under her when Tripp threw her into the cave.

****

The memory of his sneering laugh fused with the horror of what he said: he was going to take the little girl and leave Alisa to rot in the cave. That poor girl. She was even younger than Alisa was when Tripp took her.

This was how it was going to end. How she was going to end. But she had one last chance to live, and she took it. She marshalled everything in her—eight years of anger, fear, disgust, and hate.

Pure fire and rage powered her. She smashed his crotch with the rusty can of corn she'd found in the kitchen and hidden in her sweatshirt. That was enough to bring him to his knees, but not enough for her to escape him. He held her with one hard hand while he punched her ferociously with the other.

Then he howled and fell onto her, twisting and clutching behind him. He rolled onto his side. The wide-eyed, terrified girl stood next to him. They stared at Tripp's back, where a dark stain blossomed around a large kitchen knife jutting from between his shoulders.

Alisa barely hesitated before she grabbed the handle and jerked it out of his back. Blood gushed from the open wound. She held the knife high in both hands. She roared and used all her weight to drive it back into him, then yanked it out, grabbed the girl's hand and ran.

She grasped the knife, her forearm against the wall to steady herself as she and the girl crept down the hall. Dim light fell from the room behind her, the room where she had feared she was going to die, where they would both die. The air whispered of fear and evil.

Alisa gave the girl's hand a little squeeze. "Sh. Shh. I've got you."

There were four doors in the hallway, two on each side, all closed. At the end of the hall, blue television light flickered. The girl clenched Alisa's hand with both of hers.

"Stay here, honey."

The child held on tighter, shaking her head *no*.

"I need to make sure they're not keeping anyone else here."

The little girl's whole body shook *no, no*. She mewled a tiny, sharp sound.

"Sh. Shh. It's okay. I won't leave you."

Outside the front room, Alisa dropped to a crouch, bracing herself for whatever was to come. She pulled the girl close and forced herself to give her a reassuring smile. Television light danced dimly across the smears of blood that defiled the child's face. Laughter and the electronic tones of a game show almost drowned out her whimpers.

Alisa peered through the doorway. No one there. The TV was under the only window, which was shrouded with ancient brown curtains, across from a dilapidated sofa and two chairs. Several beer cans stood on a side table. The front door was closed.

"Stay close," she whispered.

They crept silently down a short hallway to the kitchen. A miasma of rotting food and old beer hung in the air. The light above the stove fell on dishes piled in the sink. A large pizza box sat on the kitchen table, along with more beer cans and dirty dishes. An overflowing trashcan stood near the kitchen door.

She crept to the kitchen door and tried the knob. Locked. She used her knife hand to part the curtain. Darkness. She murmured, "I'm going to check the other rooms, then we'll get out of here."

The girl pulled back as they approached the first door in the hall. The sliding bolt of the heavy-duty latch was open. Alisa's heart pounded. The door groaned as she opened it and peered into the small, windowless room. The air smelled old.

Light from the hall fell on two single beds, mattresses bare. Alisa exhaled. The girl gulped before resuming her tiny high-pitched moan. They crept to the next room. Also empty but for two beds. The third was the same. Blankets were piled on one bed in the fourth room, where Tripp had raped Alisa for the last time.

The girl sobbed as they inched toward the end of the hall. Alisa grasped the child's hand tighter. She took a deep breath, her knife ready. The girl's mother might still be alive. And she needed to find anything she could use on the run.

Alisa was still breathing hard from the fight and escape. She called on her battered body to do just this one more thing. She had to go back into the cave.

The closet door was wide open, the false back wall panel propped against a pile of boxes. She took deep breaths as she looked at the second, inside door. It was a safe, an old-timey one, with faded fancy gold lettering. It was as tall as her, its back cut out to create an entrance.

The heavy metal door was still partly open, the way

Tripp had left it when he thrust her into the cave, the way Alisa left it when she and the girl had escaped into the house. That door opened into the hell she and the girl had fled, how long ago? An hour? Ten minutes? A lifetime. Did she really need to go back?

She stepped into the closet, next to the safe door. The child whimpered and refused to follow. Alisa spoke urgently, then harshly. She wrenched away from the trembling child's hands. "I'll be back. Just wait here. I'm going to check on your mama."

She had to know whether, by some miracle, the girl's mother was still alive. The man hadn't come back with the van, but Tripp had a flashlight and wallet. She could use those.

The girl grabbed at Alisa, who jerked away. "I have to go in, you can stay right here. I'll be right back." She pushed the girl away a little roughly, then stepped quickly through the safe into the cave.

The light was dimming, flickering. The battery was fading. Tripp's hulking form lay face down to the right of the door, thanks to that little girl. *Where the hell did she get a knife?*

Alisa took the lantern from its hook. The girl's mother lay crumpled on her side across the cave, where the ceiling slanted sharply downward.

She set down the light but held onto the knife as she knelt next to the woman. She shook her gently, then touched her neck. She could feel no pulse. Her fingers came back sticky. Alisa checked the woman's coat and pants pockets. She found a small wallet and a hair clip, which she slipped into her jeans.

When Alisa softly rolled the woman onto her back, she jerked back with a stifled shriek. She spun her head toward the door, hoping the girl had not seen her poor dead mother's crushed and bloody face.

That move saved her. Tripp half-lunged, half-fell on her. She yelled, "Run! Go!" as his flashlight slammed her head. It knocked her flat, hammering out what little breath she had. She desperately held onto the knife as he dropped his knee on her forearm and grappled for the blade.

But despite all his fury, Tripp was done. He collapsed to the ground, expelling the last of his life with harsh grunts that weakened, then stopped. Alisa picked herself up and edged around him, now an unmoving mound seeping dark fluids. Her throbbing head felt hollowed out as she wobbled to the door. She wasn't surprised Tripp's last act in this world was full of hate; that he died trying to murder her. Served him right he was dead. But she wasn't free yet.

Alisa staggered through the metal door, then turned to close it. It squealed and barely budged, but she somehow found the strength to push it shut. She wasn't taking any chances Tripp might wake up again.

She softly called for the girl. No answer. What that poor child had been through. Alisa went out the half-open back door. There. A small footprint. Another. Alisa used a branch to brush them away along with her own as she headed to the woods.

Trees and bushes tore at her as she ran, tripping, falling, dragging herself back to her feet, crashing to the ground. The rush of adrenaline dissipated, leaving her dizzy and faint, her heart and head pounding. She had to rest, to catch her breath. Where was the little girl? Alisa was afraid to call out to her. No telling who else was around. Alisa sobbed as she fought her way through the thick brush.

Finally, she had to stop, her lungs aching, her breath pained and shallow. Alisa collapsed onto a fallen log, gasping, gulping, shuddering, her body aching from the blows she'd suffered at the hands of that evil man. But Tripp would never touch her again. Or anyone else.

The dark was becoming light. Morning. A new day. She opened the dead woman's wallet. A few bills and an Arizona driver's license. Marsha Sutton. Good. She would need ID to start over. Alisa folded the money around the license and tucked it in the heel of her sock. She slipped her shoe back on. She hid the wallet under a bush, covering it with dirt and rocks. She almost fell over when she stood up. She rested on her hands and knees before forcing herself to get up and go.

****

Marsha clenched her jaw. Her knuckles whitened as she gripped the steering wheel. A decade later, she could still feel the fear, the panic. How she hated that evil Tripp. She still thought about that brave little girl who saved their lives and wondered where the child got the knife.

And who was that strange, kind man who'd helped her, who gave her food and a leather bag, and hid her in the woods. She remembered going to the woman's house when he didn't come back. Joan. Her name was Joan and she said she would take her to someone who could help her, but after a terrible bumpy ride in the back of a pickup, Joan gave her twenty dollars and dropped her, all alone, at the bus station in St. Louis.

Marsha grasped the wheel even harder, squeezed her eyes shut and screamed until she was out of breath. She inhaled deeply, then tilted the rear-view mirror to look at herself. Time to move on. She was Marsha Sutton now. She had a presentation to make. Best focus on that.

Whatever was going on in Missouri had nothing to do with her. It must be a different cave. She could never let anyone find out she'd helped Tripp grab the real Marsha Sutton and her daughter. And that they had killed him.

Enough. Time to get to work. That part of her life was dead, entombed with the bodies in the cave.

Chapter Forty-Two

Monday Evening, Walkers Corner

It was late afternoon by the time Sheriff Linden left the diner. Sam followed him out. Vicky craned her neck to watch them through the window. They stood on the sidewalk and hugged for a long moment before he left.

When Sam returned, Vicky still had her injured leg stretched out on the bench seat. She had taken another pill and was finally released from pain, tension, fear. She often talked to reduce stress. Now, with tolerant listeners plus added relief provided by a potent prescription, she rambled on, stalling, putting off whatever was going to happen with Pete. She sometimes found it easier to say things in a group.

"There's a quote, I don't remember who said it, about the second Iraq war, something like 'we don't know if Iraq's the way it is because of Saddam Hussein, or if Saddam's the way he is because Iraq's the way it is.' Something like that. Anyway, I wonder if I'm the way I am because I'm a reporter, or if I'm a reporter because of the way I am. If that makes sense."

No one responded so maybe it didn't, but she kept going. "It used to be journalists had to keep our personal views to ourselves. It was perfect. I got to ask people their opinions but didn't have to share mine." She scoffed ruefully. "Guess that's probably not the best approach in a relationship."

She looked directly at Pete. He did not appear to notice, much less respond to her subtle, roundabout acknowledgment of one of her flaws. He seemed distracted, distant—even physically, sitting two people away from Vicky, on a chair facing the booth.

She veered back to the week's events. "I got so much wrong. I thought whoever Sam escaped from took Rose, that those events were connected. Guess they were, but with about a dozen degrees of separation. Not directly." She took a sip of coffee. "Guess I'm glad about that."

Pete leaned back in his chair, eyes drilling into Vicky's. "Why glad?"

She hadn't met this side of Pete's personality before. He was usually so easygoing.

"I should have done something after seeing that subpoena."

Liz Ann lifted her hand. "Wait, is this about the cop you told us about? You saw his papers? He thought you were hitting on him?"

Vicky reminded herself she didn't have to explain. But then, why not? "Okay, yeah. Rick Carr knew his father was being investigated. I didn't tell anyone about that, or his story about the smugglers. And Mike, the pickup at Rick's house I told you about? That was Joan. She had Alisa in back. Was she bringing her to Rick? I don't know. I should have at least told someone."

"Why didn't you?" Sam's voice was entirely level, no lilt or drop to add to the meaning of a perfectly fair question.

"I was pissed off, humiliated. I just walked away." Words tumbled from Vicky, uncharacteristically uncontrolled.

"That's understandable," Liz Ann said briskly. "Vick, no matter what happened years ago, you did some real good here. You might not have gotten every detail exactly right, but your instincts were dead on. Sam only remembered the cave because you kept asking questions. And listening. And you homed in on Joan and rescued Rose. Lighten up, darlin'."

She hugged Vicky, then motioned to Mike to let her out. "I need to get going. Here." She handed Vicky a key. "You stay at my place however long you like. I love company."

"I left my rental car at your place and walked here," Pete said. "I'll be by to pick it up later."

"No rush." Liz Ann opened her mouth like she was going to say more, then pressed her lips together and got to her feet.

Mike remained standing. "I've got to go, too."

Vicky leaned forward to get up but was relieved when he waved her back. "No, sit, it's fine." He clasped Vicky's hand. "I had my doubts about you, but you did all right. You don't let go. Glad to know you."

Vicky almost choked. For Mike, that was almost gushy. Sentimental. He followed Liz Ann toward the door. Sam said she had things to do in the kitchen.

That left Pete and Vicky. He put his daypack on the bench between them as he slid into the booth.

"Alone at last," Vicky joked.

He leaned over and kissed her cheek. "I'm glad you're okay."

Oh boy. The old kiss on the cheek.

Pete gave her a long, serious look. "I think I

understand you not telling me about your folks. That's a sad and terrible thing to keep bottled up, though. What I don't get is this thing with Dallas. What were you going to do? Call me from Texas and tell me you started a new job? I deserve better."

"I wasn't thinking about you—"

"No kidding. You're not the only one trying to make plans. Why'd you have to keep that to yourself?"

"It wasn't that I had to—"

"It's better you just wanted to? Privacy's one thing, you know I like it as much as you do. But it's something else, keeping that kind of thing to yourself. Especially when it might involve me."

"We don't know it might invol—ouch. That came out wrong. I mean, we were on a two-day camping trip. I didn't know all this was going to happen."

"Remember that long drive here? Seventeen hours? You couldn't have found a few minutes to mention you might be moving to Texas?"

"I wasn't ready to talk about it."

"And we might have had a little down time in the last two weeks when it could have come up. That's what I really don't understand. You talk all the time, about everything, but you don't say a word about something like that."

Vicky didn't answer. What could she say? It was true.

Pete got to his feet. "I think we could both do with some time to think." He picked up his pack. "I'm glad things worked out here. You did good work. Let me know what you decide. You know how to reach me."

Pete leaned in and kissed her, like he was just going to the store. It was enough of a kiss that

Vicky definitely wanted him to stay, but apparently not enough to change his mind. She sat in silence, watching him stride away, bag over one shoulder. Her shoulders sagged. God, she was tired.

Sam reappeared, coffeepot lifted in silent offering. She poured refills and smiled. "Don't take this the wrong way, but I hope you don't feel as bad as you look."

"Even worse. You look good, though."

They chuckled. They were both in serious need of rest and physical grooming. It would take more than a quick shower and change of clothes to undo the cumulative effects of the last forty-eight hours.

Dark circles around Sam's bloodshot eyes highlighted her exhaustion.

Vicky assumed she looked even worse. She'd earned it. It had been a rollercoaster two weeks. And now this thing with Pete. At least Rose was safe, and Sam had some closure. Vicky disliked that cliché but was too tired to think of a different way of saying it.

"Don't minimize what you did," Sam said. "You were the catalyst. You heard about the bag, tracked down Joan, stirred up the right people. Made the right connections. Without you, Joan might've gotten away with Rose."

"Yeah, but I should have put things together years ago. I was selfish. I was about to be out of a job. I was embarrassed about the audition and pissed at Rick. I knew about that subpoena and smuggling. Suspected, anyway. I should have followed up. Maybe they would have found your mom. Maybe you could have grown up with your family."

Vicky's voice cracked when she said the word *family*. Dammit, she better not cry. It's not like she knew what growing up in a normal one was like. And she wasn't all that sure that having *regular* parents would have been better than foster homes or institutions. Might have been hell. Probably would have been.

"My mom was dead before I left her." Sam put her hand on Vicky's. "But we would never have found her if you hadn't poked around so much. Including in my head. So, thank you. I might have kept everything buried inside me the rest of my life."

Vicky squeezed Sam's hand gently. "I know it's not over for you yet."

"Yeah. But at least I know something about who I am."

"There's that." After a moment, Vicky shook her head. "It still kills me that I never found out what all Rick knew and did."

Sam shrugged. "We never get to know every single thing about anybody."

"True. Or anything. There's always something, another angle, another layer, left out of any story."

Sam eyed Vicky skeptically. "Are you going to keep digging?"

"No. Really not. Anything to do with Rick has nothing to do with me. I'll leave that to Kerry. She's his boss, and now she knows he's not all he claims to be. She promised she's going to dig deep into his past. And so will Linden." Vicky lifted her eyebrows and grinned. "By the way, speaking of the sheriff—"

"Yeah. Forget Rick. But if you are going to investigate anything, I want to know more about my mom, if I have any family. I'd love your help."

"I'll do everything I can." Vicky closed her eyes and drew a deep breath for four slow counts, held it at the top for four beats, then exhaled at the same slow, controlled rate. She counted four again before saying, "You know, I never talk about what happened to my folks. Telling y'all about them the other night practically ripped my heart out."

Sam tilted her head slightly, almost a nod. "I could feel your pain. That's why you told us, isn't it? So I'd know you understood how I felt."

Vicky swallowed. She attempted yoga breathing again, then gave up. "I guess at some point I need to say the rest of it. I'm going to now, before I stop myself again. I always hold back. Okay. Here goes."

Vicky paused to squeeze her eyelids.

Sam said, "Talk."

Vicky chuckled through her tears. Her jaw clenched. "Yeah. Okay, you know about the wildfire and me being saved because my parents gave me to some people hanging onto a pickup truck."

Vicky blocked the swell of fear, sadness, and guilt that threatened to overwhelm her. She lowered her voice to deaden its annoying tremble.

"What I failed to mention is it wasn't just me. My little sister was with me. Everything was so confusing. People were running and screaming. Trees were on fire."

Vicky counted another sixteen-beat breath. "I was on the truck. I don't know who was holding me. My mom was running after us, lifting my sister up to someone next to me. Mama was crying, saying she loved us, telling me to take care of my little sister, to stay together."

Vicky's carefully constructed dam gave way. She let out one sharp sob. "I don't know what happened to my sister." She wiped her eyes with a wadded-up napkin.

"She was three. Shit."

Sam was crying, too. She got more napkins from the holder and gave some to Vicky, who pressed them to her eyes. Vicky's shoulders shook as she wailed, gut-level weeping, primal pain bursting through what was left of her control.

Eventually she looked up. "Sorry. I'm a blubbering mess. This is why I don't talk about any of this." She took another napkin and blew her nose, then added it to the growing pile in front of her.

"I ended up in an emergency shelter. I found out later it was at a Catholic church hall. Everything smelled like smoke. Crowds of upset and panicky people. You know what it's like when you're a kid and can't even begin to understand what's going on. And you don't know a single person? I know you do."

Sam took a deep breath and nodded. The tears in their eyes deepened the understanding that flowed between them.

Vicky exchanged her napkin for a fresh one. "I screamed and went wild. I'm told I hit a few people. Bit a couple. I barely knew my name. No one said anything about my sister, and I didn't say anything either. I didn't tell anyone about her. I was confused. I felt bad about not taking care of her. I never saw her again."

"Jesus."

"Yeah."

"That's a lot."

"Yep. But no more than the past you're lugging around. And you're doing great, Sam. You're building a really good life."

"Even so. Have you looked for her?"

"I've been searching for years. That's how I got into

news. There are no records of an unidentified girl from that fire. I had nothing to show she even existed."

Vicky exhaled. She breathed out pain, guilt, fear. She visualized exhaling memories and emotions that served no good purpose. When her lungs were empty, she took in clean fresh air, and new resolve.

"But she existed. I can picture her little face as well as if I saw her this morning. She's always in my heart. I'm going to re-start my search. I'll use DNA to see if I can find any family." Vicky pursed her lips. "Okay, enough. Sorry to dump all that on you."

"Don't be silly. Damn, and here I thought I was a mess."

They smiled through their tears, then fell silent for several minutes before Vicky said, "Moving on."

Sam leaned forward to take Vicky's hands. "All right. Can I just say something? You're nuts. You and Pete are good together."

"He's the one leaving."

"He'd stay if you asked him to."

"He's angry I didn't tell him about the Texas job offer."

"He's probably more hurt than angry. Why didn't you tell him?"

"It's something I needed to decide for myself. Anyway, he wants different things."

"Like what?"

Vicky lifted a shoulder. "A commitment. I'm not looking for that."

"Just because you're not looking doesn't mean you should turn your back on it. Not everything has to be a fight."

"It's not that."

"What then? You have something else going on? Something to prove? Everyone knows you can take care of yourself."

"It's an act, being capable. Inside I'm an insecure mess." Vicky's joke fell flat, possibly because they both knew it was at least partly true.

"I'm not saying you need someone to feel complete or anything, but why on earth would you throw that away? You two are great together. And your heart is breaking. For what?"

"It's not. I have a nice strong shell guarding my heart."

"You're good at getting people to open up to a different way of thinking. Look at me. Turn that on yourself." Sam gave a look of exaggerated horror. "Good Lord. I'm starting to talk like you."

"Hey, you sound good. Ah, Sam. This is not easy."

"I know. But it can be if you want it to be."

"I'm not going to run after him." Vicky glanced toward the door, jaw tight.

"I will. Just wait here. He's heading to Liz Ann's. I bet I can catch up with him."

"You don't have to." Vicky reached into her pocket. "He'll be back. I swiped his keys."

Epilogue

Traffickers Cave
Walkers Corner, MO
By Vicky Robeson

Travelers driving between St. Louis and Jefferson City, Missouri, might think there's no good reason to take the exit for Walkers Corner. And that's understandable, with its ordinary highway sign pointing to an ordinary-looking little town.

But those who drive on by will miss the prettiest library in the state of Missouri, and Sam's Corner Table Café, with the best cinnamon rolls in the entire Midwest. Those who stop will see the places that connect decades of dark and terrible crimes, and learn the story of a mystery woman who risked everything and saved a little girl…

A word about the author...

Maria Lynn Barrs is one of thirteen children—the first girl, with three older brothers—a birth order she believes shaped her essence by the time she was eight.

A girl's gotta be a bit pugnacious to get along in that environment. Amid the chaos of fourteen people living in a mobile home (not a double-wide), she turned fifteen, dropped out of school, and ran away from home. Being homeless, then working minimum wage jobs quickly grew old. She earned a high school equivalency diploma, went to college, where she met her husband, the father of their two wonderful now-grown children. She started in television news as a reporter, eventually working her way up to news director and general manager before deciding what she really wanted to do is write mysteries.

www.ingramcontent.com/pod-product-compliance
Lightning Source LLC
Chambersburg PA
CBHW051133030726
47504CB00004B/852